'I did not ch...
to be a bride...

'You and my father arranged it between you. Why, I believe you are nothing but an adventurer. You may be my husband, but you have yet to gain my love.'

Hal's face seemed to freeze and his hand around the flask clenched so tightly that his knuckles showed white. 'Perhaps I should make you love me. If not with your heart then with your body.'

In one, swift, lithe movement, he pushed Nicol back against the grassy bank, one hand holding her wrists above her head while he rolled across her, pinning her to the ground. She gasped and glared up at him, defiance mixed with fear. Discarding the flask he began to stroke her throat and shoulders then slowly bent to kiss her. Instinctively, she turned her face away so that his lips brushed her neck, turning the kiss into a caress that was even more unsettling. Then, quite suddenly, he drew back, a hateful, cynical smile on his lips.

'Lust and love are not so different,' he purred. 'You may not love me, my dear, but with a little training you will serve me well enough in bed!'

Truda Taylor grew up in Okehampton, Devon and now lives in Desborough, Northamptonshire, with her husband John, and children George and Amy, and a selection of cats and hampsters. She teaches seven year olds and enjoys encouraging them to use their imaginations and write.

Five years ago, she made her first visit to the Vendée and it was her fascination with the history of that area that eventually led to this book.

To John, George and Amy
for their love
and encouragement.

HAZARDOUS MARRIAGE

Truda Taylor

MILLS & BOON LIMITED
ETON HOUSE   18-24 PARADISE ROAD
RICHMOND   SURREY   TW9 1SR

First published in Great Britain 1989
by Mills & Boon Limited

© Truda Taylor 1989

Australian copyright 1989
Philippine copyright 1989
This edition 1990

ISBN 0 263 76697 7

Set in Times Roman 10½ on 12 pt.
04-9001-69623 C

Made and printed in Great Britain

PROLOGUE

Cholet, the Vendée, October 1793

HENRY GRANTLY looked out across the shallow valley and caught his breath; this time the columns were even more tightly packed. Like some menacing, unstoppable monster they crossed the valley and began to climb the rise.

'Fix bayonets!' ordered Jacquelein, and Grantly repeated the command.

Ragged cries of, *'En avant! Vive la révolution! Aux baïonnettes!'* floated up from the enemy vanguard.

The hill slowed the Republicans' progress but as soon as they were within range the Vendeans opened fire. A deadly volley decimated the front ranks, to be followed almost simultaneously by another. The blue columns seemed to slow, then came on at a trot, those in front being carried forward by the enthusiasm of those behind.

The Republicans fired wildly. Grantly heard his friend Philippe cry out but had no time to help him, continuing to load and fire as rapidly as he could. Soon his cheek began to sting and the metal of the gun was hot in his hand. The ground before him became littered with blue-coated bodies, and still they came on, threatening to swamp the Vendean line. There was time for one last volley and mercifully it was enough. The Republican advance wavered.

With perfect timing young Jacquelein, his voice hoarse from yelling encouragement, urged his men forward. He was like a young lion with his hat gone and his fair curls blowing around his face in disarray. Following his example, the Vendeans, their peat-cutters dripping blood, pressed ferociously on so that the enemy was forced to give ground and, for a while, the tide of battle swung in their direction.

Grantly turned his attention to Philippe and an agonised groan escaped his lips. There was a ragged hole in the boy's chest and he was barely alive. Knowing it was futile, he pulled off his stock and pressed it against the wound, adding the boy's own when the first cloth became soaked with blood. He had scarcely finished when the Republican cannon thundered and roundshot crashed into the nearby trees.

Lifting his friend in his arms, he staggered down from the hilltop. Two stretcher-bearers came forward to help, and with a heavy heart he relinquished his burden, knowing it was the last time he would see Philippe alive. As he watched them walking away through the powder smoke, he felt utterly alone, somehow stranded in that place of insanity and death.

A gentle breeze brushed his cheek and, like a curtain, the mist momentarily parted so that he was able to see his friend being lifted into the second of two wagons. The girl driving the first wagon glanced towards him, and his stomach contracted painfully. She was Philippe's younger sister and she would have no idea that her brother was within her reach.

Grantly silently cursed the old Comte for allowing her anywhere near the battlefield, then acknowledged that he might not have been entirely to blame. It was certainly a departure from his usual protective attitude and from all accounts the girl had a will of her own. She also had a body that would tempt the most saintly of men, and Grantly, for all his lack of a permanent female companion, was no saint. As he looked at her, he felt a stab of desire so strong that it both surprised and disgusted him. There he was, standing amid carnage and destruction, and he wanted her, a mere child. Perhaps it was her resemblance to the young mother he had so adored. Certainly she had the same creamy skin and rich, dark hair, but it was more than that. She was so full of spirit, somehow so alive. In fact it was years since he had felt so drawn to a woman.

She glanced towards him, and their eyes met in a moment of shared disillusionment and sorrow, but she gave no sign that she recognised him. He didn't tell her about Philippe. The boy was unlikely to regain consciousness and he was just too much of a coward.

The sound of the guns was calling him back to the battle and, like a zombie, he retraced his steps. He had seen war before but had forgotten how it aged and drained a man. The beauty and youth of the girl he had just seen contrasted sharply with the jaded image he had of himself, and he knew that such a fresh flower was not for his picking.

CHAPTER ONE

FOR a second day the rumble of the distant guns rolled across the Normandy countryside. The sound was oddly at variance with the peaceful scene viewed from the château windows. Nicolette rubbed the condensation from the inside of the pane and peered out across the formal lawns, their wide expanse broken only by a single, walled fountain. For the first time in her nineteen years of life, she was afraid, terribly afraid, not for herself but for her father and the cause she held dear.

The door opened and the Marchioness de la Roche Jacquelein came into the room, her anxiety apparent in her lovely face.

'There is still no news,' she sighed, moving over to warm her hands in front of the roaring fire.

'If anyone can bring us victory then it is Monsieur Henri,' Nicol replied, using the peasants' name for the young Vendean general.

The Marchioness smiled and reached for the other girl's hand, pride in her husband momentarily dwarfing her fear. 'I know, but it is such a great responsibility. I swear he has aged years during these last weeks... and Louis' dying affected him deeply.'

She was referring to the death of the Marquis de Lescure, Henri's cousin and the previous commander of the Royalist Vendean army, who had died of his wounds following the battle at Cholet—a battle that had changed all their lives irrevocably.

Nicolette's brother had died there, and her face clouded as she remembered the aftermath. Accompanied by her father, she had collected a few possessions from their home and fled to join the remnants of their army on the bank of the Loire.

It had been something of a miracle, the way young Jacquelein had rallied the men and finally managed to have the whole miscellaneous multitude ferried across the wide river and into Maine. Old men, women and children had accompanied the soldiers, and stately coaches had waited alongside farm carts and gun-carriages. Never had Nicol seen such an assortment of people, and Madame Jacquelein had likened the scene to the gates of Heaven on Judgement Day.

Now the Vendean army had reached the Normandy coast and, their confidence boosted by many victories en route, were attempting to take the coastal town of Granville. The previous day had not been a success, and today they were committing everything in one last determined assault.

In the middle of the afternoon the sound of the guns finally died away, and the two ladies waited in a fever of anxiety for news of the battle. As dusk was falling and smudges of dull red were spreading across the winter sky, a lone rider galloped under the ancient, arched gateway and into the château grounds. He dismounted stiffly outside the front door, and Nicolette, who had watched his approach from her bedroom window, recognised him as one of her father's friends.

Throwing the brush she had been using down upon the bed, she raced for the stairs, her long, dark hair flying untidily behind her.

'What news?' she cried, then, seeing his expression, halted, her hand resting lightly on the banister.

Defeat was etched into every line on his face, was apparent in each weary gesture. He was covered in dirt, from the top of his dark head to his once shiny boots, and a bloody bandage was wrapped carelessly around one hand.

'Monsieur Henri?' the Marchioness asked, entering the hallway, her face ashen.

'He is well, my lady,' Henry Grantly replied, a tired smile cracking the grime on his face. 'We have lost some eight hundred men, but your husband is safe, despite being in the thick of the fighting for most of the two days. General Stofflet too is uninjured.'

When he turned to face Nicol there was pity in his grey eyes.

'Papa?' The word was wrenched from her.

'You must be brave, Nicol. He is sorely wounded. I'm afraid he's going to die.'

Her heart seemed to lurch and her stomach turned over. 'What?' she asked rather stupidly, sitting down on the stairs before her legs gave way.

'Your father is dying,' he repeated softly.

She had heard him the first time but somehow hadn't quite understood. In that same terrible instant, images of her father were kaleidoscoping through her mind—her father encouraging her as she learnt to jump her first horse, patiently explaining the intricacies of a musket or the steps of the minuet.

'Are you all right?' Grantly asked, moving closer.

'Yes,' she replied, and, reminding herself that she was a de Carrie, proudly lifted her head. 'I must go to him.'

He nodded. 'It's why I've come. You had better get ready as quickly as possible; I'm afraid time is short.'

Regaining some control over her limbs, she stood up shakily and hurried back upstairs to fetch her cloak. Grantly sighed and drew a tired hand across his eyes. He was obviously nearing the end of his endurance and, seeing this, Madame Jacquelein guided him into the drawing-room.

When Nicol joined them, well wrapped against the cold, she found him ensconced in a comfortable chair beside the fire. He was holding a glass of Calvados in his right hand while the Marchioness bound a clean cloth around his left, with all the efficiency of one well versed in such matters.

Having finished his drink, he stood up stiffly, his tall, travel-stained figure looking completely out of place in the elegant drawing-room.

'We'd better get started,' he muttered.

'You could take my carriage,' the Marchioness offered.

He gave a brief smile and shook his head. 'The roads are poor. We shall make better time on horseback.' Then, catching hold of Nicol's arm, he almost bundled her from the room.

As they galloped through the night, Nicol glanced often at the tall, taciturn man riding at her side, thinking how little she really knew of him. He was the English grandson of one of her most respected neighbours, the Marchioness de Courcy, as well as being the brother of a prominent English Earl. Arriving in the Vendée the previous spring, he had been only too willing to throw in his lot with the Royalist insurgents.

According to her brother, he had spent several years in the British Army and was respected even by Stofflet for his initiative and tactical acumen—but then

Philippe had been prone to hero worship and, in the months before his death, had come to admire Grantly very much indeed.

From a purely physical point of view, she had to admit that he was handsome, but with an arrogance and coldness of manner that she found rather disconcerting. He carried himself well and could be charming when he chose—which was not often. Most of the time he appeared serious, almost brooding, his dark brows drawn together in a forbidding frown. He seemed to prefer the society of men, and, when he did exert himself to be pleasant with a female, it was usually some plain, insipid soul from whose clutches he presumably felt perfectly safe.

She was not sure of his age, but judged it to be somewhere between thirty-five and forty—too old to make a likely husband and yet not ancient enough to pinch her cheek with impunity. Not that she could imagine Henry Grantly doing such a thing; he had probably been born serious and middle-aged.

'Are you warm enough?' he asked solicitously, turning towards her so that the hard lines of his face were picked out in the moonlight.

'Yes, thank you ... Is there much farther to go?'

'Half a league, maybe more.'

She nodded and took a deep breath, desperately trying to steady the churning in her stomach.

Overhead the stars were bright pinpoints of light in a seemingly velvet sky, and the moon was almost full, its light making the frost on the ground and trees sparkle like a myriad fairy crystals. Only a smell of smoke served to remind her of the fighting, an acid smoke that still seemed to cling to her companion's clothes.

After a while Grantly led her off the road and down a broader, trodden track that wound between the trees. It was hard going and the horses' hoofs crashed against the ground like steel hammers. Then the Vendean camp was before them, its many fires breaking the darkness. It was an untidy conglomeration of rough shelters and wagons, camp followers and soldiers, and Nicol had to concentrate as her companion guided her through the clutter towards a group of farm buildings.

'They've made the barn into a kind of hospital,' he told her. 'Your father is being well cared for.'

They dismounted outside the mud-walled farmhouse and a couple of men came forward to take their horses. Grasping her arm, Grantly led her towards the barn, pausing a moment before the worn door.

'Does he look so very bad?' she asked, sensing his reluctance to enter the place.

He shook his head as if impatient with his own thoughts. 'No, as a matter of fact, he looks quite well. Apparently his spine is damaged but he feels little pain ... Come; he'll be waiting.'

A single oil lamp filled the barn with a comfortable yellow glow, its acid fumes blotting out the less pleasant smells of cowdung and human sweat. A peasant girl came forward to greet them, her shadow large and distorted against the floor and walls.

'So you have arrived at last,' she sighed. 'The Comte has been asking for you.'

Nicol's stomach was churning as she made her way to the figure lying in the furthest bed. Throwing herself on to her knees, she took her father's hand and held it against her cheek.

'Nicol?' His voice was much weaker than she remembered it. 'There, child! It's not so bad. I'm not afraid to die... I've missed your mother these last few years and the world holds little for me now.'

His acceptance of death frightened her and she cried out, 'But, Papa, I need you. Don't give up, Papa, please!'

'Oh, Nicol,' he sighed, lifting his hand to stroke her hair. 'In some ways you are still such a child. I'm sorry you have to see me this way, but there are arrangements to be made... Hal, are you still there?'

'Yes, sir.' Grantly answered, in a surprisingly gentle voice, and moved closer.

'Now you've had time to consider my proposal, are you still agreeable to it?'

'If it's really what you want, and, of course, if your daughter is willing.'

The Comte gave a grunt of satisfaction and seemed to relax. Sensing a conspiracy between the two men, Nicol felt suddenly uneasy.

Her father caught hold of her chin and forced her to look into his face. 'I must know that you are safe, my dear. I cannot leave you unprotected at such a time. If Philippe were still alive then it would be different. As it is, I would like to see you suitably married before I die... Hal has consented to make you his wife.'

'Hal has consented...' Stupidly she repeated the words. 'But I have no wish to marry him!'

The older man laughed, regretting it immediately as an unexpected stab of pain pierced his insides. 'It is my wish, child...the only sensible thing to do. Your inheritance has gone and you have no means of supporting yourself. I have not spoken of this before because I did not want to worry you, but wars cost money and, by now, most of ours has gone. True, the château lands remain, but who knows how long it will be before you can claim them? And running an estate is no job for a woman on her own. Hal has a family and a fine house in England. You will be comfortable and safe with him. In a few years all this will seem like a bad dream.'

'No, Papa!' she protested.

Her father looked a trifle embarrassed and, glancing across her shoulder, apologetically asked Grantly to leave.

'It's not very flattering for him that I should have to persuade you,' he continued once they were alone. 'He's doing you an honour, Nicol; the marriage is all to your advantage. It's fortunate that he is willing to surrender his freedom so lightly.'

She did not reply, and for a moment he studied her, noting with pleasure her large dark eyes and glossy raven hair. She had always been a charming child and now she had become a strikingly beautiful woman. It was a pity her emotions were not so mature.

'Trust me, my dear,' he told her. 'I'm sure I've chosen wisely. You can't fight alongside a man without getting to know him well. Henry Grantly will be all you could wish for in a husband. He has courage and integrity, combined with an odd streak of compassion that he would really rather hide, and he's not ill-looking, is he?'

'No, Papa. It's just that I'm not in love with him.'

He chuckled. 'That will come, my child, believe me. Now, go to him. Tell him that you agree.'

Looking into his pale, strained face, Nicol found it impossible to continue the argument. If it would make his last hours easier, then of course she would agree.

'Very well,' she answered simply. 'If it is really what you wish then I will do it.'

'And tonight,' he insisted. 'If I am to see it, then it must be tonight.'

She found Grantly leaning against the outside of the barn, virtually asleep on his feet. He straightened as she approached, his head turning towards her expectantly.

'I will do as my father wishes,' she told him.

'You're quite sure?'

She thought there was a hint of disappointment in his voice, and for the first time it occurred to her that he might be regretting an agreement made with a dying man.

'More to the point, sir, are you sure?' she demanded, proudly lifting her chin. 'I would not be wed out of pity.'

He smiled then, his teeth showing white in the darkness. 'I wouldn't presume to do such a thing. The suggestion was your father's, but I'm willing enough.'

'I bring you nothing, no dowry, no property, nothing.'

She did not expect a romantic declaration, but she still found his answer disappointing.

'My family have been pressing me to marry. You will do well enough.'

He was implying that choosing a wife was no more important than choosing a dog or a horse and, stomach sinking, she wondered if all Englishmen were that prosaic.

Less than an hour later she was married, not as she had always expected, in a church wearing a flowing gown, but in a lowly barn, clothed in a mudstained dress and to a man she hardly knew, a man so tired he could not repeat his vows without making a mistake. Only the presence of the priest seemed right, and she was relieved that Hal had made no objection to a Catholic ceremony.

'It was my mother's religion,' he told her. 'It will serve well enough, as long as our children are brought up in the Protestant faith.'

It was only then that she realised just how intimate she was going to be with him, and it took all her resolve to go through with the ceremony.

After the marriage the same priest turned sadly to her father and solemnly administered the last rites. Nicol choked back her tears, and in spite of Hal's coaxing refused to leave, spending the remaining hours of darkness at her father's side.

He died just as the first grey fingers of light were stealing into the barn, slipping away peacefully in his sleep without sign or murmur. For a long time afterwards she continued to hold his hand, marvelling that it could remain so warm and apparently alive. She still couldn't quite believe it; then, as the truth slowly made itself felt, she began to cry, great choking sobs that felt as though they would tear her apart.

She was hardly aware of her husband leading her gently but firmly across to the farmhouse and easing her down into a chair.

'There's nothing more you can do,' he said quietly, pressing her hand and then drawing away.

She had never felt so empty and alone, and tears, silent now, continued to run down her face. Someone pressed a cup of coffee into her hand and, glancing up, she saw Hal and again felt the shy, momentary pressure of his fingers on hers. He did not speak again, but at that moment his tactful silence was worth much more than any amount of fulsome sympathy. Words could do nothing to lessen her despair and, sensing this, he offered her none. She was thankful for that.

Her father was buried only a few hours later in the consecrated ground of a small cemetery. It was a bleak and colourless day that exactly matched her mood. Since morning the ground had remained covered by a heavy white frost and even the small church was dusted with it. The earth was iron hard and the men had to struggle to dig even a shallow resting-place, their shovels ringing hollowly through an otherwise unnatural stillness.

As the shrouded body was slowly lowered, Nicol stared down at the white, flattened grass and tried to pray, feeling cold and empty and finding not the slightest comfort in the ritual of her faith.

Hal stood close yet refrained from putting his arm around her, and she did not want him to. He was still an outsider and she felt that any great show of grief on his part would be a presumption. In fact her marriage was no comfort at all, merely something else that would have to be endured.

Her life was changing drastically and she was not sure she could cope with it. She longed for the comfort and security of her home, the peaceful place of her childhood, and yet childhood was far behind her now. It was as if another person had lived in that ancient château and wandered blithely through the private woodland, a beautiful innocent completely untouched by squalor and pain. Now there could be no returning; all her loved ones were dead, and she was experiencing a feeling of desolation that was more than she thought she could bear.

Just as they were leaving the cemetery, Henri de la Roche Jacquelein approached them. He was still holding his hat in his hands, revealing a profusion of soft curls that any female would have envied. Nicol found it hard to believe that he was only eighteen months older than herself, for his light eyes held a strange, sad maturity. She remembered that he too had lost those he loved, and somehow that helped.

'You know how sorry I am,' he told her, taking her hand and squeezing it gently. 'Unfortunately, there is little time for grief, and for a while at least I must claim your husband.' Turning to Hal, he added, 'I have important decisions to make, my friend, and I'd value your opinion as an Englishman. Perhaps Nicol would like to return to the château with my wife and you could join her later.'

Hal nodded, then glanced at Nicol. 'Is that all right with you?'

She had not expected to be consulted, and surprised herself by saying, 'I think I would rather wait at camp for you. I really need to keep busy, and from all accounts there is plenty to do. There are so many wounded to be looked after.'

He hesitated for a moment, then nodded. 'It's not a pleasant job, but it shall be as you wish.'

He said nothing more and yet surely there was a light of approval in his eyes. Suddenly, surprisingly, it was important that he should think well of her. He might have married her solely to please her father, but she would soon show him that he had not made such a bad bargain after all.

CHAPTER TWO

HENRI JACQUELEIN crossed to the window of the small farmhouse and looked out at the camp with something like despair. From a chair beside the fire Hal Grantly watched him sympathetically. The red glow from the setting sun picked out the deep shadows on his face, making him look much older than his twenty-one years.

'The people won't take much more of this,' he confessed. 'They want to go home, and I can't say that I blame them. Many of our officers agree with them; I know Stofflet does.'

'The Republicans will be expecting such a move,' Grantly reminded him. 'Westerman is poised to cut you off.'

When Jacquelein turned back to face the room, his eyes were dark with trouble, appearing almost violet in the fading light. He was a handsome young man, slim and fair with a fine-featured face saved from being too pretty by a strong nose and thick, straight eyebrows.

The war had certainly brought out the best in him, changing him from a high-spirited courtier to a general of determination and flair. He possessed a natural charm and that rare, indefinable quality that made his men willing to die for him. 'Monsieur Henri', they called him, affectionately mocking him for his youth, and at the same time respecting him for his intelligence and courage. Grantly was as much under his spell as any man, and hated to see him looking so despondent and drained.

'The people are losing their trust in us,' Jacquelein continued. 'They are afraid we shall follow the example of other aristocrats and make our escape across the Channel. It's a demoralising rumour and I would love to know who started it.'

Walking over to the table, he poured two large glasses of Calvados and passed one to the Englishman. 'How much help can we really expect from your Government, Hal?'

Grantly met the General's concerned look and felt ashamed. He sipped the wine, then said, 'Not a great deal, I'm afraid. Although Pitt's sympathetic enough in principle, it's really a question of finance. Whatever he does, he requires the backing of Parliament, and there are many who are still not convinced of the necessity of war. We were certainly ill-prepared for it, and our incompetent allies have been a continual drain on our resources.'

'If we could have taken Granville, then it would have made help from across the Channel so much easier.'

'I don't think it would have made all that much difference. My countrymen are notoriously slow to act.'

Jacquelein drained his glass and walked restlessly across the room, his emotions obviously in turmoil. 'You were always against the attack on the town, weren't you? In fact, you've never been anything but pessimistic about your country's support. If Stofflet returns to the Vendée, the majority of the army will follow him. Myself, I'm inclined to move into Brittany and bide my time there.'

'I rather think that is what Pitt would advise. It would certainly give him more time to do something, and you'd be more accessible than in the Vendée.' Hal frowned and ran a hand through his hair, obviously as concerned as the younger man. 'You know why I'm here, don't you, Henri?'

Jacquelein smiled wryly. 'Although you haven't actually said so in as many words, you haven't exactly made a secret of it, and quite honestly I see no real conflict between your country's interest and our own.'

'There may not be conflict, but I wish they would do more to help you. I intend to plead your case most strongly when I return home, although I doubt that it will do much good. Look, I know you would like something more definite. Recently I sent off a report. There could be a reply waiting with my contact. It will be a gruelling ride but I think it's worth finding out.'

Jacquelein brightened. 'I can provide an escort.'

'No, I'll make better time on my own and draw a lot less attention.'

'Whatever you think best,' replied the young General, holding out his hand. 'Just take care. I can see that you're tired, and tired men make mistakes. I should hate Nicol to be a widow before she's properly a wife!'

Romance was the furthest thing from Hal's mind when he went to look for his young bride. In fact, he was already beginning to regret falling in with her father's suggestion, and knew he would not have done so had she not been so damnably attractive. It was at least ten years since he had thought seriously about a woman, and he feared that he was too old to change his solitary ways.

As he was traversing the yard, towards the barn, he caught sight of her and, in spite of his misgivings, felt a spurt of pleasure. Regardless of the cold, the sleeves of her dress were rolled up and she was wearing someone else's apron. The bucket of water she was carrying looked much too heavy for her slender figure and, as he watched, she set it down, pausing to brush a disorderly strand of hair back from her forehead.

A warm wave of affection rose up inside him, but he forced it down. Their marriage was one of convenience and he would be a fool to let his feelings get out of hand. She was so much younger, too, and that in itself made him feel vulnerable.

He was still frowning as he approached her and took the heavy bucket from her hand.

'I've an errand to run for Jacquelein,' he told her, falling into step at her side. 'I shall have to find someone else to escort you back to the château. I'm sorry, but it's rather important.'

Nicol was already regretting her decision to help nurse the wounded, and lack of sleep was beginning to tell on her, making her short-tempered and inclined to self-pity.

Our marriage means nothing to him, she thought; he can't wait to get away from me. Lifting her head proudly, she said, 'Please don't concern yourself with me. I'd rather stay here. There's no need to bother anyone else.'

The practical side of him saw the sense of her argument, but he was still unsure. 'I shall be away all night. I think I'd feel happier knowing you were safe at the château.'

'I shall be perfectly all right here,' she insisted. 'The other girls need help. It's time I made myself useful.'

'Where will you sleep?'

She already knew that the other girls had made up beds behind the sacks and boxes in the barn.

'I can sleep with Michelle,' she replied shortly, then, relenting in the face of his obvious concern, added, 'I will be all right, truly I will.'

He shrugged and set the heavy bucket down by the barn door. 'As you wish ... I should get back some time tomorrow.'

For a moment she thought he was going to kiss her and, without being aware of it, she tensed. His frown deepened and he stepped back.

'Take care,' she told him self-consciously.

She watched him thoughtfully as he walked off towards the horses, a tall, athletic figure with the undisguised bearing of a soldier. He was so sure of himself, so incredibly self-sufficient, that she doubted that she would ever get to know him well. He would be kind to her, as he would be to anyone, but his life would remain his own and she would not be permitted to interfere in it.

At least he hadn't kissed her, pretending an affection he did not feel. Then, irrationally, she felt a pang of regret, wondering what it would be like to feel his well-shaped mouth against her own. If she was honest, she had to admit that she found him attractive, but it was going to be desperately hard to feel anything else for a man so uncommunicative and cold.

With a sigh, she picked up the bucket and entered the barn. The stench of sweat and sickness hit her like a wall, turning her stomach and making her shudder. She walked resolutely across to where the peasant girl called Michelle was tending a young man with a mutilated arm, and, setting down the water, bent to help. The arm was cut to the bone and the sight made her gag.

'It will have to be stitched,' Michelle said tightly. 'It really should have been done before.'

As the other girl worked, Nicol wiped the sweat from the young man's face and held his other hand comfortingly. She felt so useless in the face of his pain, and was glad when he fainted before the operation was completed.

Over the next few hours she gradually came to realise just how much her father had sheltered her from the realities of war. She helped to change dressings and saw sights so dreadfully gory that, had it not been for her natural compassion, she would have turned and fled. Michelle worked quietly, her lips pressed firmly together, and Nicol knew that the girl's stomach was really no stronger than her own.

There were so many wounded that not all of them could be accommodated in the barn. Many lay beneath rudely constructed shelters with little to protect them from the cold. Blankets and dressings were in short supply and laudanum virtually nonexistent. The two girls in charge of the wounded worked ceaselessly, helped by the occasional visits of a village doctor.

Nicol learnt to clean and bind wounds, working harder than ever before. She fetched water and emptied slop buckets and, when she was too exhausted to do anything else, sat comforting and soothing dying men. Most of them were peasants, many no older than herself, and they were all so pitifully grateful for her incompetent help.

If the day seemed interminable, the night that followed was even worse, and it was almost dawn before she could creep away to her pallet and rest. Even then, she found it difficult to sleep with the groans of the wounded filling her ears, but she was desperately tired and, eventually, her body demanded its due.

When she awoke, it was to find the place filling with light from the single, unglazed window. Michelle was shaking her shoulder gently; more water was required and, without a word of complaint, she went to fetch it.

Outside the camp was slowly coming to life as people dragged themselves from uncomfortable sleep and began the business of maintaining life in such squalor. In the early morning light, the ragged shelters and churned-up mud looked particularly depressing. The place smelt unwholesome, too—of acid smoke and stagnant water. It was like one of the worst nightmares she had ever experienced, with the added horror of knowing she was not going to wake up.

She was struck by how gaunt everyone looked, and there was a listlessness in the children's faces that really pulled at her heart.

This can't go on indefinitely, she thought, conscious of a man coughing uncontrollably as he huddled outside his tent.

A young officer came out of one of the more sophisticated shelters to place a billy of water over the smouldering fire. She recognised him as Jacques Marchmont, the son of one of her neighbours, and impulsively called out a greeting. They had often played together and she felt a rush of pleasure at the sight of his pleasant, familiar face.

'Nicolette! What on earth are you doing here?' he exclaimed, with a mixture of surprise and concern.

Like most of the men he had lost weight, and there was a new sadness behind his youthful charm. Then he smiled, the same boyish, encouraging smile she knew so well.

'I'm helping with the wounded,' she told him, and he nodded approvingly.

'I'm sorry about your father. I wanted to come to the funeral, only I was ordered to lead a foraging party.'

He seemed so genuinely upset by the matter that she reached for his hand. 'Papa wouldn't have minded, you must know that. It's this awful war—it controls us all.'

'You're a sweet girl, Nicol . . . and now you're married! I must say I was surprised, but Hal Grantly is a decent man and at least he'll be able to offer you security.' His eyes ran over her appreciatively, noting the way she had matured, and his smile held a hint of regret. 'In other times I might have cherished ambitions that way myself. We always got on well together, didn't we?'

His wistfulness seemed to release all the pent-up emotion inside her and her eyes filled with tears.

'Oh, lord! I didn't mean to upset you,' he groaned. 'You're not going to cry, are you?'

'No, of course not,' she protested, but nevertheless found it impossible to prevent herself.

With a grunt of embarrassment, he pulled her to him, unconsciously rubbing his hands across her back.

Having once begun to cry, she found herself quite unable to stop; there was just so much to weep for— the loss of her father and the home she treasured, the suffering of the wounded, and, of course, their cause, so noble and yet so unlikely to succeed. There was also Jacques who held her so tenderly, his own youth and happiness slipping away. Somehow, he represented all that was familiar and dear, and she realised just how little she relished escaping to England with a man she hardly knew, no matter what comfort and wealth he had to offer her.

'I don't want to go,' she confessed. 'I belong here with you and the others. If I had been a boy Father wouldn't have dreamt of sending me away.'

Jacques drew a surprisingly clean handkerchief from his pocket and offered it to her, smiling awkwardly. 'It's not that bad. When all this is over you'll be able to return to La Vendée. Hal's very fond of France—besides, he's the heir to his grandmother's property now.'

He was so sympathetic and kind, something much more than a dear friend, and, although she did not believe his words, she was grateful for them. Impulsively she reached up to kiss his cheek.

She had no idea how appealing she looked with her lips slightly parted and her eyes bright with tears, and somehow Jacques could not help himself. Bending his head, he kissed her full on the lips. It was no childish peck but the full-blooded kiss of a man for a woman; it was also a kiss of goodbye. Nicol recognised it for what it was, and not only permitted it but responded shyly, finding comfort in the circle of his arms.

'You will come and see me before you leave?' he asked, drawing away, his voice unusually husky.

She nodded and smiled a little tremulously. 'Yes... I'd better get back to work... I only came out for some water,' and, picking up the forgotten bucket, she hurried across the farmyard.

The pump had seen more use over the past few days than it had since it was built and was not working at all efficiently. In spite of the cold, Nicol found herself sweating as she laboured away at the handle. Finally she paused and, brushing a strand of damp hair back from her face, scowled in disgust at the small amount of water in the bucket.

'Allow me, *madame*,' said a smooth voice at her elbow.

Turning, she saw a slim, dark-haired man of about her husband's age. He was smiling broadly, revealing a row of immaculately white teeth, and, if his attitude was a little familiar, then she failed to notice.

'We live in sad times when a lady such as yourself has to labour like a common skivvy,' he continued. 'If you were my bride then I should be taking better care of you.'

A sharp retort was on her lips, but he stopped it with a laugh. 'No, I should carry you off to my castle and shower you with all kinds of delights. With that hair you remind me of a fairy princess and should be treated as such.'

In spite of herself, she smiled.

'There, it is full,' he said, glancing down at the bucket, 'and now I shall carry it for you.'

'That's really not necessary.'

'But, *madame*, it is,' he told her, his eyes twinkling engagingly. 'It will be my good deed for the day, and after it I can engage in all kinds of villainy with a clear conscience.'

'You're outrageous!' she chided, struggling unsuccessfully to conceal her amusement. 'Who are you?'

'Maurice Mathurin,' he replied, bowing extravagantly over her hand. 'The last of the noble and impoverished de Cruzats, and very much at your service! Now, if you will give me your arm, I will assist you across this unspeakable mud!'

Almost against her will, Nicol found herself responding to him. He was good company and his mocking courtliness was a refreshing contrast to the grey squalor that surrounded them.

'Do you know my husband?' she asked, anxious to remind him of her married state.

'Who does not know the estimable Hal?' he answered, a little sharply. 'He shares the confidence of our young General, and was he not wounded defending Monsieur Henri's back at Château Gontier? But, tell me, what is your noble husband doing that is important enough to keep him from his bride?'

She shrugged. 'Something for Jacquelein. It seems his duty comes first and I must learn to be patient.'

'He rode out alone, you know, a most unusual circumstance, and his men have no idea where he has gone. You must find it rather disconcerting.'

'I hadn't really thought about it,' she replied honestly, 'but I'm sure he can take care of himself.'

'Oh, undoubtedly.'

By this time they had reached the barn and, turning, she reached for the bucket. 'Thank you for your help, *monsieur.*'

'It has been a pleasure, my dear.' His hand touched hers and he maintained the contact a little longer than was necessary. 'I have enjoyed your company and shall look out for you again. Your husband is a fool to leave you so soon.'

She thanked him, this time more coldly, not quite sure whether she liked him or not. Hal was her husband and, rightly or wrongly, it was not de Cruzat's place to criticise him.

He must have read her mind, for he gave her the most charming smile and said, 'I'm sure he knows his friends will look after you. It is probably only his English background that makes him so unromantic.'

That was certainly true and she could not help wishing that it were otherwise. De Cruzat, or even young Jacques, would surely have been more aware of how to treat a new wife. In fact, when she returned to her work, she found it impossible to banish her handsome new acquaintance from her mind.

CHAPTER THREE

FOR the next few hours Nicolette continued with her self-imposed drudgery. With time she became accustomed to the smell and the suffering, and yet she still could not match the stamina of the other girls. Eventually she was forced to rest and sat dejectedly on one of the packing-cases at the side of the barn.

'Go outside and get some fresh air,' Michelle told her. 'You're just not used to such heavy work.'

'You and Marie have done far more than I,' she replied, despising herself for her weakness. 'I shall be all right in a minute.'

The peasant girl shrugged and turned away, leaving her feeling more inadequate than ever. Depression settled over her like a dark cloud and she felt so utterly alone that she would have welcomed even her husband's company. Self-pity welled up inside her, and with it came the warning of tears. She swallowed hard and reached for her cloak, deciding that it would be better to go for a walk than disgrace herself in front of the other girls.

It was a welcome change to get out of the barn and into the fresh air. The wind was bitterly cold but at least it smelt clean. She gathered her cloak more closely around herself and breathed deeply, lifting her head to look up at the scudding clouds. In spite of her tiredness, the position of the pale sun showed it to be not yet noon.

Some peasants were roasting a rabbit over one of the fires. She had not eaten for hours, but the smell still turned her stomach. Maurice de Cruzat seemed to appear from nowhere and fell into step at her side.

'You're looking pale, my dear,' he told her. 'I hope you're not working too hard.'

'Oh, don't you start!' she snapped. 'I'm doing no more than anyone else!'

He held up his hands in mock horror. 'Peace, *madame!* I did not mean to offend you. I was simply showing a little friendly concern.'

She made the effort to look at him and found her irritation melting under his amused and sympathetic gaze. 'I'm sorry. I'm afraid I'm tired.'

'And hungry, too,' he guessed.

She shook her head.

'When did you last eat?' he asked sternly.

'Not since yesterday, but I'm really not hungry. There was food in the barn, only I couldn't face it.'

'Eating in there! I should think not! I've fresh bread and cheese in my bivouac and I insist you share it with me. You've gone past hunger and that can be dangerous.'

'But Hal might not . . .'

'He would thank me for taking care of his beautiful young wife. I'm a friend.'

When it was put like that she could see no reason to refuse, and she let him take her arm and guide her off towards his tent. His touch was strangely comforting, and she relaxed as she sat down with him and began to share his simple meal.

He was thoughtful, witty and sympathetic, and at a time when she needed friendship as never before, and inevitably her heart warmed towards him. Her father's death had left a great gap in her life, and, although she was unaware of it, she was desperate for someone to fill it. De Cruzat flattered her, but not overtly, drawing out secrets and gaining her confidence with consummate ease.

'I first noticed you several months ago at the St Fleurants' ball,' he admitted. 'I wanted desperately to speak to you, but you were always surrounded by so many wealthy young men. It seems that war has its compensations, after all.'

Nicol was surprised, thinking that if she had seen him before then she would surely have remembered. He was a little below average height, but even so had the kind of good looks that would have stood out in a crowd.

'I ought to be getting back,' she told him hesitantly.

He smiled sadly. 'I suppose so, but first let me show you my latest acquisition. You've said you like horses, and my Audace is a really superb beast, beyond anything I could normally afford. He's not easy to control, and after his master's death the widow was only too willing to exchange him for my own beast plus a ridiculously small sum of money... Do you know, some of the peasants are actually eating their horses?' He saw her pale, and shrugged. 'I don't like it, either, but the poor devils are starving. To them the oxen that pull their wagons are worth far more than a single worn-out horse.'

Taking her hand, he led her between the trees to where a rough pen had been constructed for the officers' mounts. Audace was certainly an impressive beast, completely black with a high, arched neck and rippling muscles.

'His name suits him,' she said, as she rubbed his silken nose.

Her own mare was also in the pen, and she laughed as the little roan came forward for her share of the fuss.

De Cruzat could not take his eyes from the girl at his side and was all too aware of the frustrating weeks since he had made love to a presentable woman. When she started back towards the camp, he walked with her, his hand resting lightly beneath her elbow.

Nicol was very conscious of his proximity, and the fact that they were alone made her feel suddenly uneasy. Surreptitiously, she tried to draw away but he caught her hand and, laughing softly, drew her to him. She knew a shameless moment of pleasure as his arms enclosed her. Part of her enjoyed the warmth and security of his embrace, but her conscience could not be stilled.

'Please, no,' she muttered, struggling gently to free herself. 'This can't happen. Remember that I'm married.'

'Married be damned!' he growled. 'Grantly doesn't really care for you or he would not have deserted you so soon. It was a marriage of convenience; the whole camp is aware of that. Take my advice—enjoy the security of his name, but find your pleasure elsewhere. Grantly certainly will. Lovely Nicol, let me show you what love is all about.'

As he spoke, his hand was roving down her back and across her hips with an intimacy she had not previously experienced.

'No,' she choked, appalled. 'Let me go or we shall both regret it.'

She tried to pull away but, in spite of his apparent gentleness, he held her securely against him.

'Please, Maurice, let me go!'

In reply, he bent to kiss her and against her will she began to respond. There was something comforting in the soft movement of his hand across her back.

'Maurice...' She opened her mouth to protest again and he took the opportunity to deepen the kiss, his hard, lithe body pushing her back against the tree.

Aware of his rising passion, she began to panic but, when she tried to pull away, his arms imprisoned her like bands of steel. She did not know at what point she became angry, but suddenly she was and she began to struggle in earnest, desperately trying to turn away from his demanding mouth. She felt sure she would die of suffocation, and wondered how on earth she had let herself be manipulated into such a position.

She was just beginning to realise that she was going to have to resort to something drastic, when suddenly she was free. She heard a bone-crunching blow, and the next moment de Cruzat was sprawled at her feet, his eyes glazed and his mouth pouring blood.

Her husband's face was a mask of fury, his eyes blazing with an almost fanatical light.

'Keep your lecherous hands off my wife or I'll kill you, so help me I will!' he grated.

For a moment Nicol felt weak with relief, then, as she realised her situation, shame and embarrassment overcame all else. Hal glanced at her without the slightest hint of tenderness or compassion; in fact she thought she had never seen eyes so hard. He did not even ask if she was all right, but, taking hold of her arm, dragged her roughly back towards the camp, not stopping until they reached a secluded spot behind the barn.

'How dare you, *madame*?' he choked, ashen-faced and almost beside himself with rage. 'How dare you encourage the likes of de Cruzat? The man's a renowned lecher! You may regard our marriage as simply one of convenience, but I have given you the protection of my name and will not have it dragged in the gutter. I'd have thought twice about it, I can tell you, if I'd known you had the makings of a whore!'

She gasped at the word and swung her hand up to strike his face, the force of the blow making him wince. For a moment she thought he was going to hit her back but, instead, he reached out to grasp her arms, letting his fingers bite cruelly into her flesh.

'If you ever do that again, I shall knock you flat!' he snarled, shaking her until her teeth rattled.

'You're detestable,' she managed to say. 'I hate you and wish I'd never married you!'

'But you have, *madame*, and now you'll damned well do as I say. I'm going to find someone to escort you back to the château immediately. Obviously, you are too immature to contend with the hazards in camp!'

She was going to protest but, at that precise moment, de Cruzat came storming around the side of the building, his face contorted with fury. 'You'll give me satisfaction for that blow, Grantly!'

Hal's reply was not at all gentlemanly, short and very much to the point.

The Frenchman flushed to the roots of his hair and his hand clawed at his sword. 'Do I have to call you coward?'

Hal turned to face him, suddenly much calmer, a warning sign to those who knew him well. 'As you wish. Name your seconds!'

'Rochais and Claviere will act for me.'

Hal nodded curtly. 'I will send my own seconds to them within the hour. I trust you have no objections to swords.'

Nicol was horrified by this turn of events and tentatively reached out to grasp her husband's sleeve. 'Hal, you must not...'

'Must not?' His hard grey eyes swung in her direction, piercing her like spears. 'It is my duty to protect my wife. Come on, you're going back to the château this instant.'

Seizing her hand, he dragged her off towards the horses, oblivious to her difficulty in keeping up with his long strides.

'Don't fight him, Hal, please,' she pleaded, pulling against him with all her strength.

For just a moment he paused, his expression coldly considering. 'You should have thought of the consequences before you began flirting. I wonder who you are more concerned for, Maurice or myself?'

'I don't want either of you hurt because of me,' she replied truthfully, stung by his implication. 'Maurice is nothing to me, but he doesn't deserve to be killed.'

She was also desperately worried for Hal, yet found it impossible to voice her feelings, and his mocking laughter didn't help.

'You're forgetting, my dear, that *he* challenged *me*. My God! Have you any idea how good he is with a sword?'

'Then you mustn't go on with this foolishness,' she faltered, embarrassingly close to tears. 'I...I'm sorry, truly I am. It meant nothing... I'll get Maurice to apologise, too. He mistook my friendship for something more. It's certainly not worth risking your life over.'

By this time they had reached the horses and she was almost sobbing with frustration. 'Please, Hal. Let's just leave. We could be in England before anyone realises it.'

He did not bother to answer and, retrieving her tackle from the nearby lean-to, began to saddle her horse. Deciding that she needed a warmer cloak, he sent her off to fetch one of his own and, all the time, his attention did not waver from his task. Only the stiffness of his movements betrayed his continuing anger.

When Nicol returned, young Marchmont was waiting with him, mounted and obviously ready to ride.

'Jacques will take you back to the château,' Hal informed her coldly, then turned abruptly and went striding off towards the farmhouse.

She had no option but to follow her appointed escort, and rode off feeling very much like a chastened child. A little innocent fun had blown up in her face and the likely consequences were beyond anything she wanted to contemplate. She knew she had placed her husband in an invidious position, and had to admit that no honourable man could have acted differently, but what a disastrous start it was to their marriage. She felt foolish and somehow diminished and doubted that she would ever be forgiven.

'How good a swordsman is de Cruzat?' she asked after a while.

Jacques snorted, his previous cold silence making it quite clear what he thought of her behaviour. 'Too good!'

'And Hal?'

'He's capable enough and he keeps a cool head. I wouldn't like to put money on the outcome, if that's what you want to know. For heaven's sake, Nicol! What possessed you? De Cruzat's known as a libertine and a rake.'

She wanted to deny that it was her fault; certainly she hadn't meant any harm. Unfortunately, she wasn't entirely sure in her own mind that she hadn't encouraged the fellow.

'Hal, of all people, didn't deserve such treatment,' Jacques continued.

'You're obviously on his side!'

'Yes, as a matter of fact, I am! He's risked his life for me on more than one occasion.'

'I find him pompous and overbearing,' she replied defensively, 'and quite, *quite* unfeeling.'

In spite of her words she was more than a little concerned for him and she certainly did not want his death on her conscience. The duel had to be stopped, and it was only a matter of minutes before the solution occurred to her. She had simply to report the matter to Jacquelein. He was already short of officers and unlikely to tolerate such a foolish waste of life.

'I'm going to see Monsieur Henri,' she declared, turning her horse.

'No! Nicol, wait! You can't interfere in a affair of honour...' Then, with an exasperated oath, Jacques turned back, too.

It was strange, but in the past hour any envy he had felt for Grantly had disappeared and he was now inclined only to pity him for possessing such a self-willed and troublesome wife.

He watched Nicol gallop ahead of him, her hair spilling behind her like a dark cloud, and wondered why he had never before noticed the arrogant tilt of her head, the pride in her ramrod-stiff spine. She was a beauty, all right, and still a little naïve, but there was a passion in her and a steely determination that he found more than a little daunting. He would never have been able to handle her, he admitted, and decided that even the quietly confident Grantly was going to have a difficult time.

Having come to a decision, Nicol felt much better. She was still plagued by an uncomfortable feeling of guilt but was convinced that she would be able to put matters right; even to the point of visualising Hal thanking her for her intervention.

A weak, winter sun was beginning to melt the frost on the grass and trees and its brief warmth seemed to add to her optimism. Besides, she had known Henri Jacquelein for years and felt none of the trepidation another might have on approaching him about such a delicate matter.

They reached the camp in the middle of the afternoon and rode straight up to the ancient farm-house, Nicol on tenterhooks in case her husband should notice her before she had accomplished her mission. She was also filled with an inexplicable sense of urgency, although Jacques had declared that the duel was unlikely to take place until the morrow.

Having rehearsed exactly what she would say to the young General, it came as something of a shock to find he was out, and close questioning of the sentry did little to discover his whereabouts or when he was likely to return. She was forced to wait in a fever of anxiety, pacing restlessly up and down before the hard bench in front of the fire.

The time dragged interminably, one hour seeming like ten. The delay proved too much for young Marchmont, who declared he would take no part in the matter and went off, leaving her alone with her conscience and her fears. In her mind she could already see Hal lying dead upon the frost-kissed grass and she was surprised how much the vision upset her.

Jacquelein finally returned around three, accompanied by the dark-haired German, Jean Nicolas Stofflet, and another younger officer.

'Thank God, you're back,' blurted Nicol, too upset to consider being discreet in front of the other men. 'You must put a stop to it. It really is too ridiculous for words.'

'What on earth are you talking about?' the young General asked irritably. 'Why aren't you at the château with Hal?'

As she explained, his expression hardened, making him look unnervingly unapproachable.

'Dear God!' he finally exploded. 'As if I didn't have enough to worry about without my officers flying at each other's throats!' He turned abruptly to Stofflet. 'Did you know anything of this?'

The tall German shook his head, his brows drawing together over his hawk-like nose. 'I most certainly did not. We shall have to put a stop to it or there will be other such incidents. I thought Grantly had more sense. Not that he hasn't been greatly provoked,' he added, turning to glare at Nicol.

Jacquelein gave her shoulder a reassuring squeeze. 'You were right to come to me, although I doubt that Hal will see it that way. In spite of his general lack of manners, de Cruzat's a damned fine swordsman, and your husband has more courage than sense! Do you know when this affair is supposed to take place?'

Before she could reply, the third officer, a thin, sallow young Breton who had been looking increasingly ill at ease, cleared his throat. 'I believe about now, my General. Dupont and Darcy are to second Grantly.'

'Imbeciles!' growled Monsieur Henri. 'Why couldn't they have come to me? Where is it to be, Briac? Where?'

'In a clearing to the east of camp.'

With another oath Jacquelein turned towards the door. Quick as he was, Nicol was before him.

'Where in God's name do you think you are going?' he demanded. 'Show some sense, girl! There'll be enough scandal without your presence making it worse. Wait here!'

Even the most hardened campaigner knew that when the young General used that tone he was not to be defied. Nicol swallowed the protest that had been rising in her throat, and nodded.

'Well, Jean! What are you waiting for?' Jacquelein asked, rounding on the older Stofflet. 'De Cruzat is under your command, I believe, and I could do with the authority of your advanced years!'

Henry Grantly stood alone, a hard, set expression on his face as he watched the seconds walking towards him across the damp grass.

'De Cruzat wishes to know if you're willing to apologise?' Darcy asked.

'Certainly not,' he replied uncompromisingly.

The last-minute request was a mere formality; de Cruzat neither expected an apology nor wanted one.

'Then we shall proceed.' The young man gave a stiff bow and walked away.

Hal turned and stripped off his coat, watching as his opponent did likewise. De Cruzat also removed his boots but Hal decided against this, being more afraid of slipping on the wet grass. The Frenchman drew his sword and flexed it experimentally. He was good—too damned good if all the reports were to be believed.

Why had Nicol chosen to flirt with him of all men? It must be something of a record, Grantly concluded, to be married and all but cuckolded within the space of a day. The girl's air of frank innocence had fooled him completely. Women were all the same, so why, after all these years, had he been rash enough to assume responsibility for one? Like it or not, he was stuck with her, but if he survived the encounter then he would bloody well see she toed the line.

He watched de Cruzat's point describing swift silver circles in the air, and wondered belatedly if he should have chosen pistols. At least with them there was a considerable element of luck. Pride had motivated his choice and he had been arrogant enough to think he could match the Frenchman, in spite of his awesome reputation.

'Are you ready?' one of the seconds asked.

He caught de Cruzat's eye and nodded grimly. The Frenchman gave an ironical salute and they began, tentatively at first, each feeling their way. Hal's jaw tightened as he realised how much skill and stamina he was going to need to win through.

Gradually the pace increased as they thrust and parried with a vengeance, moving rapidly backwards and forwards across the small clearing. It soon became obvious to everyone watching that de Cruzat intended more than to just wound. Several times his point swept towards Hal's chest, only to be parried at the last minute.

He's certainly better than I, thought Hal with commendable detachment, but he's not as fit. If I can keep him off long enough then I may yet have the advantage.

De Cruzat lunged, feinted and his point slipped through Hal's guard. Only the Englishman's speed saved him as, with a swift downward stroke, he swept the blade aside. It slipped across his arm, tearing his shirt but failing to draw blood.

De Cruzat laughed unpleasantly. 'Nearly, my friend . . . nearly!'

Over the next few minutes, the world ceased to exist for Hal, and he was aware of nothing save his opponent's sword-tip and the schooled movements of his own right arm. Like thin bars of light, the swords flashed in the sunshine, the clash of steel on steel the only sound above the hissing and sobbing of his laboured breath. His throat felt scraped and his arm began to throb, but miraculously de Cruzat too was tiring. The Frenchman was finding his opponent worthier than he had thought, lacking in flair perhaps, but fast, strong and irritatingly cool.

'What's it like to have a wife who's a whore?' he asked suddenly.

Apart from a slight tightening of his jaw, Hal gave no indication that he had even heard the taunt.

'Of course, her reputation was known to me, or I would not have acted as I did. You should have seen her draped all over young Marchmont!'

'Shut up and fight,' hissed Hal, going into the attack with renewed ferocity.

'The face...of...an angel. How unfortunate she...has...the soul of a harlot!'

In his desire to taunt, de Cruzat let his concentration lapse. The words had barely left his lips before Hal's point was through his guard and into his upper arm. Immediately, the Englishman drew back. He might have felt like murder but the tradition of fair play was too strong in him, drummed into him in the nursery and reinforced on the playing fields of his school.

De Cruzat was labouring under no such disadvantage and, as Hal's point dropped, he leapt forward. Only with the most clumsy and unorthodox stroke was his blade swept aside, but his charge overbalanced him. His feet slipped on the wet grass and down he went, sprawling helplessly on his back. Cold steel was at his throat, and yet he remained defiant to the last.

'English pig!' he grated. 'I wish you joy of your overheated bitch!'

Hal did not really see the man at his feet for a red haze of fury filled his mind, highlighting memories he had thought long forgotten. Hurt and anger spread through him and, for one brief, heart-stopping moment, present and past became one, and for one angelic face he saw another. With a strangely animal groan he drew back his arm and thrust with all his might burying his point deep in the ground within an inch of de Cruzat's neck.

Jacquelein and Stofflet had arrived just in time to witness the end of the conflict and even the usually inscrutable German breathed a sigh of relief. Turning away, Hal collected his coat and walked past them, his face set in a grim mask.

Nicol was still waiting at the farmhouse. She was watching anxiously out of the window and saw him come striding across the grass.

'Thank God, you're all right,' she muttered, moving hesitantly towards him.

'Are you, *madame*?' he grated, and, glancing into his face, she thought she had never seen anyone look so cynical and hard. 'What the devil are you doing here, anyway? Can't you be trusted to do a thing you're told? I don't want you here!'

'I was worried,' she admitted. 'It was all my fault and I asked Henri to stop the fight.'

A mocking smile touched his lips, in no way reaching his eyes which remained like chips of glass. 'So you have a conscience. How novel in one of your sex! Doubtless you will soon outgrow it.'

Pushing past her he entered the room where he had left his bedroll and his few possessions, returning a moment later with a bottle in his hand. 'Jacques shall take you back to the château immediately, and this time stay there! Now you're my wife you will damned well do as you're told, even if I have to take a horse-whip to you!'

Nicol lifted her head defiantly, resentment and anger overcoming all else. 'Will I see you again? It's a matter of complete indifference to me.'

He gave a harsh laugh. 'Don't worry, *madame*; I'll honour our contract. I'll take you to England, away from all this...but, by God, you'll learn to behave. I've given you my name and I'll not have it tarnished. If you so much as look at another man, I'll kill him! I spared de Cruzat because the Army needs him. Next time I shall not be so lenient.'

Then, turning on his heel, he went out, leaving her feeling stunned and unsure. There had been such anger in him, and something more...a kind of empty despair. He had looked like a man who had faced death and was sorry that he had been able to walk away.

For a moment she remained where she was, trying to come to terms with conflicting emotions of sympathy and fear. It was as if there was a weight in her stomach and she felt more ashamed than ever before. Worst of all, she was aware of an overwhelming desire to burst into tears. She, who usually had no patience with crying women, wanted only to cling to her husband while he comforted her and dried her tears.

Damn him! she thought, taking refuge in anger. If he wasn't going to forgive her then she certainly wasn't going to crawl.

When it became obvious that he was not returning, she did the only thing she could—collected her cloak and went to ask Monsieur Henri to find her an escort back to the château.

'Is Hal all right?' the young General asked when he came to see her off.

'He's very angry,' she replied.

Jacquelein smiled gently as he ran his hand soothingly across the neck of her restless horse. 'He's a good man, Nicolette. Don't let your pride come between you. Don't be afraid to apologise.'

Nicol could only wish that it was as simple as that. Her husband's feelings ran more deeply than she felt comfortable with. In fact she had found the repressed violence in him positively awesome. Why couldn't he have been as easygoing and predictable as young Jacques? she asked herself. Why, oh why, had her father married her to such a complicated and hostile man?

CHAPTER FOUR

THREE days without her husband only served to make Nicol dread her next meeting with him the more. In her mind she went over and over the events leading up to the duel, and with each reconstruction saw him as a more formidable figure than before.

The weather had deteriorated, becoming increasingly stormy and somehow complementing her mood. As she walked through the woods, she lifted her face to the sky. Heavy storm clouds swirled dizzily above her, pushed along by the same bitter, rushing wind that ruffled the dead leaves and tossed them playfully across her feet.

Taking advantage of her solitude, she indulged in tears, weeping until she felt completely drained. Then, because she wanted to keep her weakness a secret, she continued to walk, not turning back towards the château until the evidence of her unhappiness had faded from her face.

What a lecture Madame Jacquelein had given her on hearing what had happened at the camp, and, put into words, her actions did sound both immoral and immature. She sighed deeply as she headed back across the lawns towards the ancient house, acknowledging that there was nothing she could do but reconcile herself to her new life and make her peace with the rather frightening man she had married.

She was quite unaware of the dampness of her coat or the thick mud that clung to her boots, conscious only of the wind and losing herself in its roar. When the gardener's Brittany spaniel bounded forward to greet her, she patted it and absently pulled its ears, not at all concerned that its great paws had soiled her clothes. It was only when she saw the mud smearing the hall floor that she realised her state and, aware of a lack of servants, guiltily removed her boots. As she was doing this, she heard voices coming from the drawing-room and her stomach turned over. *He* was there.

'You must be patient,' she heard the Marchioness say. 'She is really only a child and her father spoilt her abominably.'

'There speaks Methuselah!' Madame Jacquelein was scarcely older than herself, and Nicol could almost hear Hal's smile.

'My case is quite different; I've been married longer and I have a child ... She's a fine girl, Hal. Just give her time. Her behaviour was simply the result of being too closely confined. Her mother died when she was very young and her father was always over-protective. She's had no experience of men like de Cruzat. You should never have left her on her own, you know.'

He sighed. 'I've no experience of young women. I only hope I haven't taken on too much.'

'You'll manage, I'm sure, and she'll soon grow to love and respect you.'

Nicol had to pass the open drawing-room door in order to reach the stairs. For a moment she considered flight, but common sense told her she would have to face Hal sooner or later. With shaking hands, she removed her coat, and after attempting to brush the mud from her dress, resolutely walked forward to make her presence known.

Grantly was standing with his back to the fireplace, an almost gentle look on his lean face as he contemplated the Marchioness.

'Monsieur Henri is a lucky man,' he told her, with the air of one who has made a surprising discovery.

She laughed. 'Coming from you, Henry Grantly, that's quite a compliment!'

As she entered the room, Nicol was uncomfortably aware of her dishevelled appearance and wished with all her heart that she had taken the time to change. Her husband turned towards her and it was as if a shutter had come down behind his eyes.

For a moment or two they studied each other, each trying to see through the other's reserve. She noticed that he was no longer in uniform but was wearing a dark coat and rather nondescript breeches. The lace at his cuffs and throat was unusually modest, so that, had it not been for his naturally imperious bearing, he would have passed for a lawyer or a clerk. He seemed a trifle pale and the grey eyes that regarded her were smoky with tiredness.

'Good afternoon, Nicol,' he said, bowing coldly. 'I trust you are pleased to see me.'

'That depends on the state of your temper,' she replied, and afterwards could have bitten her tongue.

Surprisingly, it was he who apologised, although she could see the effort it cost him. 'I'm sorry, Nicol, perhaps we should begin again...I hope you are keeping well.'

That broke the ice somewhat and, in spite of herself, she responded with a smile. If he was willing to make the effort, the least she could do was to meet him halfway.

'I'll leave you two alone,' Madame Jacquelein muttered, moving tactfully towards the door.

'No!'

Hal frowned at Nicol's outburst.

'What I mean is, I'd rather go and change,' she stammered, glancing appealingly at her friend. 'You stay and entertain Hal.'

She felt gauche and childish and was sure she looked a sight. She had no way of knowing that her husband was desperately trying to harden his heart against her lack of guile. Her clothes were dirty, her hair a tangled mess, and yet her beauty shone through it all—surely he had never seen such deep brown eyes!

The Marchioness smiled. 'Of course, Nicol. Go and make yourself pretty while I tell Hal all about the château and our remarkable hostess.'

Nicol sorted frantically through her modest collection of dresses and wished that she had not had to leave so many behind. After much heart-searching, she selected a rather sophisticated dress of light green crêpe, and, trembling with apprehension, put it on. The low neckline was extremely flattering, and, after brushing her hair vigorously, she arranged the shining curls on top of her head.

She worked quickly and efficiently, wanting to look well but in the minimum of time, her instinct telling her that it would not do for Hal to realise that she had taken so much trouble on his account. As a finishing touch, she fastened a green velvet choker, adorned by a single cameo, around her neck, and, after pinching her cheeks to enhance their colour, hurried downstairs.

By this time her husband was seated comfortably on the sofa, a glass of cognac in his hand. He stood up politely as she entered and complimented her on her changed appearance.

'I'll leave you to talk,' Madame Jacquelein told them and, after glancing compassionately from one strained face to the other, tactfully left the room.

'Come and join me.' Hal's smile seemed a little forced as he gestured towards a chair, not sitting down himself until Nicol had settled back against the soft cushions.

She had to force herself to meet his eyes. 'I . . . I'm aware that I owe you an apology. I behaved badly in the extreme.'

'Let's forget it, shall we?' he replied sharply. 'There is nothing to be gained by raking over what is past.'

But she did not want to forget it. She wanted, in fact needed, to explain, believing that only when he understood would things really come right between them.

For a moment she sat seething in silent resentment, then asked, 'How are things at camp?'

He shrugged. 'You saw for yourself. As a matter of fact, I feel the lowest kind of animal for leaving now.'

'I hope you're not doing so on my account,' she replied quickly. 'France is my home. I'd much rather remain here.'

'You must regard England as your home now. We shan't be able to return to France for some time.' With a sigh, he stood up and, after refilling his glass, returned to stand in front of the fire. 'It's time I went home. Monsieur Henri has entrusted me with a letter for Pitt. We must leave tomorrow.'

Tomorrow! She thought she was prepared for such an eventuality, but her stomach lurched. 'So soon...? Couldn't we put it off for just one day?'

'Putting it off won't change how you feel...and the letter is important.'

'In that case, I'd better go and pack.'

'It shouldn't take you long,' he replied with almost a hint of pity. 'We can only take hand luggage, I'm afraid—jewels, washing things and perhaps a change of clothes. This part of the country may not be wholeheartedly Republican, but travel is still danger- ous. You're an aristo, my dear, from the top of your head to the ends of your pretty little toes, and if we are taken we shall probably lose our lives.'

When she paled, his expression softened a little and, walking across to her, he tilted her face to look up at him. 'I shall take care of you. Just trust me.'

'I do,' she replied, for whatever she might think of him he certainly inspired confidence.

She remembered something her father had said about natural leadership and realised that Hal had this quality in abundance. When she smiled, he re- turned it with one of surprising warmth.

'That's better,' he said. 'Now, considering I'm a guest here, don't you think it's time I met my hostess?'

Nicol laughed. 'Madame Lamarte is expecting you. She's a real character, you know, almost ninety and dreadfully frail, and yet she has the courage of a lion. I do believe she regrets not being able to fight alongside you men. As it is, she's opened her château to us... I only hope she won't suffer for it later.'

He opened the door for her and followed her up the imposing staircase, his hand resting lightly be- neath her elbow. She was disconcertingly aware of him, of his size and strength, and her breathing quickened as she felt his thigh brushing against her hip. At the top of the stairs, he turned to glance down at her and she felt herself blushing. He frowned slightly but made no comment as she guided him along to the old lady's door.

'Come in, my boy,' commanded a surprisingly vibrant voice. 'Don't stand on ceremony. Come in and let me get a good look at you.'

Nicol wondered how anyone could call Henry Grantly a boy, and yet he was grinning like one as he went forward to kiss the old lady's hand.

Hortense Lamarte was small and bird-like with thin grey hair and a parchment-coloured complexion. Her face was incredibly lined, reminding Nicol of a wizened monkey. Only her eyes remained young and alert, with an impish humour in their depths that not even ninety years of life could extinguish. She had not lost her appreciation of handsome young men, and, glancing down at Hal's dark head, she nodded her approval.

'I knew your grandmother,' she told him, playfully tapping his cheek with her fan. 'You're not at all like her. Take after your father, do you?'

Hal nodded, his own eyes glittering with amusement. 'So I'm told.'

She sniffed. 'No wonder your mother lost her heart. Your father was several years her senior, I believe?'

'Some twenty years, ma'am, but it was a good marriage for all that.'

She then said something that Nicol couldn't quite hear, but it certainly made him laugh. His face, that she had always considered so cold and haughty, suddenly revealed an unexpected warmth and charm. He talked with the old lady for some time, courteously drawing Nicol into the conversation, and he seemed like a different man, open, relaxed, and undeniably appealing.

'She liked you,' Nicol told him as they made their way back downstairs.

He turned to her with an amused smile. 'Occasionally people do.'

'I...I...didn't mean...' Confused, she looked away, and when next she glanced up at him, the usual inscrutable mask had settled on his face.

To everyone's surprise Madame Lamarte joined her guests for dinner, dressed almost regally in a gown of dark green silk. Nicol was particularly grateful for her company, for she kept up a steady flow of conversation and all but monopolised Hal. Noticing that he was eating little, she chided him strongly.

'I'm just not used to such rich fare, ma'am,' he admitted, 'or such striking company.'

'And what's your excuse, Nicol?' The old lady's eyes swung in the girl's direction. 'You're not eating enough to keep a fly alive. No wonder you're all skin and bone.'

'Oh, I wouldn't say that,' Hal commented, giving his wife a smile of such unbridled amusement that it was impossible not to respond.

It was the nearest he had come to paying her a compliment, and she was surprised how good it made her feel.

After dinner he escorted Madame Lamarte back to her room while the other two ladies returned to the drawing-room.

'I've had Hal's things taken up to your chamber,' Madame Jacquelein told Nicol.

'Surely that's not necessary! I mean...' She stopped short in confusion.

'*He* did not complain,' laughed her friend. 'Honestly, Nicol, you're such a child. You've already spent the first two nights of your marriage apart. You can't expect the poor man to wait forever.'

The rest of the evening proved something of a strain on them all, and after a while Nicol offered to play the spinet. She had always loved music and was able to lose herself in it, forgetting all about Hal until he came over to turn the pages of her score. When she looked up to thank him, he did not return her smile and she felt a new surge of anxiety and fear.

Eventually, Madame Jacquelein cleared her throat and announced that she would retire. She ignored Nicol's look of reproach and instead kissed her on the cheek and wished her well.

'Won't you play something else?' Hal asked.

Not wanting to be alone in his company for another minute, she panicked. 'No, no, I'd rather not ... I'm tired, and I'd like to go to bed.'

His eyebrows rose quizzically and she flushed as she became aware of the significance of what she had said.

At first she thought he was going to tease her, then he shrugged. 'As you wish. If you don't mind, I'll have another couple of drinks and join you later.'

My God, he's going to get drunk, she thought, closing the door of her room behind her. It's going to be awful!

She undressed with indecent haste although she was all fingers and thumbs, then donned the most un-romantic nightdress she could find. It was made of flannel and buttoned right up to her chin. Once in bed, she tucked the covers tightly around her and lay rigidly, staring up at the old-fashioned canopy. In a moment Hal would come and expect to make her truly his wife, and she couldn't even bear to think of it. He was a virtual stranger, attractive perhaps, but too hard and unapproachable for her to feel at all easy about such intimacy between them. She glanced at the candle flickering on the table beside the bed and contemplated snuffing it out. Then, deciding that it would appear too obvious, she concluded that the only thing she could do was to feign sleep. In fact, he was such a long time coming to her that she really did begin to doze.

The opening of the door disturbed her and she heard him walk lightly across the room. She knew he was watching her, could sense it with every fibre of her body, yet she continued to lie quietly, her eyes tightly closed. Cloth rustled as he began to undress. The bed gave beneath his weight and she heard the thud of his boots as he tossed them upon the floor.

When he stood up again, she risked a peep. His back was to her and after removing his breeches, he stood as naked as the day he was born. She found she liked the sight of his broad shoulders and lean hips, and felt a quite unmaidenly desire to run her hands across his well-muscled thighs.

He's beautiful, she thought with surprise, like a Grecian hero from one of Homer's tales. His dark hair was tousled and, when he turned, she saw that there was more on his chest and . . . hurriedly she looked away.

'So you are awake,' he said softly.

'You disturbed me.' Then, as he turned back the covers, she gasped. 'Surely you're not going to get into bed like that?'

He smiled. 'Why not? It's the way I always sleep.'

As he climbed in beside her, she edged away. He did not lie down but propped himself up on one elbow, regarding her speculatively. The hard lines of his face were picked out in the candlelight, making him appear even more arrogant and hard. Reaching out a tanned hand, he eased the sheet down from her chin.

'Good God! What's that?' he demanded, catching sight of the old-fashioned nightgown. With an exasperated sigh, he bent to kiss her and it was one of the most heady sensations she had ever known.

Damn him, she thought. He shall not have me as he would any camp follower, and she forced herself to lie still and unresponsive in his arms.

He took a deep breath and drew back to study her, his thumb drawing a molten line across her cheek. 'Oh, come now, Nicol; this is not easy for me, either. The least you can do is to meet me halfway. I won't hurt you, I swear.'

When she did not reply, he tried again, kissing her tenderly, his gently probing tongue tracing her lips and his free hand stroking her hair. Her senses were full of him. Her heart was pounding in her breast and almost of their own volition, her arms crept around him. Then, as he playfully nuzzled her ear, her neck, her hair, he expertly unfastened the buttons at the neck of that abominable nightdress and slipped his hand inside to feel her breast.

She stiffened at such intimacy and pulled away, more than a little frightened of what would follow and angry at what she considered his lack of romance. He hadn't whispered one single endearment.

'I . . . I can't,' she whimpered. 'Oh, please! I need more time . . . time to learn to love you.'

'Since when has love had anything to do with it?' he demanded, his face like flint. 'You're my wife. I could take you with less finesse if I chose.'

'That would be no better than rape!'

'I very much doubt it.' His lips twisted in a contemptuous smile. 'I can usually make a woman respond to me. It would just be a matter of forcing you over your initial reluctance.' When she stiffened, he gave a bitter laugh. 'Oh, don't worry. My taste has never been for reluctant virgins. You are my wife and I shall expect children, but my pleasure I can find in more willing arms!'

He was still holding her hands and, as if to prove his point, bent to kiss her hard. This time his lips bruised her mouth, demanding a response and yet almost defying her to make one. She could scarcely breathe and, when her lips parted, he took advantage and deepened the kiss. Finally, he drew back, leaving her feeling bereft and shaken.

'I could have had you had I wanted,' he told her coldly, climbing from the bed and beginning to pull on his clothes.

'What are you doing?'

'Dressing, madam! Then I shall sleep on top of the covers. I'm not made of stone and if I lie with you I'll not be able to answer for my actions.' His voice was tight and controlled but she could sense the fury bubbling beneath the surface of his composure.

She felt inadequate and extremely immature and knew her actions had added to the bad feeling that was already between them. Turning away, she lay quietly in the darkness, crying and yet determined that he should not hear the faintest snuffle. She was still engaged in this futile struggle when, despite everything, she fell asleep.

It was just beginning to get light when she awoke, feeling gritty, heavy-eyed and conscious of a weight across her stomach. Whether by accident or intent, Hal had moved closer in the night. His face was within inches of her own and one strong brown arm was draped possessively over her. He looked much younger with his expression relaxed in sleep and his mouth slightly parted to reveal the tips of his straight, white teeth. His shirt was open at the neck, the sleeves pushed up to his elbows, and a blue-black stubble shaded his jaw. He smelt pleasantly musky, his breath still fruity from the wine, and she found his dishevelled state rather appealing. Even when she lifted his arm and slipped out of bed, he did not stir.

She had dressed and was sitting brushing her hair when she first became conscious of his eyes upon her, and she felt the colour rise to her face.

'Good morning, wife,' he said huskily, swinging his legs over the side of the bed and running his hands through his tousled hair.

'Good morning.' She wanted to apologise yet knew it would only annoy him. After a moment's uneasy silence, she asked, 'Would you like some coffee? We're short of servants but I could get you some while you wash.'

'Yes, I'd like that,' he answered with a surprisingly sweet smile. 'Perhaps there are advantages in having a wife, after all.'

She wasn't quite sure how to reply to that and, after studying him uncertainly, headed towards the door. 'I'll have some hot water sent up so that you can shave.'

With her hand on the knob, she paused, suddenly wondering what had happened to the young Vendean who had been Hal's only servant. 'You will miss Georges. I suppose he had no desire to accompany you to England.'

'Yes, I shall miss him,' Hal replied bitterly. 'He died during the first assault on Granville. I didn't want him to fight alongside me but he insisted. He was only eighteen.'

Although he managed to keep his face and voice devoid of emotion, she could see the pain in his eyes. That, after all he had experienced, he should feel such sorrow for a peasant boy both touched and surprised her.

'I'm sorry,' she replied, knowing that a more elaborate show of sympathy would only embarrass him.

He forced a smile. 'You have enough grief of your own, Nicky. You can't share mine, too. I never asked if you have a maid or anyone special you would like to take with you to England. Quite honestly, it would be better if we travelled alone, but if there is someone then I'd agree to them accompanying us.'

'There's no one. Most of our servants either remained at our château or followed their husbands to war. By the time we left the Vendée, all our able-bodied men had joined the Army, and Madame Lamarte is only being served by three elderly retainers. I've got quite used to looking after myself.'

'That's probably for the best,' he admitted, standing up and stretching languorously. 'You can have servants aplenty when we reach England.' Again that bitter smile. 'It's like a different world.'

'You shouldn't feel guilty about what you have,' she said, 'but I understand why you do. I feel badly about leaving France too... Couldn't someone else take that letter?'

Her perception surprised him and for a moment he felt exposed and unsure.

He shook his head and answered her more sharply than he intended. 'I've already told you that it's time for me to return. I can serve the cause more effectively at home and, besides, I promised your father that I would take you to safety.'

'So I must suffer for your sense of honour!' she snapped. 'It's ridiculous when we both want to remain here.'

'We rarely get what we want,' he told her, attempting to defuse what had suddenly become an explosive situation, 'even coffee. I could really do with a cup now.'

With an exasperated sniff, she flounced from the room, almost slamming the door behind her.

'Spitfire,' he growled as he thoughtfully removed his creased shirt. He was going to have to be careful of her. He had always known that she was spirited, but that she should be so astute was more than he had bargained for. He liked to keep his emotions and motives well hidden and he didn't feel comfortable with the idea of another person, especially a young woman, understanding him so well.

CHAPTER FIVE

THEY began their journey straight after breakfast, and by midday were travelling through a countryside that was becoming increasingly wild and wooded, more rugged than Nicol's beloved Vendée. Up hill and down they trailed, along a track that was thick with fallen leaves. A smell of autumn was in the air, one of damp earth and rotting vegetation, becoming spicier as they rode among pines.

Nicol pulled her cloak more tightly around herself, but the wind still seemed to find a way under it. Her fingers and toes were numb with the cold and her back ached from being too long in the saddle. She wished fervently that she had taken Hal's advice and donned breeches to ride astride. She had often done so on the long trek from the Vendée, and it was pure obstinacy that prevented her now.

Her present mount was not nearly as pretty or as lively as her own beloved mare but Hal had insisted that Cleo be left behind, declaring that such an expensive piece of horseflesh would be sure to give them away. She was only slightly mollified by the fact that he had left his own impressive stallion behind and instead rode a heavy chestnut with more stamina than grace.

They had scarcely spoken all morning and the tension lay between them like a high, unscalable wall. Hal rode a little in front, answering when spoken to but initiating little conversation himself, making it abundantly clear that he resented being saddled with such an uncooperative wife. Occasionally, he turned to make sure that she was all right, but there was not the slightest warmth in his gaze. He seemed harder and more unapproachable than ever and her stomach contracted at the thought of being tied to such an uncompromising man.

Around noon, Nicol's horse cast a shoe. Hal swore foully and then had the grace to flush under her haughty stare. Swinging lithely from the saddle, he walked back to inspect the hoof, swearing again as if in defiance.

'It's nothing we can do for ourselves, even with the help of a farmer,' he growled. 'We shall have to go into the nearest small town. It will be a long walk, so we might as well stop and eat now.'

'I can't see why you're so cross,' she muttered as he ungraciously helped her to dismount. 'We might even be able to get a hot meal and a bed for the night.'

'We could also find ourselves arrested,' he snapped, leading the horses off the track and into the trees. 'You'll hardly pass for a *bourgeoise*!' He tied the reins to a convenient gorse bush and, lifting his bag from behind his saddle, tossed it down at her feet. 'There's some bread and cold chicken in there.'

Nicol sullenly helped herself, then settled down in the lee of a tree-trunk to eat. It was even colder sitting still and she couldn't prevent her teeth from chattering. Hal reached inside his coat and, withdrawing a silver flask, uncorked it and passed it across. She took a swig and promptly choked, gasping as the fiery liquid burnt her throat and stomach.

For the first time in hours he laughed, his eyes regarding her almost fondly. 'I can see you're not used to the stuff!'

'I've had brandy before,' she told him, 'but that's horrible!'

He grinned. 'It is a little rough, but the better stuff was in short supply.'

'I'm sure Madame Lamarte would have provided some.'

'It wasn't that important,' he replied and, after thanking her for the food she had passed him, again lapsed into brooding silence.

In an attempt to draw him out, she asked about his home.

'Do you mean where I was born, or the place I actually own?' he queried.

She shrugged. 'Both, I suppose.'

'Ashton Hall belongs to my brother now, although he still encourages me to think of it as my home. It's where I was born and where I spent most of my time until I was sent away to school. It's quite a place and Arthur keeps it in excellent order. The estate is more profitable now than it ever was under my father. The house itself dates back to the time of Henry VIII and was built on the site of a ruined abbey. My family were willing enough to embrace the new faith and did well under the Tudors, even managing to keep out of trouble during Mary's reign. The actual title goes back much further, to the time of Henry V, but it was under the Tudors that our fortune was made.'

'And your brother is the present lord?'

'Lord Ashton, since Father's death, but he remains as unpretentious and approachable as ever. Not that he doesn't enjoy the life and he's forever making speeches in the Lords... I keep telling him that he's too fond of the sound of his own voice.'

Nicol was surprised by the unusual warmth in his tone. 'I can see you're very fond of him.'

Hal's eyebrows rose quizzically. 'Are you surprised? What an ogre you must think me, devoid of all fraternal affection!'

'No, of course not,' she replied, annoyed that he had again succeeded in putting her in the wrong.

He shrugged and took another swig from his flask. 'Oaklands is where we shall be living. It's mine, and although it's only half the size of Ashton it's still an impressive place—all tall chimneys and gables. It was built by one of my ancestors specifically to accommodate Elizabeth I on one of her processions around England. My bailiff will be pleased by events; he's always wanted me to settle down and take a greater interest in the estate.'

'Papa felt all landowners should take their responsibilities seriously,' she told him rather pompously.

For some reason that seemed to catch him on the raw and his jaw tightened. 'I am well aware of my responsibilities, and certainly need no lecture from my child-bride!'

Nicol was conscious of a stab of disappointment. For a short while she had begun to relax with him, but it had been nothing more than a temporary truce. Her thoughtless remark had spoilt it all, but need he be quite so touchy? He had moved closer so that he could speak above the wind, and now every instinct urged her to move away.

'I did not choose to be a bride at all!' she responded angrily. 'You and my father arranged it between you. Why, I believe you are nothing but an adventurer! You may be my husband, but you have yet to gain my love.'

His face seemed to freeze and his hand around the flask clenched so tightly that his knuckles showed white. 'Perhaps I should make you love me. If not with your heart then with your body!'

In one swift, lithe movement, he pushed her back against the grassy bank, one hand holding her wrists above her head while he rolled across her, pinning her to the ground. She gasped and glared up at him, defiance mixed with fear. Discarding the flask, he began to stroke her throat and shoulders, then slowly bent to kiss her. Instinctively, she turned her face away so that his lips brushed her neck, turning the kiss into a caress that was even more unsettling.

Sensing a response in her, he began to make subtle little adjustments. His mouth softened and persuaded, and his left hand, no longer needed to restrain, wandered up her side and across her breasts. Somehow, Nicol could not help herself and, in spite of her anger, pressed her body against his. Then, quite suddenly, he drew back, a hateful, cynical smile on his lips.

'Lust and love are not so different,' he purred. 'You may not love me, my dear, but with a little training you will serve me well enough in bed!'

'That was despicable,' she choked, aiming a blow at his face.

He laughed and caught her wrist. 'I think I have made my point.'

'You've done nothing but reveal your strength and ruthlessness. God, how I hate you!'

'So that's what you were demonstrating a moment ago,' he jeered, his eyes running insolently over her.

'You must hate me more often, you really are exceptionally good at it.'

'I'm learning,' she grated, pulling away and attempting to regain some control over her trembling body. 'You're a good teacher and you've never bothered to hide the contempt you feel for me.'

He had turned and was moving towards the horses, but at that he swung back, his eyes alight with anger and something more—could it possibly be hurt pride? 'Why should I disguise it, madam? Why? When I find myself tied to a woman who prefers anything in breeches to myself?'

Although she despised herself for her weakness, a lump rose in her throat and tears stung her eyes.

'Oh, hell!' he growled. 'For heaven's sake, don't cry. Look, you can ride my horse and I'll walk. That way you won't even have to touch me!'

A couple of hours later, they entered the sleepy, old-fashioned little town of La Chauvier, a place disturbed only by the grunts of pigs and the clucking of scrawny fowl. It consisted of a dozen or so houses all facing a single square with one or two other dwellings crammed in behind.

Hal asked for the blacksmith and was directed through what looked like a farmyard and into some outbuildings. He reappeared a few minutes later and signalled for Nicol to bring the horses. Having spoken to the smith, he informed her that she was to wait in the warm while he set off in search of food. When she protested, he answered her shortly, telling her that she must do as she was bid or he would not be responsible for the consequences.

She had never been in a forge before and, in spite of her chagrin, found it interesting to watch the smith at work. He was a large, dark man whose age could have been anywhere between thirty and fifty. The sweat poured from him as he worked and whistled cheerfully, occasionally flashing her an amused glance as she sat primly on an upturned barrel.

She was intrigued by the tools and strange pieces of metal that covered the walls, and thought it incredible that such places had always existed and yet not been part of her sheltered and rather artificial world. It had never occurred to her that a plough might need mending or a hoe-head replacing, and when one of her horses had needed new shoes then someone had miraculously managed it.

Soon the warmth and the steady beating of the hammer began to make her feel drowsy, and, not wanting to shame herself by toppling from her perch, she decided to go outside. She was curious, too, and resented Hal's high-handed order to remain inside.

'I need some fresh air,' she declared, glancing haughtily at the smith. 'If my husband returns, please tell him that I shan't be long.'

'Best not,' he replied gruffly. 'He wants you to wait here and he knows what he's doing.'

'He's my husband, not my keeper!' She was furious that he should have dared to argue with her, and only just prevented herself from telling him so.

Nevertheless he did not try to stop her and, after muttering a few choice words about foolish and independent young women, returned to his work.

As she wandered across the square, she thought how seedy and depressing it looked and it smelt unwholesome, too, of a ripe mixture of pigs and rotting manure. She could not help comparing it with her home and all the comfort and elegance that had once been found there, and she was filled with a deep melancholy for all that was passed. Her presentation at Court was to have been that very autumn, and now Versailles had been desecrated and both Louis and the frivolous Marie Antoinette lay dead.

A dark-coated man came out of the nearest house. He looked intently at her, then, straightening his shoulders, came over. She was too wrapped up in her thoughts to notice how incongruous he looked amid the mud and ploughshares.

'Who are you, *citoyenne*?' he demanded. 'I have not seen you before.'

Looking up at him with just the right mixture of hauteur and surprise, she replied, 'I expect that is because I've never been here before. Now, if you will excuse me, it is not my custom to talk to strangers.'

His dark eyes narrowed suspiciously. 'Where are you from? Could it be Paris or Nantes?'

A warning sounded at the back of her mind, but she ignored it. Somehow she just could not bring herself to be respectful to such a lowborn and unpleasant individual.

'It's none of your concern, *monsieur*,' she replied tartly, and experienced a spurt of pleasure at the slow flush that crept up his face.

'I am a member of the municipality, *madame*, and it is the duty of all good Republicans to take an interest in travellers. There are too many aristos trying to escape across the Channel.'

Hate for him and all he stood for overcame what remained of her caution, and with a stinging contempt she told him to go about his business and leave her alone.

Hal, entering the square, a newly baked loaf under his arm, recognised his wife at her most imperious, and swore roundly.

'What's the trouble, citizen?' he called, lapsing easily into the Breton patois. 'Is my bitch of a wife causing trouble?'

The Republican glanced in surprise from Hal's sober dress to Nicol. 'I thought perhaps she might be a Royalist, *monsieur*.'

Hal laughed unpleasantly and, gripping Nicol's hand, dragged her roughly towards him. Then, as if to humiliate her, he kissed her hard, his hand moving up to squeeze her breast.

'Oh, she was once,' he snarled, still holding her firmly by the wrist, 'until I began to show her the error of her ways. She's a comely bedful, and under my tuition will soon learn to appreciate our Revolution. She'll bear me fine Republican sons!'

The danger of the situation had finally become apparent to Nicol and she struggled to control her temper.

When she tried to pull away from Hal, he twisted her arm viciously, making her cry out. 'Won't you, my dear?'

'Yes!' She barely managed to answer him, wanting desperately to slap his face.

The other man gave a coarse laugh, obviously beginning to enjoy the situation. 'I can see you're a man after my own heart, *monsieur*. Punish her for me when next you bed her!'

'It will be a pleasure,' Hal sneered. 'Once she was too proud to look at me, but she's glad of my protection now. I see she earns it, too. If we weren't in such a hurry, I'd let you try her for yourself.'

'How dare you?' gasped Nicol as he dragged her back towards the smithy. 'I know you were trying to help me, but was it necessary to be quite so crude and humiliate me so completely?'

'Surely it was a small price to pay for your freedom? Besides, you're not humiliated, you're just angry. In fact, a little less arrogance wouldn't go amiss. God! I wish you'd learn to do as you're told. The blacksmith's was safe enough, but you had to exercise your ignorance and independence and come dancing out here!'

'I'm not a child,' she snapped, 'and I resent being treated like one.'

He turned, letting his eyes run insolently over her. 'No, Nicol, you are not a child, but there are times when you act like one—and at those times I shall respond as if you were.'

She raised her hand and dealt him a stinging slap across the face.

'I think you have just proved my point,' he hissed. 'My God, but you can be a real bitch when you put your mind to it!'

'And you are no gentleman!'

'I never professed to be one,' he snarled. 'I don't think a gentleman is what you deserve or need. In fact, I think it's high time you were put in your place, beneath me in my bed!'

Once more she raised her hand, but this time he was ready for her, blocking the blow with his left hand and bending the loaf in the process.

'Damn it! I told you not to do that,' he declared, slapping her back.

He was careful to control his strength, but the blow still made her cheek sting and her eyes filled with tears.

Furiously, she launched herself at him, swinging with her fists as Philippe had once taught her. With an oath, he caught her and pulled her against him, pinning her arms to her sides. She continued to use her feet and he winced as her boots made contact with his shins.

'Stop it, you little hellion,' he growled, with a mixture of humour and exasperation. 'For God's sake, calm down. There's no reason to come at me like that.'

When she relaxed against him, his hold gentled. 'What am I going to do with you?' he sighed, stroking her hair.

The anger drained out of Nicol, leaving her feeling foolish and tired. She felt thoroughly ashamed of her behaviour and could only marvel that he should affect her in such a way.

'I'm sorry,' she muttered. 'I don't know what came over me. I know I've got a vile temper but it doesn't usually get so out of hand. Nobody else makes me so angry.'

He laughed, a little shakily. 'Well, at least you're not indifferent to me. I suppose anything is preferable to that.'

'Did I hurt you?' she asked.

'Only my pride. I don't usually have that effect on women.'

'I'm sorry, I wanted us to be friends.'

He glanced quickly around the yard in front of the smithy. 'Then we'll kiss and make up. You owe me that much, and you're going to have to get used to kissing me sooner or later.'

She was surprised by his answer but allowed him to draw her into his arms. His lips brushed gently over hers before settling in a deep, rewarding kiss. He tasted

of wine and smelt of the outdoors, and the feel of
him was really rather exciting. Locking her hand in
the thickness of his hair, she gave her instincts free
rein, returning his kiss with an inexperienced passion.
When they finally drew apart, they were both surprised; he by the depth of his feelings and she by her
response.

Hal felt an unexpected stab of tenderness and, in
an attempt to conceal it, spoke more harshly than he
intended. 'It's time we were going before you get into
any more trouble . . . and if you meet anyone else for
God's sake try for a little humility. It's attitudes like
yours that caused the bloody Revolution in the first
place.'

By the time they left the village it was already late
in the afternoon and, with so much low cloud, beginning to get dark. Nicol knew that their destination
was Cancale and wondered miserably if Hal intended
to push on through the night. She felt a little better
after her stay in the smithy but, if anything, the wind
was even colder and she soon felt chilled. She wanted
nothing more than a hot drink and a warm bed but
she determined not to influence Hal in any way. When
he glanced up at the sky and then kicked his horse
into a brisk trot, she resolutely followed.

In some strange way the howling of the wind was
almost soporific, and in spite of her discomfort she
began to doze. In the fading light her horse put its
foot into a particularly deep rut and nearly fell. Had
she been more alert, she could easily have righted
herself, but as it was she pitched headlong, gasping
as all the breath was knocked from her and her hands
were skinned by the hard ground.

For a moment, she lay still, winded and half stunned; then hands seized her, feeling ungently along each limb before their owner gave an exasperated sigh of relief.

'Damn it, Nicol,' growled Hal ungallantly. 'Why didn't you tell me you were so tired.'

'I'm all right,' she protested and was surprised how weak her voice sounded.

His arm was around her shoulders and she opened her eyes to find him watching her with a sympathy that had not been apparent in his voice.

'There are no bones broken,' he said gently, 'and, if you feel up to it, we'd best get on. The blacksmith has a brother with a farm near here. He was sure we'd be given lodgings for the night.'

Disregarding her protests that if he gave her just a little longer she would be able to walk, he slipped his arms under her and carried her to his horse.

'You'd best ride with me,' he said, putting her on the animal's back. Then, collecting the reins of the other beast, he swung up behind her.

As she turned her face into his shoulder, she felt his grip tighten and thought she heard him swear beneath his breath.

'That's better,' he said when he kicked his horse into a trot and she slipped an arm around him to steady herself.

There was something very comforting in his hardness and strength and, almost of its own volition, her arm tightened.

'Poor Nicky,' he whispered as she began to doze, and she thought she felt his lips graze her hair.

The Durands turned out to be a nice couple, only too willing to admit the travellers into their home.

They tactfully asked no questions, yet Nicol was quite sure that they knew how matters stood. Politics were not mentioned, although Madame Durand spoke critically of the Republicans' attitude to religion and called their local representative a 'godless savage'.

With her own children grown up and gone, she seemed happy enough to fuss over Nicol, bathing her hands and encouraging her to drink a bowl of hot, nourishing soup.

When Hal saw his wife beginning to droop, he suggested that they retire, taking it as a measure of her exhaustion when she nodded unprotestingly and even managed a grateful smile. She was hardly aware of being led into the bedroom or of lying back on the bed. She must have dozed because the next thing she knew was that someone was undressing her.

Immediately, she stiffened, but Hal's voice, both gentle and mocking, said 'It's all right, my love. I shan't bother you tonight ... The bed is all yours. I shall be comfortable enough on the floor.'

'What an unpredictable man you are,' she answered sleepily.

As he tucked the quilt around her chin, a tender smile touched his lips and he marvelled at his own forbearance. With an almost superhuman effort he moved away and glanced ruefully at the hard floor. The girl was definitely beginning to get to him. While she was being spoilt and wilful he could harden his heart against her, but the courage she was beginning to exhibit, and her fierce determination not to reveal her weaknesses, somehow pulled at his heart ... and her body was so soft! He could still feel it against him, her arm enclosing him as they rode his horse.

With a low growl, he pulled the second pillow from the bed and tossed it upon the floor, then lifted the spare blanket from the bottom of the bed. His body ached with tiredness and he wanted nothing more than to creep in beside her and draw her close, but he would not be able to stop at that, and he could no more take advantage of her vulnerability than he could fly.

CHAPTER SIX

NICOL awoke to a room filled with winter sunshine. She felt warm and relaxed, and stretched languorously, luxuriating in the feel of the soft sheets against her skin. With the realisation that she was naked came the memory of Hal undressing her and tucking her into bed.

'Good morning, wife.' His voice cut across her musing and, turning, she saw him wipe the remains of the shaving lather from his face. 'I must say you're looking much better.'

She felt embarrassed under his steady gaze, and, as if aware of it, he smiled, his eyes lighting up with amusement.

When she pulled the covers more closely around her, he laughed. 'It's too late, my dear. There's no point in hiding what's firmly imprinted on my mind forever.'

He sat down on the edge of the bed and reached for the shirt he had carelessly tossed there. The movement revealed a raw scar running from under his arm to almost his waist. She felt a rush of almost maternal compassion.

'Were you badly hurt at Château Gontier?' she asked.

He shrugged. 'It was painful enough and put me out of action for a couple of weeks. It's one of the hazards of my trade.' He had the shirt in his hands but, instead of putting it on, bent over the girl. 'Do

80

you find me less of an ogre now?' he asked, reaching out to stroke her cheek.

'I'm beginning to think of you as a friend,' she replied awkwardly, finding herself more than a little disconcerted by the effect his touch was having on her.

He did not reply but lowered his head to kiss her, an enticing kiss, full of promise and surprisingly sweet.

'The trouble is,' he sighed, 'I do not want to sleep with my friends.'

She realised then that, in spite of his sharp words and ready temper, he had, in fact, been more patient with her than she deserved and she felt a warm rush of gratitude. Last night he had been both concerned and kind, and even this morning there was a gentleness in him that gave her hope for the future.

'I'll try to be a good wife to you, Hal,' she told him. 'A...a proper wife. I like you, very much... It's just that I had always hoped to marry for love.'

'What a romantic you are,' he replied with surprising bitterness. 'Love is such an unpredictable emotion, there one moment and absent the next. I've had experience of it and would much rather rely on good old-fashioned lust!'

There was no answer to that and he didn't seem to expect one, but withdrew into himself and finished dressing in silence. Only when he was ready to leave the room did he speak again.

'You'd better get up, sleepyhead,' he teased. 'I want to reach the coast this afternoon. Then, with a little luck, we can sail for England this evening.'

As soon as he had gone, Nicol began dressing, but although her fingers worked busily her mind was elsewhere, pondering on what could possibly have made him so bitter.

In less than an hour, having partaken of a hearty breakfast, she was ready to continue the journey. Hal's hands were gentle as he lifted her into the saddle, and when he smiled and turned to take his leave of the Durands she saw the same charm that had so captivated Madame Lamarte.

A weak winter sun struggled through the trails of vapour and, somehow, its appearance seemed to promise well for the future. She felt almost light-hearted as she rode alongside Hal, actually enjoying the ride. He too seemed relaxed, chatting easily and pointing out anything of interest as they rode past. She found him surprisingly well informed about many things and felt a little ashamed that he should know so much more about her country than she did. He greeted any peasants they met and often stopped to talk, seeming more at ease in their company than either her father or Philippe would have been. In fact she began to suspect an egalitarian streak in him that would have made the old Comte's hair stand on end.

When they finally pulled up on a hill overlooking the small fishing village of Cancale, she got her first sight of the sea and thought that she had never seen anything so beautiful. Dimpled by the wind and glazed by the afternoon sun, it shone like golden glass.

'Haven't you seen it before?' Hal asked, already knowing the answer from the expression on her face.

'No,' she replied a little breathlessly, dragging her eyes with reluctance from the panorama in front of her. 'It was at least two days' ride from our château to the coast and there was just no reason to go. I suppose at Madame Lamarte's it must have been quite close, but Papa was worried about the situation and forbade me to ride out... Philippe went to La Rochelle once and didn't stop talking about it for a week. Oh, it's beautiful, Hal, quite mind-shatteringly beautiful, and so immense!'

He laughed, as intrigued by the look on her face as she was by the view. 'It can be brutal, too, frightening in a storm or as bleak and cold as the grave.' His eyes moved from her face to stare out across the ocean and he sighed. 'I can almost smell England.'

'Will your friend take us tonight?'

'I certainly hope so. I told him I would be returning with my wife. I think he was pleasantly surprised. His sister is married to one of my tenants. He spent a couple of years at Oaklands and still retains an interest in the estate. You'll like him, I'm sure.'

Seagulls wheeled and dived overhead as they walked their horses along the narrow quay, past a colourful assortment of fishing boats and then on, up a quaint, cobbled street. Nicol looked about her with interest, finding it vastly different from anywhere she had seen before. Most of all, she was amazed by the smell of the sea, so strong she could actually taste it.

Hal had scarcely taken his eyes from her face, intrigued by the excitement he saw there. If her eyes were normally bright, then now they positively shone, and her cheeks were flushed with more than the wind. When they came to the street where the Surats lived, he called a halt, frowning because of the unease that was rising inside him.

'What's the matter?' asked Nicol, aware of the tension in his body as if it were her own.

'I don't know. It's just a feeling.' For a moment he stared at the small terraced cottage, then up and down the street. 'There should be children. There is always at least one of Claude's brats outside . . . and the door is shut. It's the first time I've known that.'

Nicol had never seen him so worried and she laughed nervously. 'It is rather cold.'

He smiled, but when he turned to look down at her his eyes were still shadowed with concern. 'I expect you're right. In a few minutes we shall probably be drinking some of Louise's excellent coffee and laughing at my fears . . . but, just in case, I'd rather you waited here.'

She nodded. 'As you wish.'

'And if there's any trouble, Nicol, you must ride straight out of here. Go back to the Durands and then to Henri Jacquelein . . . He'll be able to advise you on what to do for the best.'

The thought of anything happening to him caused an uncomfortable feeling in her stomach. He was standing very close, that rather endearing frown on his face, and she was all too conscious that he was merely flesh and blood.

She threw her arms around him, feeling the softness of his coat beneath her cheek and hearing the steady beating of his heart. 'Oh, please be careful, Hal.'

Gently, he tilted her face between his hands, a whimsical little smile touching his lips. 'Why, wife, I do believe you're concerned for me,' he teased, then playfully kissed her.

He handed her the reins of both horses and strolled brazenly across the cobbles, whistling to himself as if he had not a care in the world. She saw him knock upon the door of the fifth cottage along. It opened, and without making any sign he stepped inside. Her anxiety made her want to run after him, and only common sense, and a desire not to let him down, kept her still, watching and waiting with every sense straining to pick up the earliest sign of his danger or distress.

It was surprisingly dark in the small kitchen and it was a moment before Hal's eyes became accustomed to the gloom. Madame Surat had opened the door for him, and his nerves were not at all soothed by her unusual reticence.

'Is anything wrong, Louise?' he asked.

She shook her head, but did not meet his questioning gaze. 'Where is your wife?'

There was still nothing definite to alarm him and yet his scalp was crawling with the anticipation of danger.

He did not answer the question, but said, 'It's quiet today. Where are the children?'

'They are staying with my sister.'

'And Claude?' He glanced around suspiciously then back at Madame Surat's pale face. 'What's the matter, Louise?'

'I'm the one who will be asking the questions,' said a quiet voice from the bedroom doorway.

Grantly turned to find himself confronting a tall gaunt man dressed in a dark ill-fitting coat and breeches. His eyes flew to the tricolour rosette tucked into the greasy hat, and then down to the cocked pistol aimed unwaveringly at his middle.

'I'm sorry, but they have Claude,' Madame Surat explained miserably. 'They have promised to spare him as long as I co-operate.'

'It's all right, Louise, I understand,' Grantly replied, before turning back to the Republican who was still looming menacingly in the doorway.

'I require information, *monsieur*,' the fellow sneered. 'You have other contacts, I believe, and then, of course, there is the letter you are carrying for Jacquelein. If you would be good enough to pass it to me...'

'Go to the devil,' Hal brazened, although he was a good deal shaken by the Republican's knowledge.

The latter jerked his head, and two burly troopers moved around him and into the room.

'When we've finished with you, you'll be only too willing to co-operate,' one of them growled.

Hal backed slowly away, measuring his opponents and calculating his chances. If they wanted him alive, then it was going to cost them more than a couple of bloody noses.

As the smaller of the two hurtled forward, Hal's fist caught him squarely on the jaw, sending him sprawling. The second man gave a snarl of fury and, ignoring a blow to the stomach, grasped Hal tightly around the waist, knocking him back against the kitchen shelves and sending glasses and crockery careering around them. The massive arms tightened, and Hal, unable to break the grip and, feeling as if his ribs were cracking, reached back to steady himself. Miraculously his hand closed over the smooth neck of a bottle and with the last of his strength, he brought it down on the bullet-like head. The fellow grunted and went down like a sack of coal, leaving Hal gasping for breath, the splintered neck of the bottle still in his hand.

'Enough!' screamed the man from the doorway. 'Stop, or I'll...!'

He got no further before the ham that Madame Surat had snatched from its hook on the ceiling smashed into his face. The sound of the pistol seemed to fill the whole room. Grantly stiffened, expecting to feel the agonising impact of lead, but it was the poor woman who went down, her hand clutching vainly at her breast.

He did not need to take a closer look, his soldier's experience told him that she was dead. Wasting no time, he took the chance she had so dearly bought and, wrenching open the door, started out into the street. In a last, desperate attempt to stop him, the Republican threw the empty pistol and it connected sharply with Hal's temple. For a moment he staggered against the doorway, pain filling his head and turning his limbs to water.

'Stop him!' screamed the Republican, though he dared not follow, and more soldiers appeared at the end of the street.

Nicol had been waiting anxiously, her body as tense as a coiled spring. At the sound of the shot she flung herself into the saddle and waited in agitation for some sign as to what she should do. When Hal staggered out of the house she gave a strangled cry and instinctively galloped towards him.

He saw her and waved, as if telling her to go away. Desperately she glanced towards the end of the street, calculating both time and distance, and suddenly the only thing that mattered was saving him. A shot whistled uncomfortably close as she turned the horses in front of him, praying fervently that he was capable of climbing into the saddle. He swung up, albeit shakily, and then they were both hurtling down the street, the horses' hoofs ringing against the cobbles. More musketballs whistled around them and she thought she heard Hal swear.

At the end of the street they turned right, back along the quay, heedless of everything except the need to reach the shelter of the rugged hills. For a while they followed the road, then Hal, who had again taken the lead, turned off through the trees, still moving as rapidly as possible. There was no time for conversation and Nicol needed all her skill as they dodged between the trunks and bushes, determined not to slow her husband down. He was hurt, how badly she could not tell, but there was blood on his head and arm, and occasionally he seemed to reel in the saddle.

After almost an hour he pulled up and allowed her to draw alongside.

'Are you all right?' she asked anxiously.

He managed a smile and, although he was dreadfully pale, his voice was strong enough. 'It could be worse. You saved my life, Nicol, although you still didn't do as you were told!'

'No, I suppose not ... Would you like me to see to those wounds?'

He shook his head and replied rather brusquely, 'No, time for that later when we're further from the town. We must keep moving west—it's more remote and the people there are less inclined to co-operate with the Republicans.'

They continued, but at a slower pace, until they came to a small stream, and there Hal dismounted.

'I'm afraid I've got to stop now,' he told her with an apologetic smile and, after looping the horse's reins over its head, walked rather unsteadily towards the water.

Kneeling on the muddy bank, he splashed his face and hair, then slumped down against a moss-covered boulder, his head resting against his bent knees.

Nicol wetted her handkerchief in the river, then went to kneel at his side, gently dabbing at the cut on his temple. He lifted his head to look up at her, his expression betraying him before he could help himself. He looked tired, drawn and incredibly sad. A pain more than physical was reflected in his eyes, revealing a vulnerability that she had not seen before.

'They were friends, Nicol,' he choked. 'They wouldn't have become involved if it hadn't been for me.'

His distress brought a thickness to her throat, making it impossible for her to speak, and tears filled her eyes. She ran her hand lightly through his tousled hair and down to rest against his cheek. It was a gesture to comfort him, to tell him that she cared, and yet the contact brought an unexpected throb of desire. She wanted to hold him, to have him hold her.

'Tears, Nicky,' he said with obvious effort, taking her hand and moving it from his cheek to his lips. 'It's a long time since anyone's cried for me.'

Subduing the desire to draw him into her arms, she again dabbed at his cut head while he closed his eyes and, resting his head back, submitted to her ministrations. The wound in his shoulder appeared to be nothing, a musketball having merely grazed the skin, but his extreme pallor worried her and she remembered her father saying how serious a blow to the head could be.

'You can lie back against me,' she said after a while and felt a pang of disappointment when he refused.

'That's tempting indeed,' he replied with a touch of his old humour. 'But we really ought to be getting on. It will be dark in another hour.'

'Do you think they'll follow us?' she asked.

He shrugged as he climbed stiffly to his feet. 'All we can do is keep moving west...and we'd better avoid the towns. I'm afraid the journey is going to be even more uncomfortable from now on.'

'I don't mind,' she told him and was surprised to find she meant it. 'At least we're alive.'

'Good girl!' He reached down a hand to help her to her feet.

'You're still treating me like a child,' she complained.

A smile of incredible warmth lit his face as he said, 'Yes, I suppose I am, and I really shouldn't, not after what you did today.'

As they continued through the trees, the sky before them became tinged with red, the clouds clustering like purple mountains above the horizon. Streaks of gold and yellow reached towards them, then slowly faded so that only a bloody-grey remained.

Nicol's eyes strayed often to the broad back of her husband and she became conscious of such a feeling of warmth towards him that it was almost an ache. When he turned back to smile his encouragement, she felt her stomach lurch and knew without a doubt that she was falling in love with him.

When it was almost dark, they came across a ruined and abandoned cottage, its roof sagging and small window boarded over. What it was doing in the middle of the forest, Nicol couldn't possibly guess. Hal pulled up and sat for a moment gazing speculatively at it.

'I wonder what it's like inside?' he mused.

Around them the wind moaned softly through trees that seemed to be closing in. Dead leaves rattled around the horses' feet and, somewhere in the distance, a night bird called. Nicol shivered and drew her cloak more tightly around her.

'I don't see that it matters,' she replied irritably. 'Do let's go on.'

'It might provide shelter for the night.' When she wrinkled her nose disdainfully, he laughed. 'We really are in no position to be fastidious. In the circumstances I can't ask any peasant to take us in.'

He slipped stiffly from the saddle and began to prowl around. A board over one of the windows was loose and, after much grunting and swearing, he was able to tear it away. Putting his head inside, he sniffed.

'It smells of mould and fungus,' he grunted, climbing over the sill. Nicol heard him blundering about inside; then he called out cheerfully, 'It could be worse. The chimney seems sound enough, so we'll try a fire.'

He scrambled out and began searching for firewood. Nicol dismounted and peered apprehensively into the dark hovel. The small window let in a little light, perhaps a blessing, but she was still not at all eager to enter the place. Hal gave her an amused glance as he slipped past her, and after a moment she saw the flicker of a fire in the ancient hearth. She heard him cough, then swear, and even from where she was standing could smell the woodsmoke filling the building.

'It will be better when the fire settles down,' he told her between coughs. 'I know what you think of the place, but believe me it will be far better than sleeping outside.'

He climbed past her again and began to unsaddle the horses. Reluctantly she turned to help. After carrying his own tackle to the window and unceremoniously dumping it inside, he reached out for hers.

'I'm not an invalid,' she told him rather crossly, refusing to let him take the saddle.

With an exasperated sigh, he took the two horses and led them around to the rear. Nicol was still standing beside the window when he returned.

'What's the matter? Can't you manage to climb in?' he growled.

'Yes . . . but it looks so dirty.'

'Oh, for heaven's sake, what did you expect, bloody Versailles?'

'I can manage,' she told him, ignoring his helping hand.

Once inside, he turned his attention to his bedroll, while Nicol glanced anxiously around. In fact the place was not as bad as she had expected. It was dusty and dank and harboured she dare not guess how many spiders, but there was no human rubbish apart from an old broken stool, which Hal promptly pulled apart and tossed upon the fire.

She laid out her own blankets and then began to rummage in her bag for some food, asking him rather shortly if he wanted anything. When he refused, she looked up at him. He was sitting tiredly with his back against the old stone wall, and in the flickering firelight looked haggard and rather ill.

'Is your head still aching?' she asked, feeling rather guilty about her behaviour, and, forgetting the food, moved across to his side.

'Like the devil!'

'I could bathe it again if you liked.'

Her concern seemed to amuse him and he smiled. 'No, it will be all right by morning. I've had this sort of thing before.' Then, thinking it would have been pleasant to have her ministering to him and regretting the missed opportunity, he said, 'You could have a look at that scratch on my shoulder, though—it's damned sore.'

'Of course,' she replied, kneeling beside him and helping him off with his coat and shirt.

So intent was she on her task that she completely missed the look of mischief in his eyes. The sight of his naked torso caused an odd little flutter inside her and she felt a strong desire to run her hands through the soft black down on his chest.

'Madame Jacquelein gave me a small jar of salve,' she said. 'It's really for aches and pains, but it might help.'

'Thank you.'

She carefully applied the cream with her fingertips, her touch as light as a feather. His skin felt warm and glowed like honey in the firelight, the shadows emphasising the contours of his muscles. He was so close that her senses were full of him and an empty ache spread outwards from the region of her stomach, encouraging every fibre in her body to draw him close.

As if sensing her turmoil, he turned and, taking the jar of cream from her trembling hands, placed it safely out of reach. Then, gently but firmly, he drew her to him, his lips brushing hers with a tenderness that surprised her. He planted soft, tantalising kisses upon her hair, her brow, her cheek, all the time whispering endearments and letting his hands run over her in a way that sent her pulse racing. Deftly he rolled her over, kissing her again, this time more passionately, as his fingers unfastened her blouse.

'Oh,' she whispered in a stifled voice, realising that this was what she had been wanting him to do for hours.

'Nicol,' he answered, very low.

'Oh, Hal,' she whispered, tangling her fingers in his thick hair. 'My dearest Hal.'

There was no need for further words between them as he held her pinned against his chest, caressing her through the opening in her blouse and breathing in the fragrance of her hair. She revelled in his size and strength and her body tingled under his palms. It was as if she were in a dream and it was not her at all lying upon that cottage floor, hearing the wind gusting and sighing through the trees. The fire crackled in the ancient hearth and, above them in the rafters, some small animal scuttered away.

He kissed her again, sweetly, demandingly, and then, as her fingers sensually followed the hard muscles of his chest, he bent to kiss her breast. A great wave of pleasure rose up inside her and she pressed herself against him, creating an ache of longing that just had to be fulfilled.

'At last, Nicol,' he whispered softly, stroking her neck with the back of his hand.

She was hardly conscious of their undressing, for his touch and kissing kept her totally entranced; then they were lying together and she could feel the warm glow of life in him and hear the rapid beating of his heart. He was her entire world, and she offered herself to him gladly, pressing her body against him with a passion that was almost primeval. Her breasts tingled where they touched him and then he was kissing them again, creating such a feeling of pleasure that it made her sigh and groan.

He gave a gasp of pleased surprise at finding her so responsive. His own heart was pounding like a drum as he whispered thickly, 'Don't be frightened, my love. I won't hurt you, I swear.'

Nicol felt as if her body moved of its own accord, responding to his proximity and his expert caress. Her heart beat faster and faster, and she cried out for him to complete what he had begun, her eager body rising to meet him. He was gentle, incredibly so in the circumstances, and if there was any pain then she failed to notice it in the face of her consuming desire. There, in that grubby cottage, wave after wave of pleasure engulfing her, she became truly Hal's wife, and, if the act of love did not commit him totally, for her it was otherwise—she was his, body and soul.

'My wife, my wife,' he whispered, collapsing against her and sighing into her ear. 'What a passionate wife I have married.'

Tenderly she kissed his brow, tasting the salt of his sweat and running her fingers through his damp hair. Her body was spent and her mind pleasurably blank, empty of all memory or thought. She was only conscious that she loved him. He had fallen almost instantly asleep, his dark head pillowed against her breast, and he looked surprisingly vulnerable. Even when she caressed the smooth line of his jaw, he did not stir. She felt her stomach contract with love for him and, remembering how her body had fired him, felt a sense of power, too. It was all so incredible; the forbidding Hal Grantly, the so estimable Hal, sleeping like a baby in her arms.

When she awoke, it was with the peculiar feeling that something was missing. She reached out for Hal and, startled by his absence, sat up. It was already dawn and in the thin grey light the cottage appeared as it really was—damp and rather squalid.

Hal, clad only in shirt and breeches, was sitting beside the open window, a notebook and pencil in his hand. He was so engrossed in what he was doing that for a moment he did not notice that she was awake and she was at leisure to study him. His frown was back, but this time it was one of concentration; in fact, he reminded her of Philippe when he had been forced to labour over his Latin grammar.

She sat up slowly, holding the blankets tightly against her naked body.

'So you're awake at last,' he commented, his smile warm and a little amused. 'I don't know why you're being so modest. It was a different tale last night.'

'Last night it was dark!'

'You'll freeze if you don't dress quickly. If it will make you feel better, I'll promise to keep my eyes on my book.'

'You've let the fire go out,' she complained.

He looked up sharply at her petulant tone, his eyes flashing annoyance. 'I'm afraid we can't risk a fire during the daylight—the Republicans are probably out looking for us. I've left you most of the food, and there's some fresh water in the pan beside the hearth.'

She was about to make known her displeasure in no uncertain terms when she caught sight of his coat, thrown on top of the two blankets that covered her. Instead, she reached out to finger it and smiled at his kindness. She began to dress and did not know whether to be relieved or sorry when, true to his word, he did not lift his eyes from his book. Picking up his coat, she walked over to place it across his shoulders.

'Thank you,' she said.

'Not at all, wife.' He took her hand and kissed it, then proceeded to nuzzle his way up her arm. 'If it was less cold and I had less to do...'

He looked up at her, his grey eyes dancing and appearing almost silver against his dark hair and rapidly thickening beard. She ran her hand over this evidence of his masculinity and he pulled her down to sit next to him, slipping his left arm around her shoulders.

'What are you doing?' she asked, staring in amazement at the jumble of letters.

'It's a code, simple enough to decipher once I'd remembered the key. It was something by Shakespeare—"Tell me where is Fancy bred, Or in the heart or in the head?"'

'Do you like poetry?'

He shrugged. 'Not romantic verse, although that particular poem does have a certain whimsy.'

She frowned, sensing some old bitterness but, before she could comment, he smiled and changed the subject.

'With a few calculations, I can find out when one of our frigates will be standing off various points along the French coast.'

'How on earth did you come by such information?'

'Just be glad that I have,' he replied, remaining pleasant yet refusing to be drawn. 'I would sooner have made the crossing with Claude, but as that option is no longer open to us...'

A shadow of pain crossed his face as he doggedly returned to his calculations. Nicol snuggled against him and waited patiently.

'Six days,' he muttered after another few minutes. 'We can do the journey in four, so it gives me plenty of time... Perhaps it's selfish of me to ask it of you, but if I don't return to Cancale then I shall never be able to live with myself.'

Her stomach turned over as she anticipated his next words, but her fear was all for him. She had to force herself to look into his tanned face, seeing the new lines of strain there and the purple bruise on his temple, but it was the anguish in his eyes that decided matters.

'There will be no chance of rescuing Claude,' he continued bitterly, 'but at least I can make sure that the children are being well cared for, and, if necessary, make arrangements for them to travel to England. I'd like to return to the village tonight, but I want you to remain here.'

Ever since childhood she had hated being alone, particularly in the darkness, and yet she would have died rather than let him down.

'If you think that is best,' she agreed, and he was never to know the effort her smile cost her.

He gave her hand a grateful squeeze. 'Good girl! I'll be as quick as I can. I shan't set off until after dark. Say two hours to get there, one, possibly two, to find out what I want to know... If I leave around seven I should get back shortly after midnight.'

With a brief nod she eased herself further into the comforting circle of his arm, feeling closer to him in spirit than she had with anyone. Whether this was because of their situation or the fact that they had made love, she did not know. She was only aware of a warm glow of happiness that seemed a little ridiculous in the circumstances. She was in love and felt sure that, after his tenderness of the night, he must love her, too.

She glanced shyly up at him and he kissed her, a kiss of such passion and desire that it seemed to set her on fire.

'God, girl!' he muttered thickly, kissing her again and then drawing away. 'I swear that when we reach England I shall never leave your bed! Now, eat what food we have left, and we'll go hunting. If I can catch us a rabbit, we'll roast it before I go.'

It was rather like being a child again, wandering on foot through the woods and crouching behind the trees. Hal's mood of mischievous humour only added to the illusion, as for a while he seemed to have set aside his responsibilities and feelings of guilt. Most of the time, he held her hand, swinging it gaily, and when at last he managed to hit a scurrying rabbit he gave a whoop of triumph like any boy.

Later she watched him as he sat on his heels beside the leaf-strewn stream, skinning the beast and whistling softly. He looked the complete peasant with his hair tangled and his rapidly thickening beard. There was even a smudge of mud on his nose. He seemed younger than she had first thought, perhaps no more than thirty. This placed him nearer to Philippe in age and explained the close friendship that had grown between them.

'What are you thinking about, wife?' he asked, apparently amused by her reverie.

'Warm thoughts.'

'Warm thoughts?' He went to wash his hands in the water, then, picking up their dinner, came to join her by the tree.

'Thoughts of summertime,' she explained, 'of being back in the Vendée and lying on the sun-drenched grass beside a stream just like this one, and listening to the crickets sing. I don't believe there is anywhere else on earth where the crickets make so much noise.'

He laughed gently and not without understanding. 'If you like crickets, I'll import crates of the things. Oaklands will positively hum with them.'

Nicol laughed, too, her momentary feeling of homesickness flying away. 'I'm not sure I like them that much. They are rather ugly. It's their sound... I suppose it reminds me of my childhood. Isn't it strange the way smells and sounds can be so evocative?'

'I find the smell of your hair evocative,' he murmured, playfully nuzzling her ear and sending shivers of pleasure through her chilled body. 'You're cold!' Immediately he was concerned, but that imp of mischief was dancing in his eyes again as he added, 'Come back to the cottage and I'll soon warm you up!'

'Hal!'

He laughed at her blushes. 'I jest not, wife! It will pass the time until dark when we can light our fire. Do you realise, we've been married for nearly six days? We've time to make up for.' So saying, he dragged her to her feet and began kissing her with a reckless abandon. 'I'm a greedy man,' he muttered, pausing to draw breath. 'I warn you, I shan't be easily satisfied.'

It was some time before they began collecting dry leaves to improve their beds and, at Nicol's request, Hal found a way of repositioning the shutter so that she would feel more secure when left on her own. As soon as it was dark they roasted the rabbit, and she couldn't remember a meal she had enjoyed more. Afterwards she sat with her back against the dusty wall. Hal lay contentedly with his head in her lap while she smoothed his lean face with her fingertips, moving them down his cheek and across his mouth. He bit her fingers playfully, then turned her hand over to plant a kiss in her palm.

'Do you still regret our marriage?' she asked.

He laughed softly, gazing up to look directly into her eyes. 'If you must know, I desired you from the first moment I saw you. I was fond of your father and of Philippe, but I married you because I wanted you, and I'll tell you something else—the reality was even better than the anticipation!'

He left for Cancale soon after dark, and it was all Nicol could do not to hold him back. The prospect of a night alone in the wilds was terrifying enough, but far worse was the worry that he might not return. He kissed her tenderly before he left, and with an odd restraint, as if too much passion would weaken him and make it impossible for him to go at all.

Nicol settled down beside the fire and resigned herself to a sleepless, nerve-straining wait. In the surrounding silence any sound seemed unnaturally loud and the low moaning of the wind almost human. Several times she thought she heard footsteps, and her heart lurched within her breast, only to steady after many painful moments of suspense. She was glad of the light as well as the warmth of the fire, even though its flickering cast grotesque shadows on the walls, and was careful not to let it die down. Desperately tired yet afraid to sleep, she moved as close to the blaze as she dared.

She felt sick and shaky with tiredness and finally could no longer hold out against sleep, no matter what horrors might overtake her in the night. Somehow her senses still remained alert for any different sound, and immediately she heard a voice, she wakened. With her heart in her mouth, she listened intently, not daring to relax until she heard him call her name, the sound barely distinguishable from the soft moaning of the wind through the surrounding trees.

When she recognised Hal's voice she gave a cry of joy and, heedless of the blankets tumbling around her ankles, rushed forward to meet him. He had hardly climbed over the battered sill before she was in his arms and holding him as if she would never let him go.

'Poor Nicol,' he whispered. 'You must have been really frightened, to greet me so.'

For a moment she was angry that he should think her so weak. She might have been frightened out of her mind waiting alone in the forest, but her relief was all for him. It was on the tip of her tongue to tell him so, but instead she drew back.

'It was unfair of me to leave you,' he admitted, misinterpreting her withdrawal. 'As it is, the children are quite safe. Louise's sister has them. I can't say I was made very welcome, for they know me to be the cause of it all, but they were willing enough to take my gold. It was conscience money and they were quite aware of it. Claude was executed this morning . . . No, it was yesterday morning.' He shook his head as if to clear it. 'I was forgetting that it's almost dawn.'

Nicol reached for his hand and found it like ice beneath her fingers. 'Come over by the fire,' she said, drawing him towards her crumpled blankets.

He sat down and pulled her to him, sighing deeply as he did so. His coat smelt of the night, and with a shiver of pleasure, she slipped her hand inside it, curling her arm around his broad back and feeling the warmth beneath his shirt.

For each of them it began as a passionless desire for comfort, and yet, within minutes, he was running his hands across her and kissing her with a passion that was bound to be a prelude to more. He did not speak, offering no endearments or protestations of love, but took her roughly, almost angrily, as if he needed to drain himself of all feeling and therefore all pain.

'I'm sorry, Nicol,' he whispered afterwards. 'That was unpardonable. I shouldn't have vented my frustrations on you.'

'I don't mind,' she told him softly, letting her fingers explore the hard, tense muscles at the back of his neck. 'It was still good, and I love you so.'

She felt him stiffen and he laughed a little shakily. 'Still the romantic child. Why, you've only known me a matter of days. I don't want you to love me, girl—don't you realise that? Love is a far too unpredictable emotion, if indeed it exists at all.'

So he wanted her body, nothing more. Nicol felt it like a slap in the face. Not that she expected protestations of love—he was not that kind of man—but need he have been quite so brutal and frank? He was leaving her no pride at all. She turned her face away and closed her eyes so that he should not see the pain in them.

'I'm sorry, Nicky,' he whispered, his voice seeming to come from far off. 'I'll take care of you always, I swear, but please don't ask me for more than I can give.'

Damn him, damn his arrogance, she thought, and she hated him for his kind concern. When he began to stroke her hair, she pulled away.

'I'll get dressed,' she muttered, reaching for her clothes. 'I want to boil some water before we have to put out the fire.'

He frowned, quite out of his depth now, and not convinced by her matter-of-fact tone.

'There's some coffee in my saddle-bag,' he said, reaching for his breeches. 'I'll fetch it and see to my horse.'

'I'll do it,' she said, still not meeting his eyes. 'You'd better rest. I assume you'll be wanting to move on today.'

'We ought to... Nicky, I'm sorry!'

'If you say that once more, I shall hit you,' she stormed, her eyes positively blazing. 'You've always been perfectly honest with me. You needn't worry; I shan't embarrass you with sentiment again!'

She stumbled outside and began to unsaddle the horse, hardly able to see what she was doing through her tears. It's not too late, she told herself. You can draw back from him if you really try.

'I hate him. I hate him!' she hissed at the surprised animal, and in the heat of the moment she was not lying at all.

CHAPTER SEVEN

AN HOUR later, having consumed Hal's meagre supply of coffee, they broke camp and continued on their way. Nicol was still simmering with hurt and resentment and rode silently behind her husband, relieved that he did not want to talk. Once again, he seemed to have withdrawn into himself. His characteristic frown had returned and he concealed his feelings behind an icy politeness.

The hours dragged as they travelled westwards through a countryside that was almost deserted. The girl found that she was very tired and, had it not been for the unpleasant cold, would have dozed in the saddle. In the late afternoon her horse nearly stumbled and Hal, having dismounted to examine the beast, declared that it was completely exhausted. He glanced around and a copse of tall beech trees caught his eye.

'We'll be safe in there,' he said, reaching up to help Nicol down and then leading both horses forward. 'I'm afraid it's going to be a pretty uncomfortable night.'

They found a deep depression amid the trees and, after tethering the horses, Hal set about constructing a windbreak of bracken and leafless branches.

He spread his cloak out across the ground and then bowed mockingly to Nicol. 'Your couch awaits you, madam.'

When he settled down beside her and slipped his arm around her shoulders, she stiffened.

'Oh, come on, Nicky,' he growled. 'If we don't lie close together, we'll freeze.'

Obviously he was right and she told herself that it was the only reason she permitted him to draw her close. It was incredible, but even in that cold place he seemed to generate a vital, animal warmth, and when he spread out the blankets to cover them both she did not protest. She finally fell asleep with her head against his chest, lulled by the steady, rhythmic beating of his heart.

When she awoke it was dark and a thin sliver of moon was painting silver patterns on the grass beneath the trees. Around her the wind whispered through the woods and, somewhere near, a night bird called. Cautiously, she shifted her position, not wanting to disturb Hal.

'Are you all right?' he asked huskily, revealing that he was already awake.

'Oh, fine!' she muttered sarcastically. 'I'm starving and freezing to death, but otherwise everything's perfect!'

She heard his deep chuckle, followed by a muffled groan as the circulation began to return to his numbed arm. He had obviously been in discomfort for some time.

'Why didn't you wake me?' she asked testily, scrambling up and beginning to stamp her feet. God! Would she ever be warm again?

'I hadn't the heart. You'd never have dropped off again. Even in the Army I don't think I've spent a more miserable night!' He stood up himself and stretched his arms to remove the stiffness. 'Are you really hungry?'

It was a stupid question and she did not bother to answer him, merely giving an expressive but unlady-like snort. He walked over to rummage in his saddle-bag and returned with a chunk of bread and some sausage.

'I was saving it for an emergency,' he told her with a look of triumph.

Nicol took the bread and broke it in half, but he shook his head.

'No, you can have it all. I had a meal in the village.'

She shrugged, her conscience salved by having made the gesture, and attacked the food with a gusto that obviously amused him.

As they were not going to get any more sleep, it seemed reasonable for them to continue their journey. The horses were rested, but Hal still thought it advisable not to tire Nicol's mount and insisted on leading it while she rode his sterling beast. Slowly the eastern sky grew grey with the coming of dawn, and laces of golden light stretched out to trace the clouds. Nicol felt sick and shaky with tiredness, and the sudden noisy singing of the birds grated on her frayed nerves.

Hal walked ahead without complaint. Uncon-sciously, the girl's eyes rested on his broad back and she felt an emotion that was almost tenderness. He was being considerate again but, damn him, she didn't want that.

'You must tell me when you're tired and we'll change places,' she told him.

'Of course,' he replied gravely.

'Do you know where we are going?' she asked after a while.

'More or less.'

She frowned irritably. 'What's that supposed to mean?'

'What I said ... I know where I want to go, and we're heading in the general direction. When we are nearer I shall have to enquire.'

'Where are we going?'

He sighed in exasperation, unconsciously revealing how tired he really was. 'To be honest, Nicky, it's probably better if you don't know. If anything happens to me you must return to Jacquelein.'

'Don't you trust me?'

'I wouldn't trust my own brother if the Republicans got hold of him. Now stop pestering me, there's a good girl. My feet ache and I'm tired.'

He was treating her like a child again, and she ground her teeth in frustration; there was nothing else she could do. When the sun came up and began to warm her back her spirits rose. Hal too seemed to feel better and he began to whistle cheerfully. In the middle of the morning they stopped by a small stream to water the horses, and Nicol climbed down to wash her face in its icy depths. Then, using her fingers, she tried to coax some order into her thick, untidy hair.

Hal was filling his canteen, but he paused to watch her, his breath catching in his throat. If he weren't such an experienced man, it would have been so easy to have fallen in love with her. Not only was she beautiful but she showed a strange mixture of vulnerability and spirit that was undeniably appealing. Her tangled hair made her seem unusually fragile and the fresh wind had lent a delicate colour to her cheeks. As for her body ... he swallowed when he remembered how she had felt in his arms.

'I don't suppose you've got a mirror?' she asked hopefully.

He shook his head and laughed, more to ease the sexual tension that was mounting inside him than for anything else. 'Trust a woman to ask for that!'

Nicol bit back a sharp retort and, after collecting her comb from her saddle-bag, began to tidy her hair. It was hopeless; as fast as she smoothed the tangles the wind whipped them back. Soon her arms began to ache with the effort.

'Allow me,' said Hal, moving behind her and taking the comb from her hand.

He was thorough and amazingly gentle, and yet his touch awoke feelings she would rather have kept suppressed.

'It ought to be plaited,' he told her.

'I know, but I don't think I can manage it myself,' she replied somewhat shortly.

He chuckled. 'I can. After all, your hair is not so different from a horse's tail.'

True to his word, he deftly twisted her thick tresses into a plait, and then fastened the end with a strip of leather cut from his glove. It was only when she turned to thank him that she noticed how stiffly he was standing, all colour having drained from his face.

'You're ill,' she exclaimed, impulsively reaching out to touch his arm.

He shook his head and smiled wryly. 'Stomach cramp, that's all. Perhaps I didn't cook that rabbit well enough.'

'But that was nearly two days ago...' A thought occurred to her, making her feel both angry and tender at the same time. 'You *didn't* eat in Cancale, did you?' When he did not reply, she knew that she was right.

'Damn you, Hal Grantly. I don't want any favours. Do you hear? I'm quite capable of doing my share. I don't want you walking while I ride. I don't want your share of the food. I'm not a weakling or a child!'

He seemed a little taken aback by her outburst, and she did not give him time to think of a reply. Instead she mounted her horse and set off following the bank of the stream. Damn the man. He really wasn't playing fair. He didn't love her. He'd made that perfectly clear, so why, oh, *why* did he have to be so considerate? She wanted to hate him and yet it was as if every action on his part was designed to make her love him more.

When she heard a horse behind her, she knew that he had followed.

'You'd better go easy on that beast,' he commented. 'She's not fully recovered.'

There was no rancour in his voice, and certainly no remorse. Nicol smothered her anger and slowed to a walk.

They kept to little-used tracks and saw no sign of human life until almost noon when they came across a small one-storey cottage whose weathered stone blended perfectly with the surrounding trees.

For a while they sat looking at it, not at all encouraged by its air of loneliness and neglect. Finally the gnawing pain in Hal's stomach decided him and he dismounted. Leaving Nicol to hold the horses, he walked resolutely around the woodpile and across the patch of cleared earth that led up to the door. He knocked loudly, waiting in vain for an answer, and was just lifting his hand to knock again when a movement to the right caught his eye. Turning, he found himself looking into the barrels of a shotgun.

His eyes lifted to the person holding it, and Nicol had never seen him look so surprised.

The old woman must have been at least eighty and looked so frail that it seemed as if a puff of wind would blow her away. The gun must have been heavy for her thin arms to hold, yet its muzzle was rock-steady. Hal smiled uncertainly.

'You can just get back on your horse, young man, and clear off,' she told him in a voice that was surprisingly strong and defiant. 'I can't abide strangers around me.'

He cleared his throat and for once, seemed lost for words.

Nicol felt that her intervention could scarcely make matters worse. 'Please, *madame*, we mean you no harm but we're desperately in need of food.'

'We're willing to work for it,' Hal added, letting his gaze roam over the sagging roof and the enormous pile of logs that lay ready for splitting.

'You don't look like workers,' the old woman commented, her bright eyes missing nothing. 'Still, you're strong enough, so perhaps we could do a trade.' She lowered the gun and nodded towards the woodpile. 'That wants chopping into manageable logs and some of it splitting into kindling. If you can do that for me, there's bread and cheese in the kitchen. You, girl, had better see to your horses, then I'll give you a basket and you can carry some of the wood inside.'

Both Hal and Nicol nodded mutely, feeling rather like errant schoolchildren in the presence of a dame.

'The chopper's there and there's a saw in the barn,' the old woman added. 'Now you'd best get on with it, because the sooner it's done the sooner you'll be able to eat.'

Moving past them, she entered the house, leaving the door open so that she could see that they behaved. Hal pulled a wry face and, stripping down to his shirtsleeves, picked up the axe and began his chore. Nicol unsaddled the horses and led them to a moss-covered drinking trough, then, after tethering them to a low fence, left them to graze.

Hal paused in his labours to look up and smile. His cravat was askew and even with his beard he looked ridiculously boyish. He wielded the axe again and his muscles pulled against the thin fabric of his shirt. Nicol felt that familiar quaver in her stomach and remembering the feel of his hands upon her, was forced to look away.

He reached for another log then paused with a grunt of pain, his hand lifting to press against his belt. He was as white as a sheet as he leant back against the chopping block and a thin film of perspiration beaded his brow.

His obvious pain frightened Nicol, and when she saw the old woman approaching she prepared herself for a fight. She was not going to let the old crone send them away, not with Hal in that condition.

'How long since he ate?' the old woman demanded perceptively.

'Two days, *madame*. He gave the last of the food to me.'

'The man's a fool,' was the gruff reply. 'He's the one who needs his strength. He'll work better when he's had a bite to eat. When the spasm passes, bring him into the kitchen.'

'She makes me feel like a child,' Hal complained as he watched their benefactress walk away.

'At least she's willing to feed you,' Nicol retorted. 'Perhaps next time you won't be so eager to play the martyr.'

'Shrew!' he hissed, but there was an amused sparkle in his eyes as he looked down at her.

The meal of bread and cheese could scarcely have been called adequate, and they rose from the table still feeling hungry. Nevertheless, Hal declared that he felt much better and, after consuming a mug of goat's milk, returned to his chore. Nicol collected a basket and carried some of the wood into the house.

Once he had chopped a presentable pile of logs, Hal asked the old woman if there was anything else he could do. The chimney smoked badly, she told him, and she was incapable of climbing on the roof to investigate. The barn door was off its hinges and he could turn over the kitchen garden if he was of a mind, for it would make it easier for her to plant in the spring.

He grinned and glanced meaningfully at the sky. 'That's quite a list, *madame*. I'll be lucky to finish before dark. I think it's worth another meal and shelter for the night.'

Unexpectedly the old woman laughed. 'Aye, boy, I suppose it is, and, to tell the truth, I'll be glad of your company. I find it lonely with my own boys away.'

Nicol spent the rest of the day helping with other household chores and it proved yet another exercise in humility. The old woman criticised continually and, by the time the meal was ready, Nicol felt sure that her ineptitude had given her away.

When she confided in Hal he dismissed her fears with a nonchalant shrug. He was in an oddly carefree mood, more jovial than she had ever seen him.

'The old girl's on our side; I'd stake our lives on it.' He grinned. 'In fact, I probably have! Stop worrying and come and help me get cleaned up. If I sit down at her table in this condition, she'll likely box my ears!'

In spite of the cold, he removed his shirt, and while Nicol worked the pump he sluiced his arms and chest in the icy water. The old woman threw him a cloth and he briskly rubbed his body before dabbing more gently at his hands. Nicol turned his palms upwards and exclaimed in sympathy at the broken blisters that covered them.

'Badges of honest toil,' he joked, reaching out to tuck a lock of stray hair behind her ear and kiss her playfully on the nose.

It was an easy, tender gesture, more loving in its way than a full-blooded embrace, and after all he had said it surprised her.

This time, they ate well of a rich vegetable stew followed by bread and home-made cheese. Hal's appetite was voracious. The old lady did not stint the food; rather she seemed to derive pleasure from seeing him eat. As the meal progressed, she unwound to the point of telling them her name, at the same time informing them that the people around called her Grand'mère, and that she would be pleased if they would do the same.

Hal's manner towards her was gentle, almost teasing, and, just like Madame Lamarte, she fell easily under his spell. Could he control such charm? Nicol wondered, or was it simply that he was only at ease with older women?

'How far are we from Cap Fréhel?' he asked after a while, pushing his chair back from the table and stretching his long legs with a contented sigh.

'Is that the headland that can be seen from Rothéneuf on a clear day? Almost two days' ride, and then only if you take the rather dangerous short-cut across the estuary at low tide.'

'We have to be at a point along that coast four days from now.'

Grand'mère appeared to consider the matter, then said, 'My daughter married a farmer from over that way. I believe they'd give you shelter for a day or two. They have no reason to love the Republicans.'

It was the first time she had mentioned politics, but the bitterness in her voice left them in no doubt as to where her sympathies lay.

Hal nodded uncertainly. 'We'd be grateful, *madame*, but we'd hate to get either you or your family into trouble.'

'Trouble!' the old woman laughed. 'I'm used to it. What with one grandson fighting for the Chouans and the other wanted by the Excise men, I've had more than my share. I've no time for this new government and their bullying ways. My Léon would have been forced to fight against his own kind if he hadn't run away to join Cadoudal. He's barely eighteen, too, and more like a son than a grandson to me since his mother died. What do I care about the politics of Paris? I only see the misery around here. We may not have been wealthy before the Revolution, but at least we did not live in fear. We'd be a lot happier if only the Republicans would leave us alone!'

While Nicol appreciated the luxury of a roof over her head, she regarded sharing a bed with Hal as something of a mixed blessing. She had still not forgiven him for his denial of love, and her pride revolted at the thought of a purely physical relationship.

Before they retired to bed Hal went out quietly to saddle the horses, just as a precaution. Then they undressed in silence, Nicol facing away from him and towards the wall. As quickly as she could, she slipped between the coarse sheets and lay stiffly, waiting for him to join her. She was a mass of conflicting emotions, wanting him and resenting him at the same time. For a while he lay quietly beside her, not touching and yet close enough for her to feel the warmth emanating from his naked body.

'Are you going to fight me again, Nicol?' he asked softly.

'No... no, of course not,' she answered uncertainly. 'You're my husband. After what has already happened, it would be pointless, but I don't expect any pleasure, not when you're so cold-blooded about it!'

He laughed softly, provocatively. 'That sounds like a challenge.'

'It is not!'

In reply, he rolled over, draping one long arm across her and pulling her against him so that she was touching him from shoulder to toe. The contact sent a wave of desire surging through her, and once his hand began to caress her she knew that she was lost. His hard, masculine body was deliciously familiar and her love for him was just too strong. For a while she allowed her conscious self to become lost in the primitive responses of her body. It was later, when they lay together totally spent and Hal drew her gently back into his arms, that she had to bite her tongue to hold back her words of love.

She drifted to sleep with her head pillowed against him and her unseen tears still wet upon her cheeks. She awakened some time later when he gently moved his arm. She felt the covers lift and heard him move quietly across the floor. Forcing her eyes open, she asked sleepily if anything was wrong.

He was peering through a gap in the shutters and it was a moment before he answered her. 'Somebody's out there. I don't like it, Nicky. I think we'd better get dressed.'

There was hardly any moonlight coming through the shutters and she had to fumble for her clothes. She gathered her few possessions by touch and bundled them into her soft bag. Then, as an afterthought, she quickly tidied the bed; there was no reason to leave such obvious evidence of their occupancy.

Hal took her cloak from the peg behind the door, and, putting it across her shoulders, lifted the hood and tied the strings under her chin. For a moment, he let his hand linger against the side of her face.

'Are you ready?' he asked softly.

He went back to the window and eased back the shutters, then bent to check his pistol in the moonlight. Stepping softly across the sill, he turned to help Nicol. Her feet touched the hard-packed earth and she shuddered as the cold air hit her face.

He closed the shutters behind them and, taking her hand, guided her towards the back of the building. Crouching low, they hurried into the surrounding trees. Nicol felt so tense that she could hardly breathe and her supper sat uneasily in her stomach. They had, mercifully, just reached concealment when they heard someone shouting loudly for the old woman to open the door.

'How could they know we were there?' asked Nicol, and felt Hal shrug in the darkness. 'What do we do now? Do we wait and hope that they'll go away?'

'Not on your life,' he answered, still hurrying her along. 'They haven't discovered our horses yet, but it's just a matter of time.'

He led her through the trees to the back of the barn, then began pulling at the timber wall. He loosened a couple of planks and wriggled inside, drawing Nicol after him.

'Be careful,' he cautioned. 'There are a couple of crates to your left.'

The soft whinny of a horse welcomed them and Hal led her without hesitation towards it. As he tightened the cinch and helped her to mount, she was thankful for the foresight that had led him to saddle the beasts.

'The door is to your right,' he whispered, leading his own mount forward. 'Be ready to ride out as soon as I open it. Meanwhile, keep your beast as quiet as you can.'

She heard the creak of leather as he adjusted the saddle, and then the shuffle of the other horse's hooves as it waited nervously.

'You'd better check the barn.' A voice filtered through the rough door, making Nicol's stomach turn over. 'And be careful. According to my informant, Grantly's an expert with both sword and pistol and will fight like a demon when cornered.'

'It seems a lot of effort for one man and a girl,' a gruffer voice complained. 'They're probably miles away by now.'

'Take my word for it; their capture will be well worth our while,' the first voice continued. 'Grantly is reported to be in Jacquelein's confidence and should be able to give us an insight into how the General's mind is working, not to mention what he'll be able to tell us of his own work here.'

Hal abruptly swung the door wide and pale moonlight flooded into the barn. The silhouettes of the two men stood out sharply as they turned in surprise. Nicol determinedly kicked her horse forward, every instinct telling her to ride them down. One man cried out as her horse bowled him over and Hal's pistol exploded close at hand.

'Bear right!' he shouted from behind her, and, obeying, she found herself on a narrow track that led between the trees. He had obviously taken time from his labours to have a good look around, yet another indication that he was no novice at the deadly game they were playing.

By now it was almost dawn and the sky was showing a lighter grey between the bare trees. They had hardly covered a hundred yards when figures materialised from the shadows to bar their way. Nicol slowed uncertainly and, glancing at Hal, could see that he too was undecided. He swore savagely—the men, about half a dozen of them, all held muskets and there was really no choice at all.

With a sinking stomach, Nicol pulled her horse to a halt. Hal reined in beside her and one of the men motioned for them to dismount. A burly fellow reached up to help her from the saddle and, as he set her down, he gave her breast an impudent squeeze. Immediately, her de Carrie temper exploded and she slapped him hard across the face. The situation was exacerbated by the laughter of his companions and in order to save face he dragged her against him and kissed her hard.

Frantically she tried to push him away, and then all hell seemed to break loose as Hal somehow managed to reach her attacker and fell him with a single blow. The others charged him and he went down in a welter of arms and legs, still hitting out in all directions.

Nicol was beyond all rational thought as she threw herself into the fray, kicking, gouging and pulling hair in a vain attempt to help her husband. Screwing up her fist, she smashed it against a man's temple, feeling the impact right up her arm. She twisted another man's ear and clawed wildly at his face but grunts and muttered oaths were her only reward. Someone gave her a mighty backhander and she was sent flying. Her head connected sharply with a nearby tree trunk and after a moment of sharp pain, she knew no more.

She felt as if she were suffocating and struggled weakly against the hands that held her. Someone spoke soothingly and something cool and damp was pressed against her face. Irritably, she pushed it away and opened her eyes to find the old woman bending over her. She wanted to speak but felt too sick, and for a moment had to lie quietly, breathing deeply and trying not to throw up all over the ancient patchwork coverlet. Finally she was able to look around and to her surprise found herself on the same bed that she had left only minutes before.

'Hal?' she managed to ask.

'He's bruised and angry but he'll survive. The men are asking him a few questions and if he answers honestly then you've nothing to fear. He was extremely worried about you, my dear. I'd best go and fetch him.'

None of it seemed to make any sense to Nicol, least of all Hal's husbandly concern.

'He only married me to please my father,' she choked out, surprising herself with the somewhat irrelevant admission.

'Hush, you're quite safe now,' the old woman muttered, wiping her face once more.

'But what about those men...?'

'It's all right, my dear. They're Chouans, a little rough in their ways, but you can trust them. Young Paul has already been severely chastised for the way he treated you.'

Nicol sniffed, determinedly fighting her tears. 'I'm sorry. I'm not usually such a watering pot.'

The old woman nodded understandingly. 'I expect your head is still sore. The last few days can't have been easy for you. I don't suppose they were for your husband, either. He was extremely worried about you and furious with the men. They said he fought like one demented and he too was unconscious when they brought him in.'

'But he's all right now?' Nicol asked with a spurt of anxiety.

'Oh, yes. He's a tough one. Now, dry your eyes and I'll send him in to you.'

Nicol did not want that. She was embarrassed by her show of emotion and had no wish to play the part of a weakling. She felt guilty, too, aware that her fierce temper had begun a fight that Hal had been forced to try and finish. If she had only thought before she had acted then neither one of them would have been hurt.

'I'm feeling much better,' she insisted, and, swinging her legs to the floor, stood up carefully. Her head still ached but it was a pain she could cope with and at least that awful sick feeling had disappeared.

Hal rose to his feet as soon as she entered the crowded living-room, and moved quickly towards her. She thought he looked tired and there was an additional bruise on one cheek.

'Are you all right?' he asked solicitously as he guided her across to a chair.

'I'm fine.'

His eyes searched her face as if to verify her statement. 'You're quite a little tiger when you lose your temper.'

'I'm sorry you were hurt, *madame*,' muttered a slim young man with serious brown eyes. 'We only wanted to find out a little about you. In fact, you have reason to be grateful to us. There were other Republicans waiting in the woods, and without our help you couldn't possibly have escaped them all.'

She glanced around the room at the other men and was relieved to find no sign of her attacker. 'It's lucky you were at hand.'

'Not really. We like to keep an eye on Grand'mère, and we weren't sure you could be trusted. It wouldn't be the first time that Republicans have posed as escaping Royalists and then betrayed the very people who befriended them.'

'I didn't ask you to interfere, Léon,' the old woman grumbled. 'I'm a good judge of character and know real fugitives when I see them . . . and why you had to

bring that oaf Paul with you is beyond my understanding. He never has been able to keep his hands
to himself!'

'Paul has his uses, even if it is only to dispose of
unwanted bodies,' Léon grumbled. 'I don't know how
you would have explained the two in your yard. In
any case, he won't be returning here. I've sent him
into Cancale to find out what is happening there.' He
turned worried eyes to Hal. 'Someone must have told
the Republicans about the letter you are carrying, and
it can only have been someone close to you. As to
what happened in the village, if you did not betray
the Surats—and I accept your word that you did not—
then at some time you must have been followed. Unfortunately, the Republicans are becoming rather good
at that sort of thing.'

Nicol was watching Hal and saw the brief shadow
of pain that crossed his face.

'I was usually so damned careful about that, but
the last time I visited them I was tired . . .' He sighed
and ran a hand through his already untidy hair. 'It's
possible that I was followed, even probable in view
of what has happened.'

He looked so miserable that it was all Nicol could
do not to go to him and take him in her arms.

It was Léon who placed a comforting hand on his
shoulder. 'It's no use dwelling on what has passed;
instead you must decide what you are going to do
now. This part of the coast has become too dangerous
for you and you'd best be moving on.'

'I think I can arrange a crossing if we can reach
Cap Fréhel in the next couple of days.' Hal did not
elaborate and the others did not seem to expect it of

him. He smiled apologetically at Nicol. 'I'd like to set out again later today if you feel up to it.'

She stifled a groan and nodded. He really didn't look any better than she felt, and if he could continue then so could she.

'Have you mentioned my aunt?' Léon asked his grandmother. 'They would be safe enough with her.'

'Of course I did,' the old woman answered. 'I'm quite capable of thinking for myself... And you needn't be cheeky, young man,' she added astutely when her irreverent grandson pulled a face behind her back. 'You're not too old to have your ears boxed.'

One of the men laughed and Hal strategically covered his mouth with his hand. Nicol met Léon's gaze and smiled sympathetically. In spite of his youth, he was coping admirably with a difficult situation, and she thought his grandmother could have been more supportive.

'My men and I will escort you part of the way to my aunt's farm,' he continued, trying to regain his authority. 'I'm afraid that's the best we can do; our resources are thinly stretched and we have business elsewhere.'

'We'd be most grateful,' Nicol told him, and this time he returned her smile with one of admiration and warmth.

They resumed their journey around noon after Nicol had managed a couple of hours' sleep. The Chouans were in fine spirits and, to her surprise, Nicol found herself responding to their teasing and laughter. Before an hour had passed, she was completely at home in their company. They were, after all, of an age, and adversity had thrown them together.

Hal, on the other hand, seemed unusually quiet, and Nicol began to wonder if he was feeling quite well. Once or twice he answered Léon rather shortly and seemed generally ungrateful for the help they were being given. Unlike Nicol, he realised that their numbers were still too small to afford any real protection and he would rather have travelled alone. The Frenchmen did, however, know the countryside like the backs of their hands, and led the way along the most remote of pathways. The land remained hilly and wooded, although the trees were now mostly deciduous and their leaves lay like brown butterflies upon the grass.

In the late afternoon they came out of the woods and dropped down into the valley of the Rance. The wide tidal estuary lay before them, tawny and empty with the low sun glinting on the film of water that covered the dimpled sand. Nicol thought it looked beautiful and said as much.

'Beautiful, but deadly,' Léon commented as he led the way down a gentle incline towards the crumbling banks. 'You must follow me exactly.'

Even Hal was grateful for the Chouans' guidance as they slowly made their way across the mudflats, between areas of hidden quicksand. At one point Nicol's horse sidled nervously, and the next moment its rear legs had sunk up to its knees.

'Hal!' she called frantically, stifling a scream.

In an instant he was at her side, taking the reins and urging the beast onwards, speaking in the same quiet, encouraging voice she had come to know so well.

They spent the night camping in the open, but this time they were better prepared. Grand'mère had provided additional blankets and both Hal and Léon thought it safe to risk a fire. They roasted some potatoes in the glowing embers and then ate them with some cold sausage. Suddenly, Nicol felt unbearably tired, and with tiredness came depression. She picked despondently at her food.

'What's the matter?' asked Hal, quietly moving closer.

'Nothing,' she lied.

He had already finished his own meal, and, putting his arm around her, drew her close. For a while she sat quietly, drawing on the comfort he was offering her.

Then she asked, 'Do we really have a chance of reaching England? You don't have to pretend with me, you know.'

'Of course we'll reach England,' he said.

'I don't know how you can be so sure. The Republicans seem quite determined to prevent us.'

'I promise you we shall reach England,' he repeated, placing a finger under her chin and turning her face towards him. 'Now stop worrying and eat your bloody potato; then you ought to get some rest.'

'Did anyone ever tell you that you swear too much?' she asked, a hint of laughter in her voice.

'Lots of people, but I'm afraid I'm too old to change my ways.'

'I don't think you're at all old,' she replied, suddenly serious. 'I did at first, but not any more.'

He gave an enigmatic smile and kissed her gently on the mouth. 'Finish your meal, Nicky.'

'All right, I'll eat my *bloody* potato and my *bloody* sausage,' she teased, attempting to return to the easy banter of a moment before, but it was too late.

Somehow he had withdrawn from her, and she wondered sadly if it would always be like that. Just one thoughtless word and he retreated behind a distant politeness. She wanted to grasp his shoulders and shake him in frustration but, instead, she masked her feelings, too.

The men sat up until quite late, smoking and discussing politics and, once again, Nicol was surprised by her husband's knowledge of French affairs. When he eventually came to join her between their blankets, she was already half asleep. He lay beside her for a while and then drew her close against him so that her spine was touching his stomach and his hand was spread across her ribs. When she curled up he did so, too, so that they fitted together like spoons in a drawer. She knew then that he needed her comfort, and she smiled sleepily as she realised that he was not as self-sufficient as he liked to appear.

'He's a quiet man and as deep as a well,' Grand'mère had commented before they'd left the cottage. 'If he's not in love with you now, then he soon will be.'

For the first time she wondered if the old woman had been right, then she remembered his emphatic denial of love and the circumstances of it, and that small ray of hope withered and died. She sighed, and with a sleepy, animal-like grunt he drew her closer against him so that she could feel his chest rising and falling against her back. Inexplicably, her own breathing regulated itself to his, and it was with an essential feeling of belonging that she finally drifted off to sleep.

The following morning the Chouans left them, and Hal and Nicol once more turned north towards the coast. She was tired and stiff from her night on the ground and several times he had to wait for her to catch up. In spite of this, he offered not one word of reproach but remained unfailingly patient, leading her on again with a gentle smile.

Oddly enough, this was more than she could stand. She became shrewish and accused him of being condescending, and they ended up having a flaming row. After that he rode in stony silence. Nicol ought to have felt satisfied, for she had shown him how little she cared, but instead she was miserable and perversely found herself missing his warm looks and encouraging smile.

Take 4 Medical Romances

Mills & Boon Medical Romances capture the excitement, intrigue and emotion of the busy medical world. A world often interrupted by love and romance...

We will send you 4 BRAND NEW MEDICAL ROMANCES absolutely FREE plus a cuddly teddy bear and a surprise mystery gift, as your introduction to this superb series.

At the same time we'll reserve a subscription for you to our Reader Service. Every two months you could receive the 6 latest Medical Romances delivered direct to your door POST AND PACKING FREE, plus a free Newsletter packed with competitions, author news and much, much more.

What's more there's no obligation, you can cancel or suspend your subscription at any time. So you've nothing to lose and a whole world of romance to gain!

FREE

FILL IN THE FREE BOOKS COUPON OVERLEAF

Your Free Gifts!

We'll send you this cute little tan and white teddy bear plus a surprise gift when you return this card. So don't delay.

Reader Service

FREEPOST

PO Box 236

Croydon

Surrey

CR9 9EL

SEND NO MONEY NOW

FREE BOOKS CERTIFICATE

YES please send me my 4 FREE Medical Romances, together with my Teddy and mystery gift. Please also reserve a special Reader Service subscription for me. If I decide to subscribe, I shall receive 6 new books every two months for just £8.10, post and packaging free. If I decide not to subscribe, I shall write to you within 10 days. The free books and gifts will be mine to keep in any case.

I understand that I am under no obligation whatsoever – I can cancel or suspend my subscription at any time simply by writing to you.
I am over 18 years of age.

EXTRA BONUS

We all love surprises, so as well as the FREE books and Teddy, here's an intriguing mystery gift especially for you. No clues - send off today!

1AOD

Mrs/Miss/Ms _____
(Block capitals please)

Address _____

_____ Postcode _____

Signature _____

CHAPTER EIGHT

'She's there all right,' Hal muttered with satisfaction. 'Look!'

He was lying on his stomach amid the long grass on the cliff-top and, without taking his eyes from the distant horizon, passed the spy-glass to Nicol. For a moment, she had difficulty focusing it; then the sails of the British frigate swept into view, squares of pristine white moving gracefully against the grey sea. By adjusting the glass, she could even make out the flags streaming from her mastheads.

'But she's moving away from us!' she exclaimed, more than a little confused.

'Don't worry, she'll put about after dark and come looking for a signal. All the same, I think they'll be surprised to see one!' Hal was beaming like a schoolboy as he climbed to his feet and then reached down to help her. 'Come on, wife, let's get back to the farm. A couple of hours' rest won't go amiss. We shall be busy enough tonight.'

They had spent the last couple of days with the Rouger family at their remote homestead just south of Cap Fréhel. The only daughter of the house was a recent widow, her lawyer husband having been unjustly executed for anti-Republican sympathies. The poor fellow had been unfortunate enough to represent the interests of a local count, sufficient to damn him in Republican eyes.

Like most people of the area, the Rougers were fiercely independent, their hatred of the Republicans founded more on personal tragedy and dislike of being told what to do than on any real religious or Royalist convictions. They treated Nicol with a familiarity she found faintly annoying, yet she suspected that had she been the Queen herself their attitude would have been no different.

Hal, on the other hand, had been unusually kind and attentive towards her, as if trying to make up in actions for what he could not feel. Several times she had thrown his consideration back in his face, despising herself and yet unable to help it, driven by her fierce de Carrie pride. Hal ignored her outbursts and maintained a rather superior calm, so that, once again, she became aware of how close love and hate could be.

She tried desperately to hold herself back from him and yet the responses of her body made any estrangement in real terms impossible. It was foolish, she knew, to give herself so freely to a man with so little heart, and yet somehow she just could not help herself. Even now, as he guided her back towards the horses, the touch of his hand filled her with a treacherous feeling of desire.

Monsieur Rouger was waiting for them by the stove in the farmhouse kitchen, his round, weather-beaten face looking unusually concerned.

'There are soldiers in the village,' he growled. 'They are on the look-out for an Englishman and a Vendean girl. I think, *monsieur*, that you are more important than you have led us to believe.'

Hal managed a nonchalant shrug. 'I cannot think why they should be interested in us, *monsieur*.

However, rather than bring you trouble, I think we should leave.'

'If our Chouans were here, then it would be a different matter...' Rouger blustered. 'As it is, I have my family to consider. My daughter has already suffered enough.'

'But it is so cold!' protested his wife.

'Don't worry, *madame*,' Hal assured her with a warm smile. 'We shall do well enough.'

'Of course they will,' her husband snapped, torn between feelings of relief and guilt. 'There's a British frigate prowling about just offshore. I'll wager they'll be aboard her by midnight. Take care though, *monsieur*; if I know of her then the soldiers do, too.'

Hal nodded and slipped a comforting arm around Nicol. Although he did not admit it, he was more than a little anxious, knowing full well that it would be their last chance of escape.

They spent the rest of the day hiding in a sheltered hollow on the cliff-top, their horses tethered in some nearby trees. Nicol felt unbearably sad—she was leaving France, and the realisation held an unpleasant finality. For a while she let her mind linger on all that had passed and found herself embarrassingly close to tears. Hal too was very quiet, showing an unexpected sensitivity to her feelings, and although he said nothing the warmth of his arm was a comfort in itself.

Below them the tide rolled against the base of the cliff with a soporific regularity, while overhead seabirds wheeled and cried. Slowly, imperceptibly, the sky darkened, and Nicol fell into an uneasy doze. She awoke cold and stiff and, struggling to her feet, stretched her cramped limbs. Without warning, Hal grasped her shoulders and pulled her back down. At first she thought that he was teasing but he gave her arm a warning squeeze and gestured frantically to the right.

She watched in horror as a company of Republican soldiers marched past them, the rugged cliff-top path bringing them to within a stone's throw of her hiding place. They were picked out in a sudden burst of moonlight, their faces gleaming like waxed linen above the glaring white of their uniform facings and webbing.

Hal cursed and continued to hold her down, his ragged breathing fanning her ear. As the soldiers moved away, she felt the tension leave his lean body and he heaved a sigh of relief. 'Let's hope that frigate doesn't put in an appearance too soon!'

She gave a shaky smile and snuggled closer into the crook of his arm. 'You're insane to be here, you know. You could be comfortable and safe in England.'

'There's more than one reason for what I'm doing,' he replied with a seriousness that surprised her. Then, catching hold of her chin, he forced her to look up at him. 'You do trust me, don't you, Nicky?'

'Of course,' she answered, perplexed.

For the next few hours they continued to wait in the cold, uncomfortable darkness. Nicol's spirits dropped along with the temperature and no amount of cheerful badinage on Hal's part could cheer her. From time to time he took his telescope and scanned the moonlit horizon, finally giving a sigh of relief.

'She's back,' he said. 'We'd better get ready to light the torches.'

As he spoke, the thin sliver of moon slipped behind the gathering cloud, throwing darkness across the cliff-top like a thick blanket. Out at sea, the silver light still played across the frigate's pale sails, making her presence frighteningly obvious. Hal swore irritably and fumbled for his tinder-box, then asked Nicol to stand in front of him to shelter him from the wind. The two torches, well covered with pitch, suddenly flared to life, filling the small hollow with a flickering orange light.

With a grunt of satisfaction, he moved closer to the cliff edge and began to signal, lifting one arm and then the other with such a look of concentration on his face that Nicol wanted to laugh. A light flashed from the direction of the frigate, once, twice.

'That's it,' Hal grunted, rolling the torches on the grass to extinguish them. 'They'll be with us in a minute. We'd better go down.'

Taking Nicol's hand, he drew her after him towards the steep path. It was a treacherous climb in the moonlight and several times she nearly slipped and fell. His hand was always there to steady her and yet he refused to slow his pace. Small stones scattered before them as they slithered and slipped on the damp earth; then they were almost down and Hal jumped the last few feet to the beach, turning quickly and holding out his hands to Nicol.

The sand was still wet from the retreating tide and felt strangely solid beneath their feet. Still Hal hurried, encouraging Nicol to run until her breath tore at her throat and her chest was tight with the sustained effort.

'Can't we slow down...? Please!' she panted.

Finally, when she felt that she could not take another step, he took notice of her and slowed to a brisk walk, slipping one strong arm around her and almost carrying her forward.

'If the soldiers are still around they'll have seen the signal, too,' he panted. 'I wouldn't have risked making it if things hadn't been so desperate. There!'

He pointed ahead and Nicol could just make out the dark shape of a dinghy rounding the headland. Hal glanced around as if he could actually smell danger. Nicol was close enough to feel the tension in his lean body, and knew that for once he was really afraid. With a muttered oath, he broke into a run again, pulling her roughly along behind him. Then, glancing to her right, she caught sight of a dozen uniformed figures hurrying along the beach towards them. Simultaneously the Republicans noticed their quarry and, with shouts of triumph, began running, too.

'Off with your skirt and we'll swim for it,' Hal commanded, pausing to divest himself of coat and boots.

Nicol had scarcely removed her own footwear before he was ripping off her skirt. Together, they ran forward into the surf, their heels kicking up bursts of freezing, silver spray. Nicol's heart was thundering in her breast as she ran blindly with a speed born of panic, almost stumbling when the water pulled at her legs.

The English boat was approaching with frustrating slowness, the sailors at the oars having to work hard to make headway in the choppy sea.

'Soldiers!' yelled Hal, dropping Nicol's hand and gesturing wildly for the benefit of his fellow countrymen.

By now the icy water was almost up to Nicol's shoulders and she cried out with the shock.

'Swim!' Hal commanded. 'If you get into trouble, I'll help.'

She struck out determinedly towards the approaching hull, blessing her brother and the times by the river when he had all but forced her to swim. It was something she had mastered well, and yet swimming in a dammed-up stream was very different from trying to do so in such a cold and heaving sea. She gasped for breath and all but choked as an unpredictable wave slapped her in the face. Her wet petticoats were dragging her down, and worse still was the icy numbness that seemed to be spreading through her entire body.

Panic seized her and she flailed her arms in desperation; then, just as she felt she would drown, Hal's hands grasped her and he was dragging her towards the boat. A dark shape loomed above her. Strong hands grasped her arms and Hal was pushing her upwards in the most unceremonious way. The side of the boat was rough and splinters grazed her elbows and her legs as she was pulled from the cold and clinging water.

Above the grunting and shouting, the roaring and hissing of the waves, she heard another sharper sound and musket-fire thudded into the wood, knocking splinters from the bulwarks. Hal was just being hauled on board. She saw him stiffen and his grip relax so that he would have fallen back into the water had not the sailor assisting him maintained a hold. Nicol screamed as another sailor leant over to grasp her husband's belt and pull him over the gunwhale and on to the floor.

'Damn it! We're in their range!' growled the officer, cringing as more shots thudded into the woodwork beside his arm. 'Put your backs into it and let's get away from here!'

As the sailors bent to their oars, Nicol threw herself down on her knees beside Hal.

'My back...' he gasped, and when the young officer eased him over she saw a dark stain spreading rapidly across his shirt.

Without speaking, the Lieutenant pulled off his stock and, lifting Hal's shirt, pressed it tightly against the wound.

'Is it bad?' she choked.

'I don't know,' he told her before turning to his men. 'Come on, you laggards, row, row!'

Taking off his coat, he placed it over Hal, who by now was shivering violently in spite of being only semi-conscious. Nicol too was desperately cold, but anxiety dwarfed all physical discomfort so that she was aware of nothing save the need to reach the ship and the services of a reliable physician.

She spent the next few minutes in a kind of fever, her emotions in such turmoil that she was scarcely aware of time or space. Hal lay with his head in her lap, his eyes closed, and all the time he grasped her hand, holding it tightly as if it were a lifeline to which he clung.

After what seemed an eternity, the English frigate loomed above them, an immense dark shape against the moonlit sky. As she looked up through the tangle of ropes and rigging, a feeling of hopelessness washed over Nicol. How on earth were they going to get Hal aboard?

Scrambling nets were lowered and some of the men began to climb. A brawny sailor knelt and, with surprising ease, lifted the injured man across his shoulders.

'I can manage him,' he told the girl. 'You just follow with Mr Graham.'

Even with the young Lieutenant at her elbow, she found the climb difficult and knew that for Hal it must have been agony. By the time she reached the safety of the deck, they had already set him down and someone was shouting for blankets. He lay frighteningly still upon the battered planking, his face showing unnaturally white in the lantern light. He was dying, of that she was sure, slipping away from her as surely as a wisp of smoke.

Oh, don't let him die. Please don't let him die, she prayed silently, pulling away from her escort and dropping down on her knees beside the one person she had come to love more than life itself.

The frigate's young Captain pushed forward and, bending over the injured man, uttered an oath of surprise. 'Hal Grantly, isn't it? What the devil was he doing in France?'

He did not seem to expect an answer but rounded on his men, barking a string of orders, and Nicol was vaguely aware of something warm and rough being draped across her shoulders. Then they carried Hal away and, rather like a mother reluctant to be parted from a suckling child, she followed. He was taken down to one of the cabins, but when she tried to enter, the captain himself barred her way.

'It's best that you leave him to the surgeon,' he said kindly but firmly, and then, turning to one of his men, added, 'Show her to Mr Browne's cabin and find her some dry clothes. If we aren't careful, we shall have two invalids on our hands.'

An elderly, weathered individual took her arm and all but forced her into the cabin opposite.

'Get out of those wet things,' he told her brusquely, 'and I'll find you something dry.'

'But I must go to him,' she pleaded.

'No, ma'am. Our surgeon is one of the best in the Fleet. You must leave it to him. I'll be back in a minute with some dry clothes. Now do as I say. You'll be no use to your man if you take an ague.'

There was a rough kindliness behind his words as well as a great deal of common sense and she reluctantly obeyed, peeling off what remained of her sodden garments and wrapping the coarse blanket around herself. When she sat down upon the narrow bunk she was still shivering with reaction and fear and had to struggle desperately not to give in to her grief, knowing that she had to be strong for her husband's sake.

After a few minutes the same stocky sailor returned with an armful of clothes.

'Put these on, my beauty,' he commanded, tossing them into her lap. 'They belong to our youngest midshipman and ought to fit you.'

'Thank you... but my husband...? Do you know...?' To her annoyance, she continued to tremble and the unaccustomed English did not come easily to her tongue. Fortunately the fellow seemed to understand.

'The surgeon's still with him. Don't worry so, my dear. I've seen men look a lot worse and be on their feet in a matter of days. Get dressed now, and I'll find a little something to warm you up.'

As soon as he had gone, she struggled into the unfamiliar shirt and breeches. To her surprise they fitted quite well, although the shoes and stockings were too large and the breeches somewhat loose at the waist. She had scarcely made herself decent before the old sailor returned with a glass of brandy, then stood, arms folded, while she drained every drop.

The liquor warmed and steadied her even if it did make her feel a little unreal, and she managed a smile. 'Now can I see my husband?'

The fellow nodded and led her across to the other cabin. He opened the door and, after speaking with someone, stood aside for her to enter. Hal was lying quite still upon the narrow bunk, his eyes closed and his breathing shallow. The loss of blood and the shadows thrown by the lantern seemed to emphasise his features. His eyes appeared sunken under heavy brows and the old bruise on his temple stood out against skin that was unnaturally pale. His hair was still damp and tousled, making him look particularly young and vulnerable.

Nicol went to kneel beside him and, without thinking, gently brushed the dark curls back from his face.

'Is he going to be all right?' she asked, turning fear-filled eyes towards the surgeon.

He was a small, taciturn man who had spent most of his life at sea and thought himself fully hardened to the misery of others.

'I can't promise anything. I'm sorry,' he replied, feeling an unexpected stab of pity. 'The ball missed the shoulder-blade but has broken at least one rib. More dangerous still, it pierced the chest cavity. I don't think it touched the lung and I was able to remove it without too much trouble, but any chest wound is serious ... His obvious strength is in his favour, so I'm hopeful that he'll pull through.'

Nicol's eyes fell upon the bowl of bloodied water. At Granville she had become used to such sights, but the fact that it was Hal's blood caused any remaining colour to drain from her face. The surgeon tactfully motioned to the offending article and the stocky sailor carried it away.

'I want to stay with him,' she declared, turning to face the surgeon and almost defying him to send her away.

He merely nodded and considerately placed a chair beside the bed. 'I've done all I can for the present,' he said quietly, 'but you can call me if he wakes.'

She nodded, not trusting herself to speak, and did not even look up as he left the cabin. She had eyes only for Hal's pale face, her whole being concentrating on willing him to live. Anxiety was like a tight knot in her stomach and she was burdened by a futile and aching regret, regret for so many things left unsaid. She had never really expressed her gratitude, in fact hadn't really thought about it until then. Hal might not love her, but somehow that only indebted her more, particularly as she knew his inability to do so had vexed him as well as herself.

For quite some time she sat there, watching the rise and fall of his ribs and at any moment expecting it to cease. Eventually she dozed, only to be disturbed by a light tap on the door and the appearance of the ship's Captain. With his fair hair and his rather patrician nose, he was very much Nicol's idea of the typical Englishman. Even in the low lamplight she could see the deep shadows on his face, and his blue eyes were full of concern.

'How's he doing?' he asked quietly.

Nicol shrugged. 'The surgeon couldn't say.'

'I'm sorry to see him like this.' He moved closer to stare down at the man upon the bunk. 'I was at school with him, you know. I heard he had joined the Army. What on earth was he doing in France?'

'He's been fighting for the Vendeans, but he decided to return home once we were married.'

'I take it that wasn't long ago.'

'Just over a week.'

Her eyes filled with tears and he reached out to give her shoulder a comforting squeeze. 'I don't suppose you know how he got hold of our signals?'

Nicol shook her head. 'He had a notebook written in some kind of code.'

'Did he, by Jove!'

The conversation must have disturbed Hal because he moved slightly and groaned, his hand trying to reach across to his left side. Before Nicol could move, the Captain had bent over and, with surprising gentleness, had tucked the hand back under the blankets.

'Take it easy, old chap,' he whispered. 'You're quite safe.'

Hal opened eyes that were shadowed with pain and blinked to clear his vision.

'Dick Burgess,' he muttered. 'What...are... you...?'

'My ship, old boy—the *Cassandra*. Just take it easy and you'll be all right.'

'Nicky...' Hal tried to sit up and stifled a gasp of pain.

'I'm here,' she whispered, 'but lie still, my darling, please.'

'I remember,' he muttered, covering his eyes with his arm. 'Damned French bullet got me.'

Dick Burgess nodded. 'If you feel up to talking, there are one or two questions I'd like to ask you... For instance, how you came by our signals. I thought they were strictly for the Navy.'

Hal managed a smile. 'Pitt himself got them for me... I gather some of your superiors weren't too happy.'

'You're working for the Government, then?'

Hal glanced apprehensively towards his wife before replying, 'In a manner of speaking.'

'Does that mean you were spying?' asked Burgess incredulously.

Hal felt Nicol's grip tighten on his hand and wished he felt more up to defending his position. 'Nasty word... I prefer to be called an observer. Jacquelein knew all... about... it, Nicky.' His lips clamped together as he fought a wave of pain, then, taking a deep breath, he continued, 'I've a letter... to... deliver to Pitt. Can you see... to ... it?'

'I'll do what I can, old chap, but I'm afraid we're not on our way to England,' Burgess answered, his face tight with concern. 'We're heading west and then down to Biscay on another lap of our patrol. However, as soon as we sight another English vessel, I'll signal her and see what can be arranged. It's impossible for me to leave my patrol area without permission, but there shouldn't be too much delay. All you have to do is get well.'

'Thanks...' Hal nodded, then swore as the pain took his breath away. 'You'll look after Nicky?'

'Of course,' Burgess answered, bending to give Hal's shoulder a reassuring squeeze before turning apologetically to Nicol. 'I'm sorry if I disturbed him. Would you like me to send someone to help with the nursing?'

'No, thank you, but if I should need the surgeon?'

'I'll leave a man outside the door,' he told her, bowing and taking his leave.

'Nicky,' Hal whispered, struggling to open his eyes and hold on to consciousness. 'I'm sorry...I... never...told you, but...'

'Hush!' She gently pressed a finger to his lips, then bent to kiss his cheek. 'We'll talk about it later.'

In fact she was burning with curiosity, but concern for him overrode all else. Uttering a small sound that was something between a sigh and a groan, he began to doze, leaving her time to come to terms with this new and unexpected development.

The word spy sprang into her mind and she shuddered with distaste. Had her father known? she wondered. Had her husband's sympathy been truly with the Vendean cause? In spite of these questions, she still loved him; the unexpected vulnerability that was responsible for that was even more apparent in him now, tying her to him as surely as any chain. She hardly knew him and yet she was committed to him, body and soul.

By morning he was in such pain and so restless that she became anxious and sent for the surgeon. The fellow came at once but did not examine the wound, thinking it better to leave it undisturbed. Some fever was to be expected, he told her, but they could try to keep it down by sponging the patient's entire body in cold water.

Nicol wrung out a towel in some icy water and laid it across Hal's burning forehead, then, with another cloth, wiped his chest and face.

'Nicky,' he said anxiously, speaking as if every word was an effort. 'If I don't get over this, you must ... go ... to ... my brother. Promise me ...!'

'You're not to talk like that,' she answered. 'I won't let you die.'

He laughed at that, regretting it at once as red-hot knives pierced his side.

'Won't you ever obey me?' he sighed, but although he turned his head away wearily his hand found and tightly grasped hers.

The next couple of days were a nightmare as Hal's fever mounted and he tossed and turned in delirium, totally unaware of where he was or who was ministering to him. Nicol drove herself to the limits of her endurance, bathing him and seeking to quieten him as she would a child. Finally he fell into an uneasy sleep and she, the last of her physical reserves worn down by the strength of her emotions, all but collapsed in her chair.

As if in a dream, she was aware of someone carrying her and of being laid down on a soft bunk. She tried to protest but the words just would not come.

'Hal ...?' she choked.

'He's sleeping,' Dick Burgess answered, pulling the covers up to her chin. 'Don't worry—we'll call you if there's the slightest change.'

She sighed then, accepting that there was nothing else she could do. Tiredness had numbed her both emotionally and physically, and all she wanted to do was sleep.

CHAPTER NINE

REALITY was slow in returning to her and for several seconds she lay staring up at the lantern swaying gently above her head, her mind in a kind of limbo. When her memory did return, it was like a blow to her stomach.

'Hal!' she gasped, almost throwing herself from the narrow bunk, her stockinged feet slipping on the polished floor.

Hurriedly she pulled on her shoes and made her way to the cabin opposite, her heart thundering with both apprehension and fear. It took all her courage to enter, but when she did she was immediately conscious of a feeling of peace.

The old sailor sitting beside the bunk, looked up and smiled, holding a cautioning finger to his lips. 'He's sleeping like a baby, my dear. The worst is over.'

Foolishly, she began to cry, great tears rolling unchecked down her face and neck. It was utterly ridiculous, and yet the old sailor did not seem to find it so. In fact he nodded understandingly as he came to slip his arm around her shoulders and guide her to a chair.

'Hush, my pretty,' he whispered, 'or you'll wake him. He's going to be fine now. You just sit down and I'll go and find you some breakfast.'

She snuffled and nodded, then snuffled again as her pent-up emotion continued to find an outlet in tears.

Later she felt almost happy as she sat beside Hal. She had been expecting him to wake soon but, even so, was surprised when, looking up from her book, she found his grey eyes watching her, clear but a little puzzled. She leant forward, and with a touch as light as a butterfly's wing gently brushed the tendrils of dark hair back from his forehead.

'How long...?' he asked huskily.

'Nearly three days, but you're going to be all right, Hal. You're going to be just fine.'

'I'm sorry if I frightened...you. Is there anything to...drink?'

Turning around, she poured some water from a jug on the table, then slipping her hand beneath his head, gently lifted it so that the cool water could trickle down his throat.

'Thank you,' he said.

She smiled then, quite unaware of the tenderness that showed in her face or the love that shone in her eyes.

Hal felt a strange stirring in his chest, quite separate from the pain of his wound. 'Kiss me, Nicky.'

As she bent over him, his arm came around her to draw her down. His lips brushed first her cheek and then her brow before finally seeking and finding hers. When her tears touched his mouth, he tilted her head back so that he could look into her eyes.

'That's the second time you've cried for me,' he told her a trifle uncertainly.

Then she bent to kiss him again, her fingers brushing his face, lingering against the bruise that still showed on his temple and losing themselves in the thick hair at his nape. His lips seemed to come to life under hers, giving to her and taking from her so that she knew no other man could rouse her so. Inevitably, just as their passion was mounting, he groaned and drew back, bringing her back to reality with an unpleasant jolt. She was alarmed to see fresh perspiration on his forehead and his breathing too seemed ragged.

'Now I've hurt you,' she choked.

'Don't cry,' he whispered with a brave smile. 'It was worth it.'

He seemed to doze then and Nicol stayed close beside him, not wanting to move and disturb him, and hardly daring to breathe. The next time he awoke, she was able to get some broth down him, feeding him as she would a child. Even the effort of swallowing seemed to tire him and, when he settled back, his face was as white as the pillow on which he lay. She found his helplessness such a contrast to his usual virility, that once more it brought tears to her eyes.

'I'm grateful for the way you've looked after me,' he told her, struggling to stay awake. 'You've done much more than you needed... Much more than I would have expected when I married you.'

The tactless surprise in his voice made her smile. 'You thought me a spoilt child—confess it!'

'Perhaps, but I never... doubted your courage. I really did not want... a submissive... wife.'

Nor one who would love you, she thought bitterly.

'I... don't deserve you, Nicky,' he continued feverishly. 'I can't...'

'Hush!' She silenced him by placing her fingers on his lips, not wanting to hear what he was going to say next. 'Go to sleep.'

For a long time after that she continued to study him, wondering just what it was about him that had captured her heart. He was handsome enough, but so were a great many other men, and yet she could not imagine another face, another body stirring her so. Laughter lines, frown lines, the set of cheek and jaw, all combined to make his face unique and infinitely adorable.

His lips were parted to reveal the tips of his strong white teeth. In someone else the small space between them might have been considered a flaw, but it was yet another thing that endeared him to her.

When she bent to kiss him he did not even stir. She gave a small smile of satisfaction; for the present he had to accept her love, and she was going to make the most of it.

Oddly enough, as he recovered, he became a much more difficult patient. The pain in his side he never mentioned and yet he moaned constantly about the food and the inactivity, submitting to her ministrations with an utter lack of grace. Nicol bore his ill humour with a fortitude that surprised even herself and occasionally found it more than a little amusing. Then he developed a cough which must have caused agony in his side, and yet of that he never complained at all. Only by the fact that he would lie quietly after an attack did she know how bad it was; then she would wipe the sweat from his brow and whisper lovingly. Sometimes she even held him during a spasm, feeling his agony as her own.

On one such occasion, he turned his head into her breast and muttered, 'How could I ever have thought you a child?' and, settling back against his pillows, he continued to regard her with a warm and rather thoughtful expression that she had not seen before.

Once everyone knew that Hal was on the mend, Dick Burgess asked Nicol to dine with his officers and she willingly agreed. It was strange to be sitting down at a table with only gentlemen, herself clad in shirt and breeches, and yet she enjoyed it enormously. The Lieutenants were all charming, personable young men, some even younger than herself, and they obviously found her company pleasing. She couldn't know that her new-found maturity had added to her beauty, or that more than one of her companions would willingly have traded places with Hal.

A great deal of wine was consumed and, although there was no impropriety, there was a great deal of joking and hearty laughter. Dick Burgess and his First Lieutenant, a tall chestnut-haired fellow called Hector Browne, she found particularly entertaining. They had both spent their time before becoming midshipmen at the same school as Hal, and were able to tell her of several escapades in which he had participated, giving her the impression of a rather open and irrepressible young man very different from the Hal Grantly she knew.

She found that individual very quiet when she returned to his cabin, where a bed had been made up for her on the floor. He seemed disinclined to conversation and was so short with her that she worried in case he was feeling worse. However, the following morning, he insisted on getting out of bed, and a couple of days later was walking unsteadily around the cabin.

The next time she was invited to dine with the captain, Hal accompanied her. The surgeon advised against it, and Nicol even contemplated not going herself in an effort to dissuade him, but to no avail.

Later, sitting around the wardroom table, surrounded by a dozen handsome young men, she had to admit that she found her husband the most attractive of all.

His face, thinner now, seemed almost alive in the flickering candlelight, fascinating her with its differing expressions—the lift of an eyebrow, the slow, reluctant smile: they were all familiar to her and filled her with a peculiar, tender warmth.

'It's not right that you should dine with us and still only have eyes for your husband,' Browne teased.

Nicol laughed. 'You will have to make allowances. After all, we've only been married for a couple of weeks.'

'He's a very lucky man.' He moved closer, not attempting to conceal the admiration in his eyes.

Hal was seated at the opposite end of the table and Nicol looked up to find him watching her, a rather tight expression on his face. Burgess spoke to him and he appeared to draw his eyes away reluctantly, finding it necessary to apologise for his lack of attention.

As the meal progressed and the wine flowed freely, the company became so jolly that Nicol did not notice her husband's silence. Burgess was the first to become aware of it and asked with concern if he was feeling all right.

Hal smiled apologetically. 'I'm fine, Dick—tired, that's all—but if you'll excuse me, I think that I'll retire.'

'Of course.' The young Captain rose at once and solicitously helped Hal to his feet. 'I think perhaps you've overdone it a bit, old man.'

Hal glanced at Nicol who was also standing. 'No, wife, stay and enjoy yourself. I'm perfectly all right.'

If he had not looked so pale she might have agreed, for it was pleasant to be complimented and teased, especially since her confidence with men had been so recently undermined. As it was, she shook her head and moved dutifully to his side, ignoring the cries of protest as the rest of the company disputed her action. She felt a little smug at having done the right thing, but if she expected any gratitude from Hal then she was sadly mistaken.

'I'm not in my dotage!' he hissed, once they were outside the door. 'I'm quite capable of managing on my own.'

Justifiably angry, she pushed open their cabin door. 'I knew it would be too much for you. Why must you always be so pigheaded?'

His face was quite grey as he sat down on the edge of the narrow bunk, almost doubling over with pain. 'Don't lecture me, damn it! The last thing I need is a nagging wife.'

When he lifted his head to look up at her there was such misery in his eyes that for a moment she was taken aback.

An angry retort died in her throat. 'Oh, do lie down!'

He scowled but nevertheless obeyed, and she was able to remove his boots. As she reached up to loosen his cravat, he caught her hand, holding it in a grip of steel.

'You're my wife,' he grated. 'Don't you forget it!'

His uncalled-for anger both puzzled and upset her and, determinedly withdrawing her hand, she felt his face. His skin felt warm and clammy and small beads of perspiration were gathering above his lips.

'Do you know, even like this I want you,' he said bitterly, then, aware of her horror, laughed. 'Oh, don't worry—I've too much pride to start something so doomed to failure . . . But you'll wait for my recovery, wife. Do you hear?'

'Oh, go to sleep!' she snapped, drawing the blankets up to his chin and then moving away to undress. Halfway through, she paused. 'You have got a poor opinion of women, haven't you, Hal Grantly? Do you think that men have a monopoly on fidelity?'

He did not reply and, turning, she saw that he was already asleep. Bare-footed, she moved across to stare down at his strong, still face with all its harshness wiped away. For a moment she wondered if he could possibly have been jealous, then dismissed the suspicion almost as quickly as it had occurred. He was possessive, that was all, and his male pride was dented by his lack of strength. Nevertheless she was still pondering on his strange behaviour when she slipped between her own blankets. Sleep did not come easily, and when it did it was only to dream of Hal, strange, tortured dreams in which he always eluded her.

In the middle of the night something disturbed her and she awoke to lie tense and listening in the darkness. She heard Hal mutter incoherently and her stomach turned over in alarm. She called out to him and, when there was no reply, struggled up and reached for the lamp. It was a moment before her clumsy fingers managed to light it and the glow revealed him tossing and turning in a tangle of blankets.

At first she thought he was in the grip of a fever but his skin felt quite cool and, after a while, she realised that he was merely having a bad dream.

Thinking it kindest to wake him, she took hold of his shoulders and softly called his name.

'Damned woman,' he muttered without opening his eyes. 'How could she...? Morals of a cat...shouldn't have followed her.'

Nicol stiffened, drawing her hands away from his shoulders as if he burned. The realisation that he had not forgiven her for her earlier flirtatious behaviour was like a knife twisting at her insides. She closed her eyes with the pain, and when she opened them again found him gazing up at her.

He still looked rather dazed and his breathing was ragged but he managed a shaky laugh. 'Sorry, Nicky...just a bad dream.'

'You ought to get out of that shirt,' she said flatly, attempting to hide her disappointment and hurt, and, suiting action to the words, began to undo his buttons. When he reached up to help her, she could feel his hands shaking. 'It must have been an excessively bad dream!'

He frowned as he struggled to sit up and she helped him off with the sweat-soaked garment. 'I'm sorry if I woke you.'

'It's all right,' she replied stiffly. 'Can I get you a drink or something?'

Still frowning, he shook his head. 'Go back to your own bed before you freeze.' As she turned away, he added, 'I'm sorry if I've been a bit of a bear recently...I'll do what I can to make up for it.'

'Why don't you just forgive me?'

'Forgive you?' He sat up again with an alacrity that made him wince and, catching her wrist, prevented her from moving away. 'What are you talking about?'

'It's nothing. For heaven's sake, let me go back to bed!'

She pushed his hand away and, still looking puzzled, he let her go. It was not until the cabin was once more in darkness and the same appalling dream was threatening to engulf him that he remembered how he had spoken as he awoke before. For a while he lay quietly, hating himself and the circumstances that had made him what he was. He desperately wanted to put things right between them, and yet he couldn't have explained, not even if his life had depended on it. Not for the first time, it occurred to him how unfair he had been to marry Nicol. She was so young and loving, and deserved so much more than he would ever be able to give.

It was agony for him to lie there feeling helpless and inadequate in the face of her sorrow, and he was filled with a bitter self-disgust. Her muffled sob was too much for him and, leaving the warm cocoon of his own bed, he went across to her, kneeling beside her to stroke her face. When he felt the wetness of her tears his throat tightened.

'Go away!' she told him, her pride too battered for her to be able to confess her hurt.

'No.' He tenderly but firmly drew her into his arms. He could not say the words but he tried to comfort her in the only way he knew how.

Appalled by her weakness, Nicol nevertheless let him draw her close, wrapping her arms around him and burying her face against his bare shoulder. He was so warm and solid, the slightly musky scent of him so deliciously familiar that she felt her pulse race. He stroked her and caressed her as he would a child, and felt the stirrings of passion within his own battered body.

Even through her sorrow, Nicol was aware of a need to care for him and, with an endearingly maternal gesture, lifted the blankets to cover him too. She let him hold her, let him stroke her, her body responding to him almost against her will. They did not make love or even talk, and yet there was a deep tenderness between them, a tacit understanding of each other's suffering that went far beyond words. Hal felt it was the closest thing to love that he was ever likely to experience.

CHAPTER TEN

HAL walked stiffly across the Captain's day cabin and leant forward to peer out of the stern windows, frowning slightly as he studied the bubbling wake. In the distance, the low shape of Noirmoutier stood out as a darker smudge against the grey sea. It was strange that so much had happened, and yet here they were within a stone's throw of the Vendée.

'Are you homesick, wife?' he asked softly.

Nicol, attempting to mend the tear in his shirt, looked up from her sewing and managed a smile. 'A little.'

In fact it was agony to be so close to her home and yet to have its comfort and security denied her. If it hadn't been for Hal, she was sure she would have pleaded with Burgess to put her ashore.

His face softened, then, as if acknowledging that there was nothing he could do to ease her pain, he thrust his hands deep into his pockets and turned back to the window.

Nicol could scarcely take her eyes from him. He was still not completely recovered and tired easily, and yet, clad only in an open-necked shirt and breeches, he seemed so intensely male and alive. Over the past week she had come to know every curve and line of his body and found that his very presence could awaken a desire in her that was almost frightening.

Since his illness, there had been a subtle change in his attitude towards her and he treated her with a new deference, as if he had finally acknowledged that she had grown up. Certainly it would have been difficult for him to treat her with the same overbearing arrogance after she had nursed him like a babe, seeing to even his most basic needs. Sometimes she wondered if he resented it a little for he was unusually subdued and occasionally, she caught him watching her, a thoughtful, almost brooding expression in his eyes.

There was a knock at the door and a young midshipman entered, saluting smartly. 'The Captain's compliments, sir, and if you feel up to it would you join him on deck?'

Hal nodded. 'Tell him I'll be up directly.'

'What do you think he wants?' Nicol asked in surprise, rising to her feet and setting her sewing aside.

Hal shrugged and reached for his borrowed coat, wincing as he lifted his arm to ease it over his shoulder. Nicol automatically moved forward to help and buttoned it up for him, at the same time studiously avoiding his eyes.

'Quite the little mother!' he teased, gently lifting her chin.

There was a strange light in his eyes and, without warning, he bent to claim her lips. His hands ran down her back, creating chaos where they touched, firing her nerves into life and releasing a torrent of desire. It was he who finally drew back, breathless and a little shaken.

'I'm sorry, Nicky. I shouldn't have done that,' he told her with a rueful smile. 'I've neither the strength nor time to finish what I started... Come on, let's see what Dick wants.'

Burgess was standing on the quarterdeck, a rather self-satisfied expression on his face.

'I think I've solved our problem,' he said, turning to Hal. 'That French frigate has been shadowing us for days, only this time she's come too close. With the help of this breeze, I can cut between her and the island and take her. She'll make a fine prize and provide the means of transporting both you and your letter to England.'

He handed Hal the telescope. 'Here, take a look and tell me what you think. She's *La Créole*, I believe, over six hundred tons and thirty-two guns to our thirty-eight.'

'You're the expert,' Hal replied, lifting the glass to his eye. 'She's a neat enough ship, but can you take her without running us aground?'

Burgess laughed confidently. 'It'll be child's play. You just watch me! Mr Browne, you will quietly and unobtrusively clear the ship for action!' He turned to Nicol. 'I know it's pointless asking Hal to leave, but you will have to go below. We shall be running out the gun in my cabin so I'm afraid you'll have to take refuge in Browne's. It's going to be a little noisy but there's nothing to worry about.'

Nicol knew it would be futile to protest and resignedly made her way below. Hal could have had the decency to accompany her, she thought resentfully, instead of selfishly indulging his own pleasure. It wasn't as if he were needed on deck.

Nevertheless he obviously still had her safety in mind, for he joined her a few minutes later with a loaded pistol in his hand.

'Just in case,' he told her, placing it carefully on the bunk. 'There's shot and powder, too. I don't suppose you'll need it, but I'll feel happier knowing you've got it here... And keep away from the window, there's a good girl.'

She found his obvious excitement both annoying and endearing and she bit back a sharp retort, instead merely telling him to take care. Then he was gone and she settled down on the bunk to wait.

It seemed an age before she heard the roar and felt the vibration as the carronades opened fire. There was a great deal of shouting and suddenly the deck tilted as Burgess put his ship about. She heard the rumble of the enemy's guns, followed by a light-hearted cheer as the shot obviously fell short. Ignoring Hal's warning, she hurried to the small window but could see nothing except the heaving grey sea.

The *Cassandra*'s guns spoke again, this time from the main gundeck, and the whole ship shuddered as if rocked by some giant earthquake or violent storm. Nicol continued to watch and finally caught sight of the French ship as she keeled over ready to make another pass. The girl waited in a fever of anxiety for the next broadside, then the roar of the guns filled the whole ship, shaking her ancient timbers and filling everywhere with thick grey smoke.

Nicol's throat was dry and she clenched her hands until the knuckles showed white. If only she had known what was happening she would not have felt so afraid, but having to guess from the sounds of the battle was almost unendurable. The thud of running feet echoed around her, mingled with the bark of orders and the squeal of tackle as the guns were run in ready to be swabbed and reloaded with their devastating shot, and her nerves neared breaking point.

Again, she heard the rumble of the Frenchman's guns and felt the hollow thud as some of the shot went home. Someone screamed horribly and there was a great deal of shouting before the *Cassandra* fired another broadside. Then the firing ceased and, even in her isolation, she could sense the air of expectancy culminating in a raucous cheer as the two vessels came alongside.

There was more shouting. The rattle of musket-fire rose above the clash of steel on steel, and when a man cried out in agony she covered her ears. She felt sick when she thought of Hal being involved in the carnage on deck and wished belatedly that she had made a scene and tried to keep him with her. Then she realised that the sound of fighting was closer, had actually spread down the companionway, and her stomach turned over.

The cabin door burst open and three Frenchmen entered with the force of a small whirlwind. Stifling a scream, she edged away until her back was against the narrow bunk. In desperation she groped behind her for the pistol, her eyes never leaving the face of the foremost intruder—a lean, rather unprepossessing individual wearing the uniform of some kind of officer. Only his eyes, dark and hard as a snake's, revealed how dangerous he really was.

As he moved menacingly towards her, she lifted the gun. 'Get out or I'll shoot!'

Her legs felt like rubber and her grasp on the pistol was precarious at best, but she was determined to carry out her threat.

The officer paused uncertainly, then, dark eyes dilating, made a rush towards her. She fired instinctively, hating him for what he made her do, and satisfaction momentarily replaced fear as she watched him stagger back. She was now defenceless, and with snarls of rage the other two men fell upon her, dragging her roughly towards the door. She continued to struggle and one of them slapped her across the face making her senses swim.

She was only vaguely aware of Hal's arrival, seeing him through a grey mist as he filled the companionway like some avenging angel. His hair was tangled, his face hardly recognisable beneath the dirt, and yet he had never presented a more welcome sight. His eyes were blazing with the light of battle, and her relief changed swiftly to apprehension as she remembered his weakened state.

One of the intruders rushed at him, steel ringing against steel as their swords came together. For a moment they fought a fast, deadly duel, until the remaining Frenchman, seeing his friend hard pressed, also entered the fray. Time and time again, it looked as if Hal was finished but his speed and skill always saved him. There was no doubt that he quite outclassed his opponents in swordsmanship, but he soon began to tire and fought with one hand pressed against his side.

With a deft upward stroke, he slipped through one man's guard and pierced him neatly through the arm, then, taking advantage of the improved odds, pressed home his attack.

Nicol seized her opportunity and, retrieving the pistol, began to reload. She was shaking so badly that it took her much longer than it should have, and all the while part of her attention was on the fight. By the time she had actually cocked it, the wounded Frenchman had again entered the fray and Hal was in grave difficulty.

The stronger Frenchman lunged. With surprising speed, Hal parried and buried his blade deep in the fellow's chest. Nicol saw the other man's sword lift and knew that her husband was not going to be able to free his weapon in time. Gritting her teeth, she fired, fighting down nausea as the Frenchman screamed and crashed down, pouring blood. For a moment the floor seemed to waver beneath her feet.

'For God's sake, don't faint on me now,' Hal hissed, slipping a strong arm around her waist.

More footsteps sounded in the companionway and, gently pushing her behind him, he turned to face this new danger.

Hector Browne's lean, freckled face broke into a surprised smile and he swore roundly. 'Been having a party of your own?'

Hal relaxed and drew Nicol back into the comforting circle of his arm. 'How's it going on deck?'

'It's all over, pretty well. Dick's in great spirits. *La Créole*'s a fine prize and taken without too many casualties.'

A loud cheer from overhead told them that the French ship had finally lowered her colours. Almost simultaneously a young midshipman hurtled into the cabin, his eyes widening like saucers when he caught sight of the bodies. 'I didn't see any of them come down.'

'No,' laughed Browne, 'but things were rather busy for a while. We weren't expecting *them* to try and board *us*! What do you want? I assume you did come with a message.'

The boy swallowed and managed to calm himself. He was still very pale, and Nicol thought privately that he was too young for such a hard life.

'The Captain's compliments, and would Mr Grantly join him on deck for a moment?' he said.

Hal nodded, and because Nicol was still clinging to his hand decided she had better go, too. She kept her eyes averted as they moved around the bodies and, aware of her feelings, he gave her hand a reassuring squeeze.

By the hatchway he paused. 'You did well, Nicky.'

She felt like throwing herself into his arms and indulging in a good cry, but she managed a smile. His eyes softened and he kissed her, briefly.

'What was that for?' she asked.

'I suppose you could call it a reward for gallantry. You've certainly got courage, and I like that.' His eyes held hers for a moment longer. They were warm with approval and perhaps something more. Before she could be sure, he had broken the contact and catching hold of her arm, guided her towards the stairs.

Dick Burgess was staring down over the starboard side, surveying the chaos below. *La Créole*'s main deck was a tangle of bodies and fallen rigging and the new tricolour flag hung dejectedly from the bottom of her mast. *Cassandra*'s marines, their red coats quite distinctive, were supervising as the unhappy Frenchmen began to clear the mess. In spite of the breeze, the air was still thick with smoke and everywhere seemed dirty.

Looking down on the *Cassandra*'s deck, Nicol noticed a number of corpses laid tidily side by side.

Burgess followed her stare and a brief shadow of pain crossed his face.

'We were lucky,' he said, before giving his attention to Hal. 'It's a job well done, even if I do say so myself. She's a fine prize and, even with a skeleton crew, will make a fast passage home. I intend to give Browne his first command and young Oaks can go with him... How are you for funds, by the way? I've gold for such emergencies. You'll have to sign for it, of course, but considering your business there'll be no problem.'

When Hal nodded and expressed his thanks, Nicol felt sickened. That he was spying was bad enough, but that he should accept payment for it was despicable. She moved away to stare down at the captured ship, not really seeing it at all, and after a moment realised that he had come to stand beside her.

'What's the matter, Nicky?' he asked, noting her set face and the way her hands were gripping the rail.

'I find the idea that you were spying a little distasteful, that's all.'

'I never made any secret of my errand,' he answered sharply. 'Both your father and Henri Jacquelein knew.'

She smiled bleakly and, because she was hurting, wanted to hurt him too. 'I've only your word for that.'

His expression froze, his mouth setting in the grim line she knew so well. 'I see, and my word is just not good enough, is that it? My God, what a doubting, sanctimonious little cat you are! Are you always so ready to believe the worst of people, or is it just me?'

Fortunately, Nicol did not need to answer him, for at that moment Burgess called him away.

'I sent for you because we've found some prisoners aboard *La Créole*,' the Captain announced. 'They're both Frenchmen, and Oaks is bringing them over now. My French is damned rusty, and I'd like to find out all I can from them.'

Hal walked over to join him, said something Nicol couldn't quite catch, and then laughed. He did not look back at her, and if he was upset by her attitude he certainly did not show it.

For a while she waited miserably beside the rail, feeling lonely and rather out of place. Oh, why had she had to speak out and shatter the fragile respect that was growing between them? She desperately wanted to escape below, but Burgess and Hal were between her and the companionway, and she dared not pass close to them in case they should see how near she was to tears.

In an effort to distract herself she studied the French ship, and was therefore the first person on the quarterdeck to notice the midshipman approaching with the two liberated prisoners. The taller Frenchman was brawny and rough-looking with an untidy thatch of reddish hair, but the other was quite definitely a gentleman. There was something disturbingly familiar about his rather precise walk. Then he glanced up and, to her horror, she recognised Maurice de Cruzat.

Oh, God! she thought. What on earth is he doing here? She closed her eyes and tried to will him away, praying that he was merely a figment of her guilt-ridden imagination, but when she looked again he was still an unpleasant reality. Her stomach sank, for his presence couldn't help but remind Hal of her earlier lapse. When she heard her husband's muttered oath, she knew that he too had recognised his late antagonist.

'*Mon Dieu!* It is the estimable Monsieur Grantly,' laughed de Cruzat as he joined them.

In spite of this exclamation, Nicol had the impression that he was not at all surprised. Of course, the sight of her would have prepared him, so why did she feel there was more to it than that?

'What the devil are you doing here?' Hal demanded, making no attempt to conceal his surprise and dislike.

'Pure circumstance, my dear Hal,' the Frenchman responded smoothly. 'I was unlucky enough to be taken prisoner and then transported aboard that hulk.' He gestured contemptuously towards the French frigate.

Burgess glanced at Hal in surprise. 'Do you know this fellow?'

'The last time I saw him he was on the receiving end of my sword.'

De Cruzat shrugged and pointedly addressed himself to the Captain. 'Monsieur Grantly and I are not on the best of terms. No doubt it would suit him better to have me remain in irons. However, I'm sure you're a fair man, and I'm willing to place myself at your mercy. Grantly knows that I work for Jacquelein, and it was on a mission for him that I was captured. The Republicans were returning me to Nantes for punishment, no doubt intending to make a gory example of me to my family and friends.'

'As if Carrier's butchery isn't discouragement enough,' replied Hal bitterly, thinking of the barbaric punishments being meted out by that particular Republican representative.

Again the Frenchman shrugged. 'Perhaps they would not have bothered, had the frigate not already been provisioned and ready to sail.'

'Then, to your knowledge, your vessel was not specifically shadowing us?' Burgess demanded.

'I really cannot say. I was a prisoner, *monsieur*, and not privy to such matters.'

'What about you?' Hal asked the other Frenchman.

'I was doing a little smuggling, that's all. The coastguard sank my boat and my cargo. As I originally sailed from Pornic, that was where I was to be tried. Officials are all the same. I have no respect for the Republicans or any other interfering government.' As if to make his point, he coughed noisily and spat on the deck.

Burgess stiffened and his mouth tightened in anger.

De Cruzat smiled smoothly. 'We are entirely at your mercy, Captain. I beg you not to be prejudiced by the manners of my uncouth friend. At present I have no wish to return to the Vendée, but England would suit me well enough.'

'I shall have to think about it,' Burgess told him shortly. 'Now, if you will go with my officer, he will provide you with somewhere to rest and some food. Whatever I decide, I shall take Mr Grantly's opinion into account!'

Having dismissed de Cruzat, he turned to the smuggler, his expression like granite. 'As a seaman you might prove useful. My bosun will find you something to do.'

When the fellow began to protest, the burly bosun stepped forward, a belaying pin in his hand. He was obviously going to enjoy using force, and, after a smouldering glance at the Captain, the smuggler allowed himself to be led away.

Burgess sighed and turned to Hal. 'Care to tell me what's between you and that de Cruzat fellow?'

'Just the small matter of a duel, but it's over and done with now and best forgotten. I don't like the man, but to be fair I've never had reason to doubt either his courage or his commitment to the Vendean cause. That smuggler I wouldn't trust at all. It's a pity you can't just toss him over the side and forget about him!'

'I certainly don't want him in my hair. In fact I'm inclined to send them both to England with you. Some ship might be short-handed enough to take him, although personally I think he'll be more trouble than he's worth. You know what they say about one bad apple, and there are several weeks of this patrol still to go. Browne can hand the fellow over to the authorities at Spit; I see no reason why his first command should be entirely without headaches!'

In less than two hours both vessels had been cleared and swabbed clean and, although jury-rigged, the French frigate was ready to sail. There was little time for farewells, but Burgess did manage to give Nicol a swift parting kiss. She felt more than a little sad as she watched the *Cassandra* fall behind, and understood something of what a sailor could come to feel for his ship.

'I shall miss the old girl, too,' Browne commented, the effect of his words rather spoilt by his excited smile.

Hal, standing at Nicol's other side, sniffed impatiently. 'I don't think it's the ship Nicol will miss!'

For a moment she thought that she had misheard him, then indignation nearly choked her. An angry retort died on her lips when she was struck by the most incredible realisation—he was jealous! He had witnessed the Captain's rather brotherly kiss and he hadn't liked it at all. Whether this feeling arose from a genuine affection or a rather less flattering dog-in-the-manger attitude was impossible to tell, but it was infinitely satisfying. Perhaps he was beginning to love her. She took that hope and held it to herself, for it was something that made the hazards and inconveniences they had suffered all worthwhile.

They had scarcely waved goodbye to the *Cassandra* when the weather worsened, storm following storm as they beat their way up into the Channel. Browne began to look quite haggard from lack of sleep and Hal, too, did much more than his share. He was not qualified to stand watch, but he spent a great deal of time with the young midshipman, his very presence seeming to steady the boy.

At times Nicol wondered if it was merely an excuse to keep out of her way. When he did come to share her cabin, he was too tired even to talk and fell instantly asleep. More than once she found herself wishing that he would make love to her, and only pride prevented her from crawling into his bed.

'They are so short-handed that even my help is appreciated,' he told her one evening, as she applied salve to his rope-burned palms. 'We're all tired.'

When her hand reached to touch his stubbled cheek, he captured it and gave it a reassuring squeeze. 'Still playing the little mother, Nicky? Wait until we have children of our own, then you'll be able to give your maternal instincts full rein.'

'Must you always be so condescending and nasty?' she asked flatly.

'I'm afraid you seem to bring out the worst in me.' This time there was no sting to his words, only the beginnings of a smile. His fingers touched her shoulders, moving lightly in an unconscious caress. 'I didn't mean to upset you. It's just such a long time since I've been able to accept a woman's love and care.'

The love she felt seemed to expand inside her and tears burned at the back of her eyes as she wondered what on earth could have turned him so completely against her sex. The emotions he expressed reached out to her, making her want to hold him to her breast and whisper words of love, and yet, instinctively, she knew that the time was not right. She had to be patient, showing him by deed rather than word that he could trust her enough to risk loving her too. In the past some woman must have hurt him very badly, she concluded, as she finished tending his hands and placed the jar of salve between them on the bunk.

Hal searched her face, seeing the gentleness there, and, unable to help himself, leant forward to brush a stray strand of hair back behind her ear.

'I'm a lost cause, you know,' he whispered.

She looked up at him, struggling with another wave of tears, and her lips trembled as he ran his fingers slowly over the curve of her cheek. Try as she might, she could not prevent the tears spilling over. The sight of them nearly destroyed him and he wiped them away with his fingertips.

'I won't be able to change in a week,' he told her shakily. 'I'm not even sure I want to try.'

Nicol sighed, aware that the years of loneliness had taught him to guard his heart as carefully as his life. He drew her gently forward and she melted against his chest. Lifting her face, he brushed his lips across hers, intending it to be a kiss of comfort and control, but she responded hungrily, giving him her heart and her soul. His sigh was soft and moist against her lips, his breath incredibly sweet. Words of love welled up inside her, threatening to spill in an embarrassing torrent of endearments and pleas, but somehow she held them back.

'I must be more tired than I thought,' she told him, drawing away and smiling bravely.

He looked at her strangely. 'I suppose we all are.'

Dragging himself reluctantly to his feet, he headed towards the door. There he paused to glance back at her, and the smile that tugged at his lips was infinitely sad. 'I haven't done a very good job of taking care of you, have I? I'll make it up to you when we reach home. You shall have anything you want.'

Yes, she thought wistfully, anything but your heart.

Nicol found it awkward being in such close proximity to de Cruzat and did her best to keep out of his way. On the evening of the third day the sea was particularly rough and the lurching of the hull violent enough to make her feel unusually queasy. Thinking that she would feel better for some fresh air, she left the sanctuary of her cabin and staggered along the narrow corridor towards the stairs. Just as she was passing de Cruzat's cabin, he came out, and an unpredictable roll of the ship sent her tottering into his arms.

He smiled and released her almost at once, yet made no attempt to move out of her way.

'Excuse me, but I'd like to get by,' she told him in her most autocratic voice.

'Won't you talk for a while?' he asked, his dark eyes boring into her like a snake's assessing its prey. 'Lying in my cabin listening to Browne snore is driving me insane. You and Hal haven't said two words to me since we came aboard. Come into the wardroom. I won't touch you, I swear.'

'I don't think Hal would approve,' she answered, 'and, after what has happened between us, I can't say that I blame him.'

'I've already been warned by your estimable husband to stay well away from you,' he admitted wryly.

Nicol shook her head. 'I'd much rather you didn't anger him. I behaved badly and I'm sorry for it. I never meant to encourage you, and Hal's been very good to me.'

'He leaves you too much alone. Even I can see that you're not well. If you're going on deck, then I really think I should accompany you—it's dangerously rough.'

There was no mistaking the concern in his face and, without being aware of it, she relaxed. 'Thank you, but I would rather go alone... Now, if you would just let me pass.'

'You think you're in love with him, don't you?'

'Yes, damn you!'

A pained look crossed his narrow face and he sighed deeply. 'What an inexperienced little creature you are. How does he feel about you? Tell me that?' When she did not reply, he laughed softly. 'Just as I thought. He's a cold fish, that one. Oh, he'll be kind to you, all right, because you're his wife and his stiff-necked morality will permit nothing else... but love? Why, I doubt he's capable of it.'

He had come too near the mark, and because of it she was angry. 'You're a fine one to talk! What you wanted from me in the woods had nothing to do with love, either!'

'Don't sell me short, my dear, just because I'm more amorous than your Hal. I cherish what is mine, like any honest Frenchman. Grantly is English, through and through. He was spying on us, you know. If our Vendean interests had clashed with Mr Pitt's, he would have betrayed us without a qualm.'

If she was surprised by his knowledge, then she was also a little relieved, for it meant Hal had been truthful when he spoke of the forthright way in which he had approached his mission.

'He was an observer, that's all,' she snapped defensively. 'He made no secret of it!'

De Cruzat smiled sadly. 'I'm sure that's what he would like you to believe, but I'm afraid he was too close to our gullible young General for it to be that simple. Our attack on Granville was misguided, to say the least, and I've heard that your husband was strongly in favour of it. Perhaps a Vendean success is not what Mr Pitt wants at the moment. It would certainly increase the pressure on him to come to our aid.'

'Now you are being ridiculous. In fact, I don't know why I'm standing here discussing it with you.' Angrily, she tried to push past him.

'Because you dare not discuss it with him!'

She paused, striving one last time to make him see reason. 'If my father and Monsieur Henri trusted him, then that should be good enough for you. I begin to think you're trying to blacken his name out of pure spite. He bested you in that ridiculous duel, and you can't stand it.'

'Believe what you like, child,' he replied with a melancholy shrug. 'I admit I may be a little jealous, but not of his swordplay, I assure you! If you need a friend, remember that you can count on me.'

She frowned as she studied his face, seeing nothing in it but kindness and concern. He drew a finger across her cheek and smiled wistfully.

'People are not always what they seem,' he muttered as he stepped back into his cabin.

The encounter left Nicol feeling miserable and confused. In spite of his rather tarnished reputation, de Cruzat was a fellow countryman who obviously had her welfare at heart, whereas Hal, much as she loved him, appeared nothing more than an opportunist and a spy.

She was still pondering the matter when she reached the quarterdeck and, glancing around, caught sight of her husband on the deck below. One of the carronades had come adrift and he was helping a couple of seamen to lash it back into place. Automatically, she scrambled down the ladder and lurched towards him.

The next moment she was swept completely off her feet by a wall of water and felt herself being propelled amid the roaring, stinging surf, to the ship's side. Rough planking grazed her knees and elbows before her outstretched hand closed around something solid and she clung to it like grim death. When the ship lifted she found herself jammed against the nettings, water cascading around her as the vessel ploughed on.

Still shaking from her narrow escape, she staggered to her feet in time to see another grey mountain of water rising towards her. Someone screamed—it might even have been herself—and she stood like one paralysed. There was just time for her to reach the comparative shelter of the mast, but for some reason her frozen limbs refused even to try. The water hit her like something solid and then she was falling, the weight of her body dragging her hands from the rail.

In the final instant someone grabbed her and, although she could see nothing, the pressure on her arms eased. She felt herself being held against something soft and heard Hal's husky, angry voice next to her ear.

'Little fool! What the devil are you doing on deck?' He coughed helplessly, and she felt herself being prised from his arms.

She opened her mouth to protest but instead was violently sick. In fact she was still retching as the two burly sailors half dragged, half carried her to the safety of the quarterdeck. When she was able to look up, she found herself staring into her husband's concerned face. Water was running from his hair and dripping off the end of his nose.

'I think I'd better get you below.' he said softly.

He wanted to carry her, and she felt so bruised and exhausted that had it not been for his wound she would have let him. As it was, she was glad of his arm and she did not protest when, after slamming their cabin door, he began to strip off her clothes.

He gently wrapped a blanket around her and then, taking a towel, began to dry her hair. Her teeth were chattering so badly that she could hardly speak, and her trembling limbs made it virtually impossible for her to do anything for herself.

'Get into bed,' he commanded, pulling back the covers and then tucking them up to her chin.

It was a moment before she realised that he was in a scarcely better condition than herself; he was shaking with cold and his lips looked quite blue. Removing his clothes, he began to rub himself with the damp towel. Nicol held up the covers and after a moment's hesitation, he climbed in beside her on the narrow bunk, reaching out to draw her firmly against his un-injured side.

'It's all right,' he whispered, stroking her back and trying to still the tremors of his own frozen body.

Somehow his tenderness set the seal on her distress and she began to cry softly for things that had nothing to do with her narrow escape from death. As he held her he sighed and muttered under his breath soothing, meaningless words that were infinitely comforting.

Nicol could not say which ceased first, her own tears or the steady, rhythmic movement of his hand. She only became aware that they were both still and, lifting her head, saw that he was sound asleep. A great tenderness overcame her and a feeling of love so strong that it was like a physical pain. He was still not fully recovered and, rather like a puppy, needed to sleep after his exertion.

She moved slightly so that her head was nestled against his shoulder, his warm breath fanning her ear. A feeling of lassitude was spreading through her, filling her mind with wool, and she was actually warm, the only discomfort being Hal's damp bandages pressed against her side. How very wet he must have been, she thought, as she drifted off to sleep.

Later she awoke to one of the most pleasant sensations of her life. She was relaxed and comfortable and warm hands were moving softly over her body, touching her in the most intimate places. Hal was wetting her face with warm little kisses and softly whispering her name. Instinctively, she snuggled against him, her awakening body responding to his need.

In the extreme darkness of the cabin she could not see a thing and, as if to compensate, her sense of touch seemed to increase. Everywhere Hal's hands rested her nerves sprang to life, creating such a fire inside her that she felt she would explode. He buried his face against her breasts and suckled gently as, sighing and squirming with pleasure, she ran her hands through his hair.

He groaned with longing for her, toying with her beautifully until her need was as great as his own. In her sleepy, almost semi-conscious state she was aware of nothing but the warm, musky body covering hers, and knew she wanted him closer still. Then he took her, tenderly, almost reverently, so that it was for her one of the best times of all.

It was over in a matter of minutes, and so soft, so perfect had it been that in the morning she almost believed it a dream. This time, when she awoke, fresh sunlight was forcing its way into the cabin, heralding the beginning of yet another day. Hal was gone and for a moment she was deeply disappointed. Then she saw that he had spread her clothes to dry and she smiled at his thoughtfulness. They were still a little damp, but she put them on and hurriedly made her way up on deck.

She was surprised to see distant white cliffs thrown into sharp relief by the sunlight. There was still some cloud in the sky and a stiff breeze was blowing, but for all that, there was a strange feeling of peace after the storm. Hal was gazing out across the dappled water, his fine eyes slitted against the glare. He turned at her approach and possessively held out his hand. She took it and allowed him to draw her close, giving a little shiver of pleasure as he slipped an arm around her waist.

'We'll soon be home,' he told her, not taking his eyes off the distant land. 'You'll like England.'

Oddly enough, his air of assurance rather annoyed her. 'How much longer?'

'A couple of hours, maybe three. It really depends on the tide.' Only then did he turn to look at her, a rather self-satisfied smile on his face.

Below them the water slapped and hissed against the hull with a soporific regularity, while overhead the wind hummed softly through the rigging, the sails creaking as they took the strain. Even the calling of the seabirds seemed strangely muted. Hal sighed with the air of a man at one with the world and Nicol also relaxed, feeling the peace in him reaching out to enfold her too.

By the time they dropped anchor it was almost midday. The wind had dropped and the sun was surprisingly warm, sparkling on the blue sea and picking out the whitewashed houses of the sprawling town. The land before them looked welcoming and picturesque and Hal was glad of it, for he desperately wanted Nicol to get a good impression of her new home. She had been so staunch and uncomplaining, and he was conscious of a need to make up to her for what he still considered his incompetence and neglect.

He did not question the tenderness he was feeling, and it showed in his face as he reached out to twist a strand of her dark hair around his fingertip. Nicol was too wrapped up in her own thoughts to notice. Her eyes skimmed over the docks and quays and on to the houses spread out like a Lilliputian village across the undulating land. She wondered about the people who lived there, who worked and fought for the country she was having to make her home. Would they really welcome her?

'Tonight we'll sleep in a proper bed,' Hal declared, and his eyes held the promise of pleasure to come.

Finally, when the last-minute details had been taken care of, the longboat was lowered to take them ashore. Nicol sat in the stern between her husband and Hector Browne and looked around with interest as the sailors dipped their oars and sent the boat skimming across the bay. There must have been at least two dozen ships anchored there, with longboats and cutters moving purposefully between the larger vessels and the quay. In fact there was an air of lively confidence about the scene that only served to make Nicol feel even more unsure.

The men were in excellent spirits and when some sailors leant over the side of one of the anchored warships to call out their congratulations on the capture of the French frigate, even Browne acknowledged them. Hal slipped his arm around Nicol and gave her shoulders a reassuring squeeze. She glanced up at him and was shaken by the love she felt. He was so handsome. His grey eyes seemed to have taken on the colour of the sea and for once seemed full of understanding.

At the steps to the quay a man came forward to help them land and exchange a cheery word with the sailors. Over the last couple of weeks Nicol had become accustomed to the use of English, but hearing it spoken by this stranger rather forcibly reminded her that she was a foreigner in that land. Panic surged through her and she wondered desperately if she would ever feel at home.

Hal must have read her thoughts because he smiled gently and said, 'You'll soon get used to it. The differences are only skin-deep, I assure you. If I can learn to feel at home in two different countries so can you.'

'But you're half French,' she replied.

He frowned as if he did not like her negative attitude. 'Just give it time, Nicky.'

As they walked along the quay, he took her hand and once more smiled his reassurance, only this time there was a shadow of concern in his eyes. Her fingers tightened nervously around his, but she managed to conceal the trepidation she was feeling. He had risked his life to bring her to his country and she did not want to insult him by showing her fear. Besides, she reminded herself fiercely, she could make anywhere her home as long as he was there.

CHAPTER ELEVEN

THE street outside the Red Lion inn was buzzing with activity. Looking down from the parlour window, Nicol was fascinated by the variety of people she saw there. Merchants and fishermen, children and matrons bustled across the cobbles, a bright moving scene punctuated by the occasional dark coat of a naval officer. The port was prosperous and somehow cheerful, with even the most humble individual able to look others in the eye. Nicol found it a sharp and painful contrast to her beloved France where suspicion was everywhere, and those not seeking trouble tried to melt into the background and unobtrusively continue with their lives.

The inn itself was enchanting, with neat windows, brasses and a roaring fire. She had even looked into the taproom, wanting to go in until Hal had explained that it was not at all the thing.

'But in these clothes they won't even know I'm a girl,' she had protested.

'Oh, they'd know!' he'd assured her, his eyes brimming with laughter. 'In fact, the next thing we must do is get you something proper to wear.'

He had already asked the landlady about dressmakers and one had rapidly been summoned, with whose encouragement Nicol had selected three gowns, two which needed alterations and would arrive later that day, and the plain blue she was wearing now. Almost against her expectations, she found she was enjoying herself. Everything was so new and exciting, and people seemed to be putting themselves out to welcome her and help.

De Cruzat was also staying at the inn, and at Hal's expense.

'No, I don't like the fellow,' Hal had admitted when questioned, 'but the business of our duel is over and done with. I've fought alongside him in the past, and that imposes a certain obligation. Jacquelein found him useful, so I intend to give him the money to return to France.'

Hal was out now, in search of clothes for himself, having insisted that he did not feel right in Dick Burgess's second-best uniform. What a strange man he was, Nicol thought wistfully, such a peculiar mixture of tolerance and unyielding temper.

She returned to the fire and settled down in one of the comfortable, chintz-covered chairs. The noise from the street seemed to be coming from a great distance, inexplicably mingling with vague images in her mind. Without even being aware of it, she curled around and, resting her head upon her arm, fell sound asleep.

Hal returned some time later, wearing a new suit of clothes. In spite of his improved appearance, he felt both hungry and tired. For a while he stood in the doorway, staring across at Nicol, a soft smile playing on his lips. How would she take the news that he had hired two coaches for the morrow, one to transport her to Ashton, and the other to convey himself and Jacquelein's letter to London? Not well, he'd warrant.

Watching her sleeping, he knew he had been right; she was obviously in no condition to make the double journey, the stress of the last weeks having drained her more than she would admit. She was pale and she had lost weight, creating a new fineness and maturity around her mouth that only served to enhance her beauty. He moved to stand over her, noting the provocative rise and fall of her breasts, the thickness of her dark lashes lying in semicircles against her soft cheeks, and he felt an almost breathtaking tenderness. He bent over her, his lips brushing her hair, his heart lurching slightly when she opened her eyes to smile at him.

'They'll be serving dinner in half an hour,' he told her. 'I thought you might like to go and freshen up. That dressmaker has delivered your other gowns and Browne is going to join us.'

'I thought he was too busy,' she muttered, rubbing her eyes in a childishly endearing gesture.

'He is.' Hal grinned. 'But he needs cheering up. That other Frenchman has jumped ship and he's not at all looking forward to reporting the matter to Burgess.'

Not until the meal was over and they were once more alone, did Hal inform Nicol of the arrangements he had made and precipitate the fiercest argument of their marriage. They were both tired, and because of that short-tempered and utterly unsympathetic.

The letter was still very much on Hal's mind and he felt guilty about spending even the one night in Portsmouth. His own and his brother's estates both lay to the west, Ashton Hall the closer by some twenty miles. London, of course, was in the opposite direction, and he refused to allow Nicol to make such a gruelling and roundabout journey. In fact, he scarcely felt up to it himself. The simplest solution was for her to go on to Ashton ahead of him, and, while he recognised how awkward she might feel about this, he knew he could rely upon his brother to make her welcome and set her at ease.

Nicol, on the other hand, did not have this confidence in Lord Ashton, and the idea of turning up on his doorstep unannounced filled her with horror.

'I won't do it!' she snapped. 'How can you even ask it of me? Let me go to London with you.'

'No,' he replied uncompromisingly, and, unable to meet her eyes, turned away to refill his glass from the bottle on the table.

'If you won't take me with you, then at least let me wait here. I won't stray from the inn, I promise . . . Please, Hal! Maurice would keep an eye on me if only you would ask him.'

He had begun to weaken, but her last suggestion only strengthened his resolve. 'It puts hours on my own journey if I have to come back here—besides, Portsmouth's no place for an unaccompanied female . . . and don't mention de Cruzat again, because I still don't trust the fellow.'

She had tried pleading, and now, unconsciously, she gave her anger free rein. 'What you mean, Hal Grantly, is that you don't trust *me*! I wonder what can have happened in the past to give you such a distorted view of women?'

His fingers tightened around the wine glass until the knuckles showed white, his eyes suddenly becoming as cold and hard as lake water. 'You are my wife, Nicol, and you will do as I say. I may not trust you and Maurice together, but that's not the reason for my decision. Ashton won't eat you, believe me!'

Nicol turned away, the anger and humiliation inside her about to trigger tears. He did not love her and was obviously beginning to find her an encumbrance, but if he thought he was going to bundle her off to his relations like a piece of unwanted luggage, he was most definitely mistaken.

'I won't go!' she shouted. 'I'd rather return to France. What's the matter? Have you some paramour in London I'm not supposed to meet?'

Hal set his glass down upon the table and, with the groan of a man goaded beyond endurance, reached out to grasp her shoulders and shake her hard. 'It's nothing like that, you stupid little fool. In that respect I'm a damned sight more trustworthy than you are! But that's beside the point—I'm sick of your childishness. You're my wife, and you're damned well going to act like it!'

'Trustworthy!' she snapped, pulling away. 'That's rich, coming from a spy. What would have happened, Hal, if England's interests hadn't matched our own?'

More than once he had asked himself that very question, and had felt guilty at the obvious answer: in upbringing he was more English than French.

The colour drained from his face and his mouth set in a grim line. 'You've been talking to de Cruzat. I ought to have killed him when I had the chance! I'll tell you this, though—you're going to Ashton tomorrow, even if I have to tie you in the bloody carriage!'

'If that's how things are done in England, then I wish to God I'd never left France,' she choked, turning and running towards the door.

Hal, an empty sickness tearing at his insides, made no attempt to stop her. With her hand on the knob, she paused, her unhappiness driving her to one last, bitter taunt.

'Why did you marry me?' she demanded. 'Was it so you could have your own private whore? It was either for that or for my inheritance! After all, we both know the Republicans won't be in power for ever.'

Then, slamming the door behind her, she raced for the stairs, desperate for the sanctuary of her bedroom. She felt so terribly alone, and France was so far away. The thought filled her with panic and, flinging herself upon the bed, she began to cry, finding that the only outlet for her misery and frustration.

Downstairs, Hal ground his teeth until his jaw ached, then with a muttered oath reached for his cloak. More than anything else, he needed to walk and think things through. The girl had certainly tried his patience, but it was more than that. Suddenly he was no longer sure of his own emotions. He only knew that all his waking hours were full of Nicol. Somehow she had managed to penetrate his painfully erected barriers, and it left him feeling vulnerable and rather afraid.

Nicol eventually cried herself to sleep, not stirring until the middle of the night. Then, finding Hal had not joined her, she felt more dejected than ever. Tiredly, she removed her crumpled dress and crawled between the smooth sheets, shivering with emotional reaction and cold. Oh, how she missed the security of Hal's arms! She had to remind herself quite firmly that such comfort was only an illusion, nothing more than an appealing but dangerous lie.

She was still awake when the first grey fingers of dawn came creeping into the room, the stark light seeming only to reinforce the hopelessness of her situation. Rising stiffly, she dressed and went haggard and hollow-eyed in search of some breakfast. To her surprise, she found Maurice de Cruzat already tucking into a plate of bacon and eggs.

'He hasn't been in all night,' he informed her, correctly interpreting her anxious look around. 'Do I gather that all is not roses between you? Last night you made enough noise quarrelling to disturb the whole household.'

Nicol nodded and turned to gaze out the window, not able to face him until she had her emotions properly under control. A movement at her side alerted her to the fact that he had left the table and was standing close to her. She faced him with a look of blank misery.

'Do you want to tell me about it?' he asked softly.

'He's quite insufferable,' she faltered. 'I don't think I've ever known anyone so self-opinionated and domineering.'

He shrugged. 'He's always been like that, I don't know what your father was thinking of to marry you to the fellow.'

'Well, I am married!'

'My dear, sweet Nicol,' he whispered, drawing a finger gently across her cheek. 'You are still so naïve. Leave him and return to France. There is no reason why you should suffer for the rest of your life because of one single misjudgement. Go back to La Vendée— the Republicans are unlikely to concern themselves with a woman on her own. You would simply have to exercise a little diplomacy. Sooner or later they'll need to pacify the area; certainly such fighting is too expensive to continue.'

'How can I return?' she asked miserably. 'I've no money, nothing!'

'I've funds enough for us both, and a passage arranged for later today. Granville or La Vendée, wherever you wish. I'll willingly escort you and expect nothing in return but your friendship... We are friends now, aren't we, Nicol?'

She nodded. 'Yes, yes, of course... It's just that it's such a big step.'

'It's a bigger one to stay. Come with me now, child, before Grantly returns. Surely anything is preferable to being tied to a man who does not really want you? Hal has always been solitary; I'm afraid wedded bliss is not his *métier*. If you stay, he'll eventually grow to hate you, and somehow, my sweet Nicol, I don't think you could take that.'

He's right, she admitted to herself. As far as Hal's concerned, I'm nothing more than a possession, and her fierce de Carrie pride rebelled, spurring her on to a decision she would not otherwise have made. It was as if someone else nodded agreement and went upstairs to fetch her things.

In less than fifteen minutes she was walking away from the inn and away from the man who had become the centre of her rather chaotic life. She knew she was leaving a part of herself behind, and realised that had Hal returned and made even a half-hearted attempt at a reconciliation, she would not be leaving at all.

As if sensing her regret, de Cruzat smiled encouragingly and possessively tucked her hand through his arm, leading her determinedly away from the main street and towards the civilian harbour.

Although it was early, the town was already coming to life and the harbour itself was quite busy. The smell of fish seemed to be everywhere, reminding her so forcibly of Cancale and that first, blissful time with Hal that once more she had to fight back tears. Oh, damn it, she thought, all I seem to want to do is cry.

De Cruzat led her on, away from the working boats towards an older, quieter part of the waterfront. Here they passed boats that looked as if they had not been moved for generations, and the warehouses behind stood empty and in need of repair. An unaccountable feeling of unease spread through Nicol and, looking around, she realised that they were the only people for almost half a mile.

'Where are we going?' she asked anxiously.

'The boat is along here. I couldn't afford a first-rate craft, I'm afraid, but it will be safe enough.' He stopped walking and turned to study her. 'Not having second thoughts, are you?'

She swallowed, remembering Hal's clear grey eyes and the way they could darken with pain. She knew then that she could not bear never to see him again, not to be able to run her fingers through his hair or feel the touch of his lips and those deep, enticing kisses. How she would miss his wry smile and the occasional, unbridled amusement that flashed in his eyes, all the more precious for being so rare.'

'I'm sorry,' she told de Cruzat, 'but I don't think I can go through with this. I can't face not seeing him again ... I'm going back to apologise ... I only hope he'll forgive me. I said such dreadful things ...' She faltered, frightened by the anger that had suddenly sprung into the Frenchman's eyes.

'But I need you, Nicolette,' he insisted, his hand reaching out to grasp her wrist.

'No!' In panic she tried to pull away, but his fingers held her as surely as bands of steel.

'I need you as bait for your estimable husband,' he continued, expertly side-stepping her kick and drawing her more firmly into his arms. 'I intend to get hold of Jacquelein's letter and you're going to help me. I've friends who will reward me handsomely for intercepting it and, if Grantly can be persuaded to give me the names of his contacts in France, so much the better. I received scant reward from Jacquelein so I've sold my talents elsewhere. I was never a prisoner aboard *La Créole*, my dear—simply a strategy I adopted when the battle failed to go our way!'

'Traitor!' hissed Nicol, struggling and kicking out with renewed effort.

She made little impression against his heavy boots, but he found her efforts annoying enough for him to have to call for help.

'Carnot!' he shouted, and the man who had been his companion aboard the French frigate emerged from the nearest boat.

Nicol tried to scream, and when de Cruzat covered her mouth with his hand she bit down with all her strength. With an oath, he pulled away, then cuffed her sharply across the ear, making her head swim and turning her legs to water. Other rough hands grasped her, and, still struggling, she was carried across to the ancient boat and unceremoniously hustled below.

'You can damned well stay there and cool off,' de Cruzat told her, standing at the top of the steps and sucking angrily at his bleeding hand. 'There isn't another way out, so you may as well save your energy. If you're sensible and you co-operate, you might— just might!—get out of here alive!'

CHAPTER TWELVE

HAL found he wasn't in the least hungry, and in fact the food was making him feel sick. With a sigh he pushed his plate away and leant forward to rest his aching head in his hands. It was like the repetition of a particularly bad dream and he groaned aloud at the injustice of it. The very thing he had dreaded most had happened. Indeed, it was as if it had been ordained, as if every word and action on his part had been perversely directed towards that end.

All morning he had walked the streets and quay, looking for Nicol, and now he had to face the fact that she was gone, running away from him like a thoughtless child. At first he had been angry, furiously so, determined to drag her back and finish de Cruzat once and for all. Then, as time passed and there was still no trace of her, anxiety had blotted out all else, leaving him with a feeling of loneliness that was more than he thought he could bear.

The innkeeper had told him that she had gone willingly with de Cruzat, without leaving any note or explanation, and that hurt most of all. In his clumsy way he had done his best for her, and was even beginning to think optimistically of their future together... As for de Cruzat, she was as safe with him as with a hungry bear!

I ought to let her go to the devil, he told himself, absently pouring himself a glass of wine, and yet already he knew he would continue his search, even if it meant returning to France.

There was a sharp knock at the door and the inn-keeper's wife entered, a folded piece of paper in her hand. 'A most unsavoury little urchin brought this to the back door.' As she handed it across, her expression told him just what she thought of a gentleman whose wife had seen fit to run away.

'Thank you.' Hal took the note, his stomach churning with apprehension. He had to force himself not to open it until the woman had left the room.

It was written in French, brief and very much to the point. De Cruzat had Nicol and was going to kill her unless Hal brought him Jacquelein's letter. He had until that evening to decide, for at nine o'clock de Cruzat would take the girl to a deserted warehouse, and if there was no sign of Grantly and the letter then she would not leave the place alive.

Hal slumped down in his chair, staring into the roaring fire and yet not really seeing it at all as he tried desperately to think things through. Slowly he withdrew Jacquelein's letter from inside his coat, reached for a knife on the table and began to heat the blade in the flames. With great care he lifted the wax seal, spread out the papers and began to read. It was a liberty, he knew, but Jacquelein would forgive him under the circumstances.

The contents were no great surprise to him, and—apart from a couple of sentences—gave very little away, certainly nothing de Cruzat could not have sur-mised. Hal gave a grunt as he came to a decision, and, standing up, shoved the letter back into his coat. What he intended to do could easily have been classed as a betrayal of trust, but, having assured himself that no harm could be done, he had no intention of sacrificing his wife for some stiff-necked ideal. His face was grim as he left the inn, for he had few illusions about the outcome of his scheme. He was going to need help, too, and he was grateful that he had at least one disreputable contact in the port.

It took him the best part of the afternoon to locate the smuggler who on other occasions had carried him secretly to France. That rather ruthless individual respected few men, but fortunately Hal was one of them. This respect, however, did not stretch to giving free information and he had to pay dearly for the name he was eventually given.

At a surprisingly respectable house he found a clever little man who on occasion forged Excise documents for those in need and willing to pay. Silas Minton glanced at Jacquelein's letter and immediately informed Hal that copying it would be 'as simple as ABC'. Selecting a suitable square of parchment, he carefully wrote a second letter. It differed slightly in content from the original, but when Hal placed the two documents side by side, superficially at least, they appeared identical.

The little forger grinned. 'It's a superb job, even if I do say so myself. I'm sure your Mr Jacquelein wouldn't be able to tell that he didn't write it.'

The second letter was closed with Jacquelein's original seal and, after paying the man generously for his unusual craft, Hal made his way back to the harbour where he found a boat to take him out to *La Créole*.

By that time the sun was sinking behind the town and the sea looked dark and oily. The tall ships swung gracefully at their anchors, their masts and rigging touched with gold. The scene before him was one of beauty, only Hal was too preoccupied to notice.

Browne welcomed him warmly but soon realised that something was wrong. Not only did Hal find it impossible to respond with a smile, but he looked positively haggard. The young Lieutenant was horrified when he found out what had happened and readily promised his support.

'It will be dangerous,' Hal admitted as he stalked across the cabin, 'and your superiors will probably say that de Cruzat's capture should come first.'

'Nonsense,' Browne replied. 'I'm with you all the way. Nicol's safety is more important. Mind, I must admit, I don't like the risk you'll be taking. Are you sure there's no other way?'

Hal shook his head. 'I'm positive, and—believe me—I've done nothing but think about it since I received de Cruzat's letter. It's the only chance we've got.'

Studying Hal's drawn face, young Browne decided there and then that he never wanted to fall in love, not if it made a man that vulnerable to pain.

'We'll make it work,' he replied comfortingly, 'and we'll teach that Frenchman a sharp lesson for dragging Mrs Grantly into his scheme.'

Hal closed his eyes to conceal the hurt. He hadn't been able to tell Browne that Nicol had gone willingly with de Cruzat. His pride just wouldn't allow it, and besides, he was still trying to hang on to the hope that such had not really been the case.

'You ought to get some rest,' Browne told him. 'If you can't sleep, at least take advantage of my bunk and lie down.'

'I will,' Hal replied, drawing a hand across his eyes, 'but first, if you'd be good enough to provide the wherewithal, I'd like to write an explanatory letter to Pitt. Then, I must ask you another favour—a reliable man to carry a packet to London. If things don't work out, then I must know that the letter will be safely delivered.'

Browne motioned to the quills and ink that sat upon the desk-top. 'There's paper in the drawer. Help yourself. You won't disturb anything of importance. I'll go and organise the men we'll be needing for tonight.'

Once left alone, Hal settled to his task. Under normal circumstances he had no difficulty in composing a letter, but this time he found it hard to explain why he had opened Jacquelein's message and at the same time not give the impression that he had placed his personal interests above those of his country. In fact, the last point was something he was not entirely sure about in his own mind.

He was still not completely satisfied with the missive once he had finished it, but he folded it with Jacquelein's original letter, sealed it, and left it on the desk for Browne to find. Removing his boots, he stretched out on the narrow bunk and tried to relax. His body throbbed with tiredness but that was nothing when compared to the ache in his heart. Resolutely, he tried to will the pain away, to isolate it and return his feelings to the limbo in which they had existed for so long. He didn't want to allow himself to feel. Over the years he had become adept at subduing his emotions, and yet now every time he closed his eyes the barricade he was constructing crumbled before the image of Nicol's lovely face.

In spite of all his previous training, he found it impossible to sleep but lay there in the encroaching darkness, feeling isolated and unsure. Was Nicol even thinking of him? he wondered. Was she even aware of what de Cruzat was doing? She might have been intriguing with the man, but she would never willingly have betrayed the Vendean cause. It was the only thing in the whole sorry mess that he could be sure of.

When it was really dark and he went to join the Lieutenant on the deck, Hal's feelings were well concealed. He appeared calm and very much in control of the situation, so much so that, for a while at least, even Browne was fooled.

Nicol waited in the grubby cabin, struggling against despair. She knew she was unlikely to reach either France or Ashton Hall, and to make matters worse she had involved Hal in her predicament. She was sickened by the knowledge of her own immaturity in fleeing from her marriage just because it had not been perfect. In retrospect she knew she should have cherished what she had.

She could only hope that Hal would be angry enough to wash his hands of her, and yet she knew instinctively that he would not. She was his responsibility and for a moment she almost hated her father for forcing that upon him. It occurred to her that, from the very beginning, she had resented the fact that he had not chosen her himself. It was her pride again, her damnable, self-destructive pride, and now it was going to be the death of them both. She desperately wanted to warn him, would willingly have given her life to save his, and yet she could only wait, frustrated and helpless, while events took their fatal course.

Already she had searched her small prison for some way of escape or, failing that, some weapon—a strip of metal, a bar of wood, anything she could use against her captors—but to no avail. The cabin had been virtually stripped, leaving only a padded chest and a single wooden chair too sturdy to be broken up. The lights over the windows were all tightly screwed and the single door was firmly bolted from the outside. The only other thing of interest was a bucket in the corner, and she could think of no use for this beyond the obvious.

Around noon de Cruzat brought her food and stopped to talk for a while, revealing that a note had already gone to Hal and that there was every expectation of his appearing at the rendezvous that evening.

'You're deluding yourself,' Nicol told him, with a confidence she did not feel. 'He cares nothing for me.'

De Cruzat laughed, regarding her with something like pity. 'I constantly marvel at the ignorance of youth ... The poor fool's in love with you, anyone can see that. It's a pity there's no future for you together, but he'll come, never fear.'

But she did fear, not so much for herself but for Hal. She now knew how vicious and unscrupulous the Frenchman could be—not a man to have an enemy at his mercy and then let him leave.

By the time it grew dark she felt sick with apprehension, and when her captors came to fetch her she put up such a fight that they were forced to handle her very roughly indeed. She would have been willing to suffer much more had it been of help to Hal, but in spite of her efforts she found herself waiting in the darkened warehouse, praying fervently that he would not appear. De Cruzat's confidence was a little unnerving, and so was the evil-looking knife being held within an inch of her throat.

They waited for what seemed an age, the silence seeming to press in upon them from all sides. Around them was as black as pitch with only the open doorway showing a slightly lighter hue. Nicol felt cold and shivered violently, almost welcoming the warmth of de Cruzat's hand upon her arm. The place was alive with rats and she could hear them scrabbling in the rafters. Then there came the unmistakable sound of footsteps, someone walking purposefully and without apparent fear.

'De Cruzat.'

Nicol would have known that voice anywhere and opened her mouth to shout a warning. De Cruzat smothered it with his hand, chuckling softly with satisfaction.

'Is that you, Grantly?' he asked.

'Yes.'

'Step into the doorway where I can see you more clearly.'

There was a moment's silence, then Hal's tall figure filled the doorway, his hands held up to show that he was unarmed. Nicol's heart lurched at the sight of him.

'Light the lamp, Carnot,' de Cruzat commanded, and the whole scene was bathed in a soft yellow glow.

'You shouldn't have come,' Nicol whispered.

For a brief moment Hal's eyes sought and held hers, but there was nothing in his expression to give any hint of what he was thinking.

'Have you got the letter?' asked de Cruzat.

'Yes... Let Nicol go, and I will give it to you.'

The Frenchman's laugh was harsh and entirely without humour. 'Did you really think I would release her so that she could go running straight to the authorities?'

'No,' Hal replied simply.

Nicol groaned, realising that Jacquelein's letter was lost, and all for nothing.

'It seems that you do understand me, Grantly. Now toss the letter over here. No tricks, mind, or your wife dies instantly.'

Hal reached slowly inside his coat and, withdrawing the folded paper, tossed it across. De Cruzat motioned to Carnot, who quickly retrieved it and with the air of a pleased dog handed it to his master.

'Now, Grantly, put your hands behind your back and face the other way.' When Hal hesitated, de Cruzat pressed the knife harder against Nicol's throat; she felt the sharp sting and knew he had drawn blood. 'I'll kill her now,' he hissed. 'Do as I tell you, and I might, just might, spare her life. It very much depends how useful you can be to me.' He laughed as Hal obediently turned, unable to resist a further taunt. 'The great Hal Grantly as docile as a lamb, brought to heel by some slip of a girl!'

'Oh, why did you come?' choked Nicol.

Hal turned his head towards her, an odd expression in his eyes. 'I'm surprised you need to ask, Nicky,' he answered softly.

She was too numb to understand his meaning, but he had come for her, that much was clear, caring enough to sacrifice himself and his honour to save her worthless life.

'Oh, you fool,' she whispered to herself. 'You dear, noble fool.'

They returned to the boat in silence, Nicol feeling as if her heart were a great leaden weight in her chest. Once or twice she glanced at her husband but it was too dark for her to be able to see his face. On one occasion he stumbled and, with uncharacteristic clumsiness, sent a stack of wooden barrels crashing over. The sudden noise carried through the stillness, revealing their presence to anyone else in the area.

De Cruzat swore and cuffed him viciously across the head. 'Take more care, damn you, or the next blow will be for Nicol.'

When they boarded the boat, Hal was pushed so roughly into the cabin that he crashed down on his knees. Before he could right himself, Carnot administered a hard punch to the back of his neck and he fell forward, stunned. De Cruzat was still holding Nicol by the arm and, as she made to follow, he held her back.

'I'll let you soften him up while I talk to her,' he growled.

Carnot looked a little surprised but made no comment, instead dragging Hal away from the door.

'There's nothing I can tell you,' Nicol informed de Cruzat steadily, although she was desperately concerned for Hal. 'Now you've got the letter, why don't you just let us go?'

'You'll have to see if you can persuade me,' he replied sardonically, guiding her across the narrow deck and into what had once been some kind of small, sleeping-cabin.

He thrust her away from him, and, pushing his pistol into his belt, reached out to light the lantern and place it back on top of the locker.

'Have a seat?' he said with mock courtesy.

It was more a command than an offer and, anxious not to anger him further, she sat down on the unmade bunk. The mattress was damp and greasy from countless bodies and the whole place smelt strongly of mould, but in her agitation she did not notice it.

De Cruzat closed the door and leant back against it, his arms folded negligently across his chest. He did not seem in any hurry to begin the conversation and, unable to bear the silence any longer, Nicol asked the question that was uppermost in her mind.

'What are you going to do with him?'

'With Grantly?' he asked in mock surprise.

'Yes!'

He laughed softly, apparently enjoying the situation. 'I thought that was obvious. We shall find out what we want to know and then kill him, quickly if he's lucky.'

'No! Please, no!'

'But yes, my dear. There's no profit in keeping him alive.'

'I'll do anything, Maurice, anything,' she sobbed, her mind desperately searching for something that might change his mind. 'There's my property in France. You can have it, and willingly. The Republicans will surely let you keep it. I know it's not worth anything to me, but it would be to you!' When he made no sign of accepting or rejecting her offer, she continued desperately, 'What about Hal's family? They're rich, very rich. They'd pay handsomely for his return. Think of all you'd be throwing away if you killed him!'

He chuckled softly and with a maddening self-assurance. 'The Republicans are paying me well enough for this venture. I have promises of property and advancement and I'm not a greedy man. True, more money would be nice but, balanced against the risks, it's just not worthwhile. Beside, I find revenge very sweet indeed. I shall enjoy killing your husband! The estimable Henry Grantly has been a thorn in my side for some time. He stepped casually into a promotion that should have been mine, and it wasn't because of his ability, either. It will be a pleasure to have him grovelling before me!'

'He'll never do that,' Nicol snapped, pride overcoming her caution. 'He's more of a man than you'll ever be!'

He merely smiled and moved forward so that he could touch her cheek. 'We shall see, my sweet Nicol, we shall see.'

She froze as he ran the back of his hand down her neck, then slipped it under her cloak. His long fingers moved beneath the neck of her dress to caress the rounded swell of her breast and she shuddered.

'He'll talk to protect you.'

'I'll do anything you want, Maurice,' she said steadily, rising to her feet.

He threw back his head and laughed uproariously. 'So you'd come to me, would you? You'd give yourself to me to save his worthless hide. How sickeningly noble! You really haven't got the idea, have you, my sweet? When this business is over, I shall take you anyway!'

As if to prove his point, he pulled her against him and kissed her ardently, one hand pulling at her hair while the other caressed her breast. She kicked out at him and, when he drew back, slapped him hard. His eyes flashed and he replied in kind, splitting her lips and knocking her back against the bulkhead.

'I'll soon cure you of that,' he said softly. 'You'll find I can hit much harder than you. If you've a taste for violence, then we'll go and see how Carnot is doing. He's not a patient man and, as your husband is inclined to be stubborn, it should be most entertaining.'

As he dragged her across to the other cabin, her stomach was turning somersaults and she was afraid she was going to be sick. She dreaded seeing Hal and prayed that they hadn't hurt him too badly. In fact, he looked surprisingly unharmed. There was a cut on one of his cheeks and he was deathly pale, but that was all. He was seated in the single chair and his wrists were tightly lashed to the arms.

'Have they hurt you?' she asked quietly, wanting to go to him, only de Cruzat was restraining her.

'I'm all right,' he answered.

He did not immediately look at her, and when she did see the expression in his eyes she was shaken. They were full of resignation, as if he had given up hope and accepted what he was going to have to endure. He was hurting and not just from the blows, and she desperately wanted to put her arms around him and comfort him.

'Go and sit over there,' de Cruzat commanded, shoving her towards the chest that stood against the bulkhead.

She dabbed gingerly at her mouth and her hand came away spotted with blood. Hal's eyes snapped angrily and that made her feel ridiculously relieved; at least he still had some spirit.

'Your quarrel is with me, Maurice,' he hissed. 'Leave her alone!'

De Cruzat chuckled unpleasantly. 'You have no say in the matter, Grantly. In any case, the girl came willingly with me. She's encouraged me in every way!'

Nicol saw the doubt in her husband's eyes and felt desolate, aware that she had done nothing to deserve his trust. He glanced questioningly towards her, looking for a denial, and when she did not make one his expression became even grimmer.

De Cruzat gave a satisfied smile, and, withdrawing Jacquelein's letter from inside his coat, lifted the seal and began to read. For a moment he was completely engrossed in what he was doing and the prisoners were forced to wait in nerve-straining silence.

Finally he turned his attention back to Hal, a look of anticipation in his eyes. 'Now, Grantly, you will tell me all about your activities in France. I want the names of your associates and the details of any confidences you received from our gullible young General—in short, anything that might be of interest to my Republican friends. Tell me enough, and the girl shall live... I cannot, of course, make the same promise for yourself, but then I don't suppose you expected me to.'

'No,' replied Hal, making it clear that he had walked willingly into the trap. 'I wouldn't want to strain your generosity too far.'

He glanced at Nicol and managed a wry smile. She had never loved him more than she did then.

'I don't want you to tell them anything,' she said, her voice harsh with defiance.

His eyes showed a momentary flash of pain. 'Brave words, Nicky, but I doubt if you realise just how exacting these men can be.'

De Cruzat laughed unpleasantly. 'I see you understand me perfectly. Now tell me how long you think it will be before Jacquelein realises that his letter has not been delivered. Oh, I know he'll send another, but time is not on his side.'

'Two weeks, possibly three,' Hal replied vaguely. 'Quite honestly, you have as much notion as I.'

'Were you the only messenger?'

'As far as I know.'

'This letter implies that Jacquelein will move west into Brittany, yet we both know that the wish of the Army is to return home. The question is, will he be able to force the issue?'

Hal shrugged. 'As I've said before, I have no more notion than you. Where you got the idea I was in Jacquelein's confidence I do not know.'

'What about Pitt?' de Cruzat demanded, struggling to keep his temper. 'Will he send the Vendeans the help they so desperately require?'

'I don't know, but I would certainly have done my best to persuade him.'

De Cruzat reached out and, grasping the prisoner's hair, forced his head back. 'You are not being very helpful, my friend, but we'll leave that for a moment. Tell me about your contacts in France.'

'There were only the Surats in Cancale and the address of an empty house in Laval where I was supposed to leave a packet.'

De Cruzat frowned. 'We had been watching the Surats for some time, but I am sure there are others as yet unknown to us. You will give me their names unless you wish your wife to suffer!'

He motioned to Carnot who had been standing quietly but menacingly beside Nicol. Twisting her arm behind her back, the burly man dragged her to her feet and forced her forward until she was within a couple of feet of Hal.

'She's a dainty piece,' he growled. 'I could snap her limbs like twigs. In fact . . .' he paused to reach his left hand across her shoulder and down to touch her breast '. . . there are so many ways to hurt a woman.'

De Cruzat gave a slight nod, and in one swift movement Carnot swung Nicol around. He hit her hard across the face, and while her head was still spinning he ripped her dress down to her waist.

'You should have been kinder to me, Nicol.' De Cruzat's voice seemed to be coming from far off. 'The best thing you can do now is to persuade your husband to talk.'

Nicol could only shake her head at him. Carnot's large coarse hands were fondling her and nausea was washing over her in ever-increasing waves.

'She's quite lovely,' de Cruzat told Hal. 'Are you really willing to see her ravished in front of you, and all for some outdated ideal? Carnot is none too gentle with his women.'

The colour drained from Hal's face as he struggled vainly against his bonds.

'For Christ's sake, Maurice,' he pleaded, 'there's no need for that!'

Nicol met his frantic gaze and shook her head; hate was fast overcoming her fear. 'All this means nothing,

nothing! Don't say a word. I will not be responsible for the deaths of your friends!'

The tears of anger and humiliation that streamed down her face were too much for Hal and he kicked out in desperation, managing to catch de Cruzat across the shin. Predictably, the Frenchman spun around and dealt him such a blow that chair and everything went flying.

'Coward!' growled Hal, though his head was ringing, and followed the word with a stream of abuse more foul than anything Nicol had ever heard.

'Oh, no!' she gasped, wondering how he could be so foolish.

Then the Frenchman seemed to lose all control and, turning on his prisoner, began to kick and punch him viciously. He was like a man demented as all his pent-up hatred and anger found an outlet, pouring from him like water from a recently breached dam.

'Stop it! You're killing him!' Nicol screamed, completely oblivious to her own predicament.

She was nearly frantic with anxiety and kicked and clawed like a wildcat in an attempt to reach Hal's side.

With a sudden crash the door burst open, and Hector Browne and a handful of seamen came charging in. The sharp sound of a shot cut above the other noise, followed almost instantly by another. Carnot crumpled like a grotesque rag doll and de Cruzat ducked and swore. Still incensed, he clawed the pistol from his belt and levelled it at Hal. Browne's pistol was empty and even as he started across the cabin, it was obvious that he was not going to be in time.

For the fraction of a heartbeat Nicol watched in frozen horror, then, acting purely on instinct, she flung herself against the Frenchman, intending to drag his arm aside. It was a disastrous mistake. In an instant de Cruzat had hold of her and had hauled her in front of him, intending to use her as a shield. His pistol moved away from Hal, and its cold, hard muzzle pressed against her temple.

'Shoot her and you're a dead man,' threatened Browne from the doorway.

'On the contrary, it is Nicol who will be dead,' de Cruzat informed him coolly.

Hal was still strapped to the chair but somehow managed to struggle to his feet. He sat down because it was impossible for him to stand upright, making him appear incongruously relaxed in that atmosphere of tension and uncertainty.

De Cruzat glanced at him. 'Tell them to let us pass. One false move and Nicol dies!'

Nicol could feel the tension in the Frenchman's wiry body and the arm under her chin tightened painfully. Hal's expression could have been carved in stone, with only his eyes betraying his anger. When he answered his voice was as cold and hard as polar ice. 'If you hurt her, you're a dead man, and if you intend to kidnap her then you'd better kill me now, because I shall hunt you down no matter where you go. You're not fit to breathe the same air as decent men. You're nothing but a gutter-born son of a tinker's trull!'

Nicol gasped, thinking he must have a deathwish to taunt a man with a primed pistol. How could he be so reckless? In fact in that moment she almost hated him for holding his own life so cheaply.

De Cruzat's finger tightened on the trigger as he moved the pistol to cover Hal. His body was literally shaking with rage. For a moment hatred nearly overcame his reason, but he just could not waste his one precious shot. Browne and four of his men were still waiting in the doorway like hungry vultures.

'Oh, I know how much you hate me,' Hal continued. 'The feeling is mutual, I assure you. As we have reached an impasse, I'm willing to fight you for your freedom.'

'Don't be a fool,' Browne growled, taking a step forward. 'He wouldn't dare use that pistol.'

Studying de Cruzat, Hal smiled grimly. 'As a matter of fact, I think he would. I want you to co-operate, Hector. Give your word that if he triumphs, then he will be allowed to walk out of here.'

'I can't.' Browne shook his head vigorously, but there was indecision in his eyes. 'He's a spy and should be handed over to the authorities!' He hesitated, then swore. 'Oh, all right then, but he deserves death.'

De Cruzat nodded. 'I accept your challenge, Grantly, but the girl is to be part of the bargain. If I win, she comes with me.'

'No!' snapped Hal. 'Whatever happens, she goes with Browne. That is not negotiable!'

'Your concern for her is misplaced,' the Frenchman replied coolly, 'but it shall be as you wish as long as we fight with swords. I see that both the Lieutenant and the midshipman are wearing them.'

It was all happening too quickly for Nicol, who felt dazed and unsure. All she could think about was that Hal was risking his life again, and it seemed so unfair. She wanted to protest, but de Cruzat's arm was nearly choking her, and she realised too that by running away she had forfeited her right to interfere.

De Cruzat again placed the cold muzzle of the gun against her temple. 'You may untie your friend, Mr

Browne, but no tricks, mind. Then you and your men move over to the far bulkhead. Grantly and I will fight on deck.'

Once this was done, the Frenchman released Nicol. 'Go and collect their weapons, girl, the empty pistols as well as the swords—and remember! I'm watching every move.'

She glanced at Hal before doing as she was bid and he gave her a reassuring smile. She saw that he was rubbing his wrists to restore their circulation and she felt sure that he was not fit to fight a duel.

He took a step forward but de Cruzat motioned him back. 'Not so fast. I will go first with Nicol.'

Slowly, de Cruzat backed towards the door, feeling his way cautiously up the steps. His pistol menaced the whole room before finally settling on Hal.

'I'd shoot you now,' he growled, 'only I want to see you die slowly. You can come up and lock the door behind you.'

Nicol dumped the weapons, two pistols, knives and the swords, on the deck and glanced apprehensively at the Frenchman.

Hal bolted the door and turned towards de Cruzat. His face was that of a stranger. 'Choose your weapon.'

'You don't have to fight him,' Nicol pleaded. 'You could just let him go.'

He gave a wry smile. 'I believe we've had this conversation before, and yes, I do have to fight him.'

If she had asked him why, then he would not have been able to answer her; he did not fully understand himself. He hated the Frenchman, that much was clear, and much of that hatred was founded on jealousy and a need to protect his own, but there was more to it than that. Years ago he had sworn never again to pursue a woman, and yet here he was doing that very thing. Nicol belonged to him and he was going to keep her, whatever the cost. He felt guilty about that, and it was as if that guilt, and the unreasonable responsibility he felt for what had happened in the past, could be wiped away by the coming act of violence. In some perverse way he was putting up his life as the stake and leaving it for Fate to decide.

De Cruzat tucked the pistol into his belt and picked up one of the swords, flexing it experimentally. It was broader and heavier than the ones he was used to, but that did not shake his confidence at all.

Hal did not bother to try his own weapon but eyed the Frenchman suspiciously. 'Give the pistol to Nicol.'

'So that she can help you?'

'So that I know she will be safe even if you win!'

De Cruzat laughed nastily and shook his head. Taking the pistol, he tossed it negligently over the side. 'I'm afraid I don't trust her impartiality. We fight to the death, Grantly.'

Hal nodded and glanced briefly at his wife. 'Get off the boat, Nicky. I want you to try and find your way back to the inn. If I don't join you there, you'll have to inform the authorities. Someone will have to come and release our friends.'

Nicol couldn't bear to watch the fight but she couldn't leave either; her fate was irrevocably bound with Hal's. If the Frenchman won, her life would be as nothing and she would extract her vengeance whatever the cost might be.

'I won't go,' she choked. 'Don't ask it of me.'

Hal was completely without compassion. 'Damn it, woman, do as I say!'

'He's afraid I'll force you to come with me,' de Cruzat enlightened her, 'and who knows, with him dead, you might be glad of my company... Enough of this, Grantly. Let us begin!'

Without further warning he lifted his sword and went into the attack, leaving Hal little time to parry and step back. Nicol moved to the broken railings and watched in frozen horror as they fought like men possessed, their blades sliding and crossing, parting and clashing again with a breathtaking rapidity.

De Cruzat was still a master, his wiry body moving as quickly and gracefully as an acrobat's. Hal, on the other hand, was strong and determined, fighting as he had never fought before. They thrust and parried, feinted and withdrew, and yet neither could gain the upper hand. The Frenchman's point passed within an inch of Hal's neck, and when he drew back they both paused, Hal silently acknowledging that it had been a near thing.

Once more their blades hissed and clattered. De Cruzat circled his enemy, thrusting and parrying and lunging again, but Hal stood his ground. His face was set in a grim mask and his eyes were as cold and hard as polished glass. Their chests rose and fell with their efforts and sweat streamed down their faces, and still the pace did not slacken.

Then Hal began to tire. His movements became less crisp and his face began to mirror the strain. Nicol was terribly afraid for him and her heart hammered along with his. She watched motionless, her eyes aching as she attempted to follow the deadly dance of the swords slanting and sliding in the moonlight, and she prayed unceasingly.

The blades crashed together, then locked at their hilts as the two men strained against each other. Hal pushed de Cruzat away, sending him crashing against the cabin door, and for a moment the Frenchman was shaken. Taking advantage, Hal closed the distance. De Cruzat's thrust was ill-timed and Hal slipped his blade inside it to slice his opponent's ribs. He felt a surge of exultation that did not diminish even when the Frenchman managed to retrieve the situation and mount another attack. Now they were both tiring, and de Cruzat was losing a lot of blood. Hal's wrist and shoulder felt numb with weariness and he was finding it more and more difficult to ignore the persistent pain in his side. They were both fighting on sheer willpower, spurred on by the primeval instinct to kill.

Nicol was becoming increasingly anxious and began to look desperately around for something she could use as a weapon. She was not interested in chivalry or honour and knew she would stoop to the lowest trick if it would save Hal's life.

The two antagonists came together again, and once more their swords locked. This time de Cruzat was aware of Hal's superior strength and, before he could be pushed away, he brought up his knee. Hal doubled over with a gasp of pain and his sword arm dropped. Like a cat de Cruzat sprang. His blade struck out, and only by a miracle did Hal manage to deflect it. The Frenchman moved forward again, and, feeling sick and desperate, Hal dropped to one knee. De Cruzat was committed to his stroke and, unable to draw back, virtually impaled himself on Hal's low blade.

A horrible, gasping sound escaped him and, like a puppet without strings, he fell to the floor, rolling over to stare upwards with wide, unseeing eyes. A dark stain was spreading slowly across his abdomen and Nicol watched it with morbid fascination. It was obvious even to her that he was dead.

Reaction set in and she began to cry, great tears rolling down her cheeks as she clung weakly to the rail.

'It's all right, Nicky,' Hal whispered, desperate to put his arms around her.

For a moment he hesitated, afraid of rejection, and then he was holding her, crushing her to him as if he would never let her go. She couldn't get enough of him, could hardly believe that he was real and virtually unharmed. His warm hand was gently tangling her hair and he was almost crying, too, his strong body trembling with reaction.

Whether words of love would have followed they never knew, for their embrace was cut short by the frantic banging on the cabin door. Hal gently pushed his wife away and went to release his friends.

Browne tumbled through the doorway and glanced around.

'You bested him then,' he said, running a hand through his cinnamon-coloured hair. 'I don't think I've ever felt so frustrated in my life! We heard the fight, but we couldn't see a damn thing... I still don't see why you had to fight him. We could have worked things out some other way.'

Hal reached out to squeeze the younger man's shoulder. 'Thanks for your help, anyway. I couldn't have done it on my own.'

'You took all the risks.' Browne laughed as the tension left him. 'But I must say I've heard of less painful ways of distracting someone, and if you hadn't knocked over those barrels we'd have lost you for sure. If this adventure's done nothing else, it's made me aware of my own foolishness. Another time we shall carry more than two loaded pistols, you may rely on that!'

Nicol moved closer to Hal and he slipped his arm around her shoulders.

'You're bleeding,' she choked, wiping a thin trickle of blood from his eyebrow.

'I'm all right.' His smile was gentle and a little shaky as he surveyed her from head to toe.

She was trying to hold the bodice of her dress together with her left hand and she looked frail and extremely vulnerable.

'Come on,' he said softly. 'Let's go.'

'Do you want this?' asked Browne, stooping to remove the letter from de Cruzat's coat. It was crumpled and soaked with the man's blood.

Hal shook his head, then, at Nicol's surprised gasp, explained. 'It's a forgery, Nicky. I had Jacquelein's letter copied by an expert, leaving out anything that might have been of interest to the Republicans. The original is already on its way to Pitt, minus the seal but with a full explanation.'

As he helped her across the precarious gangplank, he added, 'The letter was mainly a plea for help. I only hope Pitt will respond. After I've seen you safely to Ashton, I intend to go to London and plead Jacquelein's case myself. You won't mind that, will you?'

'Of course not,' she replied, tightening her grip on his arm. 'In fact I'd be grateful...'

His rather strained laugh interrupted her. 'It's always been my cause, too, you know. Oh, my first loyalty is to England, but I am a quarter Vendean. I served Jacquelein faithfully, believe me.'

It was true, of course. Had he not been badly injured in the Vendean cause? The scar he carried was lurid proof of his courage and commitment and she wondered how she could possibly have forgotten. She was filled with shame and tenderness, and most of all with anger at her own destructive stupidity. In her pride and selfishness, she had spoilt something rather fine.

'I've done nothing to make you doubt me,' he continued bitterly. 'I never lied to you.'

'I know,' she answered in a voice that was barely more than a whisper.

They walked on in silence, their way illuminated by an almost full moon. Everywhere was strangely quiet and Nicol was particularly aware of the man at her side. She wanted to throw her arms around him, to confess her love and plead for forgiveness, but once again he seemed withdrawn and restrained.

Browne and his men left them at the dock gates, the Lieutenant declaring that he would inform the authorities and that all Hal had to do was to see his wife safely home. Nicol was almost sorry to see him go, for she was afraid of the confrontation she knew was coming.

As they turned into the street where the inn was situated, Hal asked the question that had been almost constantly on his mind—the question Nicol had been dreading.

'You went willingly with de Cruzat, Nicky—why?' He spoke quietly, almost matter-of-factly, and yet Nicol could sense the turmoil inside him.

She wanted to tell him that she loved him too much to be satisfied with a one-sided marriage, that she couldn't stand the fact that he didn't love her, too, but her fierce de Carrie pride was still a barrier between them. Once before he had thrown her love back in her face, and she wouldn't give him the opportunity to do so again.

'I wanted to go home, Hal, that's all. Maurice offered to take me.'

He drew an exasperated breath and, clasping her tightly by the arms, turned her to face him. 'Was he going to be your lover?'

'No!' The flames of her anger died swiftly as she acknowledged how it must have appeared. 'He was going to escort me, nothing more!'

'Dear God!' he grated. 'I don't know whether you're a total innocent or a damned fine liar. How *could* you have been so stupid? De Cruzat's Republican sympathies aside, you would not have reached France unmolested! To think you went willingly, not giving a damn about me or how I might feel! I ought to put you over my knee and thrash you to within an inch of your life!'

'Is that your answer to everything?' she snapped. Then, when he did not reply, she added, 'It's just that a marriage is so arid without love. It's not enough!'

As she turned towards the inn, he muttered an oath and pushed her back against the wall. 'Love! You don't walk out on someone you love! Your responses to me are much more fundamental.'

She looked up apprehensively and saw that familiar hard light in his eyes. Bending his head, he forced her lips apart in a kiss that humiliated her with its icy contempt, stifling her and smothering her cry. She could hardly believe that after all they had been through that evening he could be so savage. To think that she had almost begun to believe that he cared.

A struggle would only have humiliated her further so she froze, waiting coolly for him to finish. Her emotions were in turmoil, and it was all she could do to conceal her mounting desire.

Finally he drew back, laughing harshly. 'So that's the way you're going to play it. It will be interesting to see which of us breaks first. But just remember, madam, that I, at least, have the opportunity of finding my pleasure elsewhere!'

'You're hateful!' she spat, as he opened the door and almost pushed her into the hall.

She felt numb and exhausted and her eyes were so full of tears that she stumbled on the stairs. Hal caught her and swung her into his arms.

'Keep still,' he hissed. 'I'm finding this enough of a strain on my side without you struggling like a maniac.'

'I can walk,' she protested, yet nevertheless felt no inclination to pull away from him or demand that he set her down.

When he placed her on the bed and closed the door behind him, she caught her breath in panic, anticipating another scolding. She heard him swear, and when finally he managed to light the candle she saw that he was deathly pale.

'Don't worry. I shan't force myself on you tonight,' he grated, totally misinterpreting her fear. 'I, for one, am not up to it.'

He glanced at her torn dress, just visible beneath her dusty cloak, and a shadow of pain crossed his

glass. For a moment he thought she was going to make some comment, but the frown on his face discouraged her and she turned away with a slight shake of her head.

Before the bottle was half empty, he realised that the alcohol was not having the desired effect; instead of deadening the pain, it only seemed to be accentuating what he was feeling. Finally he decided to give in to his tiredness and make his weary way to bed. Then the stairs seemed to move beneath his feet and his stomach felt distinctly queasy.

He was relieved to reach the room he was sharing with Nicol, but on trying the door was surprised to find it locked against him. Swearing under his breath, he rattled the latch and called out crossly for her to let him in. She did not respond at once, and the longer he had to wait the more angry he became.

Nicol struggled from sleep, feeling dazed and disorientated, and for a moment could not think what was wrong; then, realising that it was Hal, she cursed herself for falling asleep. She had certainly not intended to do so, and had only locked the door because she had felt nervous on her own. The candle beside her bed had guttered out and the room was in darkness, so she knew he had been gone for some time. Part of her thought that it served him right to have to wait, but deep down she was afraid of the interpretation he would put on the locked door. Before she had slept, she had keyed herself up to apologise and declare her love, but now he sounded far too angry to listen.

She scrambled from the bed, completely unaware of her nakedness, and hurried to the door. It took several seconds for her to locate the key in the darkness, and even longer before her stiff fingers could turn it. The door swung open and Hal stormed in. The candle he was carrying picked out the hard lines of his face and anger positively sparked from his eyes.

'I'm sorry,' she muttered. 'I'm afraid I fell asleep. I really didn't mean to lock you out.'

He gave a snort of disbelief and pushed past her, slamming the door behind him. She jumped at the sound and her eyes widened in apprehension. She'd never seen him so tense and angry, not even after that awful duel.

'You were gone such a long time,' she told him, hoping he would apologise or at least offer some explanation. She had been so miserable, lying in that great bed alone, and she felt he should have sensed her need for him.

Ignoring her, he staggered across to the bed and set the candle down on the nearby table. He slumped down and, holding his head in his hands, tried to regain control over his churning emotions.

It was the first time Nicol had seen him drunk and she could only guess at the strain that had prompted it. He looked so vulnerable that her resentment melted and, swamped by love and compassion, she sat down beside him and reached out to smooth his hair.

'You must believe that I didn't mean to lock you out,' she whispered. 'I intended to let you in as soon as I heard you at the door.'

He jerked away as if her touch burnt, and turned to face her. Only then did he become aware of her state of undress, and he was momentarily stunned by her beauty. The soft candlelight seemed to accentuate her graceful curves and turned her skin to alabaster.

The desire that surged through him took him completely by surprise.

Dear God, he wondered desperately, is she always going to have this effect on me?

She saw the need flare in his eyes and, shaking her head at him, slowly backed away. It wasn't that she didn't want him, but passion was only going to confuse the issue. Although he knew she was unwilling, he uncharacteristically pushed the consideration aside.

What the hell? he thought, through a haze of wine. She's my wife. I can take her whenever I wish. She may not love me, but on the most basic level she responds as if she does.

Reaching out, he caught hold of her shoulders and forced her back down on the bed. His mouth fused with hers and he kissed her passionately, as if with his lips he could brand her as his own.

'I want you,' he growled, raining kisses on her neck and throat. 'We may not love each other, but, by God, we're good in bed!'

Nicol tried to turn away in order to answer him, but, curling his fingers in her hair, he forced her lips back to his own. He was being almost brutal and she cried out that he was hurting her, only he didn't seem to hear.

Just hours before, she had wanted nothing more than to be loved by him and held in his arms, but not like this. She might have understood his anger, but her pride revolted at being treated in such a way.

'No, Hal,' she pleaded, still trying to dissuade him. 'We need to get things straight between us first. We need to talk.'

'Like hell we do!' he snapped. 'We really only communicate in bed.'

She could smell the tang of wine on his breath and feel the rasp of his beard against her cheek. The proximity of his hard body brought back memories of their previous lovemaking, and suddenly she wanted him, too. She grasped a handful of his hair, intending to lift his face away, then, somehow, her body betrayed her and she was kissing him back in earnest. If he wanted it this way, she thought with a flash of anger, then she would give as good as she got. Her hands pulled at his shirt and, finding their way beneath it, began to caress the warm, hair-roughened skin across his chest.

He loved her with an angry and intense passion, seeking both to comfort and punish, and she matched him every step of the way. Their climax, when it came, was cataclysmic, shaking them and draining them utterly. When Hal collapsed on top of her, Nicol was completely unable to move. She wanted to run her hands across him, to soothe and hold him, but her arms felt like lumps of lead. Finally, he pushed himself away from her, leaving her feeling lonely and bereft. Gradually the euphoria she was feeling evaporated under the certain knowledge that something was wrong.

'I'm sorry. I behaved like a savage,' he muttered, climbing shakily to his feet. 'I think I must have been trying to punish you for someone else.'

She opened her eyes at that and was stunned by the desolation she saw in his candlelit face.

'It won't happen again,' he added distractedly, as he straightened his rumpled clothes.

When the door shut behind him, she sat up in surprise. She hadn't realised that he was leaving, not until she heard the click of the latch, and then she just couldn't believe it. She had thought that they were going to make things up between them, but he had simply taken his satisfaction and walked away. Unable to restrain herself, she rushed to the door, dragged it open, and desperately called out his name, Her voice fell on empty air.

In a haze of misery she returned to the bed and crawled under the covers, like a wounded animal retreating to its lair. Her body still ached from his lovemaking and the familiar smell of him lingered on her damp skin. She loved him, and yet she knew that she had killed any possibility that he might grow to love her, too. In fact the odds had always been against her, for he was a man whose past made it impossible for him to love and trust again.

Vehemently she cursed the woman who had made him like that, the woman who, for some dark reason, he still needed to punish. It might all be in the past, but he had not forgiven or forgotten. The look on his face as he had left the room had been heartrending to behold, so full of pain and self-reproach. It was the latter that puzzled her the most. Surely he didn't think that he had forced her? After the way she had responded to him the thought was too ridiculous for words. Once more she turned her face into her pillow and let the tears fall. She felt so lonely that she wanted to die, and only exhaustion made it possible for her to sleep at all.

Hal returned to the darkened taproom and slumped down on a chair before the dying fire, feeling quite as wretched as she. The glowing embers flickered and throbbed in time to the pain in his temples, and the sickness in his stomach now had nothing to do with the wine. In his drunken state he thought that he had all but raped Nicol, for he had been blindly unaware of her response.

Not that it mattered, he told himself bitterly. She had left him and he couldn't pretend it had not happened. She had never really loved him, and he had been right in his mistrust of the emotion. She was simply young and unawakened and had been enthralled by the lovemaking of a more experienced man. Tears pricked at the back of his eyes but he resolutely blinked them away. Damn her, he would survive on his own, just as he had been doing for so many cold and colourless years.

CHAPTER THIRTEEN

As THE hired coach rocked and swayed along the narrow country road, bouncing in and out of potholes with a bone-jarring regularity, Nicol glanced across at her husband sitting silently in the opposite corner. He was obviously in some discomfort, and whenever there was a really severe jolt she saw him wince.

He had been unusually quiet all day, whether from pain or anger she did not know; it was impossible to tell what he was thinking, and the rather bleak expression on his face discouraged conversation. He had not mentioned de Cruzat or chastised her again, but his stony silence was even more unnerving.

Last night he had not returned to her room, and that, more than anything, had told her how he felt about matters. God knew where he had slept; in fact, meeting him in the parlour for breakfast, she would have guessed that he had not slept at all. He was looking a little better now, having washed and shaved, but he was still very pale and drinking too much brandy from the flask he carried. He had certainly not forgiven her, and his male pride was still smarting. It couldn't possibly be more than that, she told herself, for his heart had never been involved. She reminded herself that he had come after her, that he had risked his life in no uncertain way, but then he was that sort of man. Hadn't he done the same for Jacquelein and her brother?

Several times she considered asking him if he would like her to leave, but she dreaded his answer too much. She felt that she had lost him, and the realisation was like a tight and sickening knot in her stomach. He might not have loved her, but he had given her his name and his friendship. Many marriages had been built on less, and had she continued to win his respect, who knew what might have grown?

How she longed to draw him into her arms and kiss away his frown, to lay her aching head against his chest and sob out her wishes and her fears, but his icy reserve was like a wall between them and her pride would not let her even try to break it down. He caught her watching him and smiled, a smile that did not reach his eyes.

'Not much longer, wife,' he said.

Nicol looked away and, glancing across the landscape of thick hedgerows and half-covered trees, thought it not so different from her beloved Vendée. A few minutes later they rolled through a small village and the quiet beauty of the place quite took her breath away. A weak, winter sun had, at last, pierced the light cloud, and it sparkled on the small duck pond. Neat thatched cottages flanked the green, and at one end an impressive church pointed towards the sky.

'Liversham,' Hal informed her. 'In another five miles we'll come to Ashton and the Hall.'

'Is it as pretty as this?' she asked.

He nodded. 'I think so, although it's slightly smaller and has no green. The thatch is attractive but in many ways it's a nuisance. It requires a great deal of maintenance.'

'Does your brother own the whole village?'

'Yes.' Hal closed his eyes and sighed as if suddenly bored with the subject.

An unruly lock of hair had fallen forward across his forehead and Nicol had to fight an almost overwhelming desire to lean across and brush it back. After a moment he did it himself, a careless gesture that was achingly familiar. Nicol wanted to slip her arm around his neck and curl her fingers in the thick dark hair at his nape.

Finally they turned off the narrow road and, after passing through a most impressive gateway, began winding their way up a long gravel drive. Rhododendron bushes almost brushed the sides of the coach while the bare branches of tall trees arched overhead. Then they were through the wooded tunnel and a wide expanse of lawn stretched before them, leading up to a mansion whose beauty impressed Nicol. For all its grandeur there was a solidity about it, as if it had grown there along with the grass and trees. The late afternoon sun lent its walls a honeyed light and sparkled like jewels on the countless mullioned windows.

Nicol drew a sharp breath of appreciation, making Hal smile for the first time in hours.

'It's quite an edifice, isn't it?'

'It's fit for a King,' she replied.

'I suppose if it comes down to it the Grantlys can trace their origins back further than our illustrious George . . . Oaklands is only half the size, but, as you can see, I really had no need of your precarious inheritance.'

She was mortified that he had remembered her words and flushed to the roots of her hair.

Oddly enough, that seemed to amuse him and he actually laughed. 'I'm sorry, that was ungallant of me. I promise I won't mention the matter again. Now, for goodness' sake, relax—you look as if you're going to an execution!'

When he turned back to the window there was a soft, rather possessive expression on his face, showing that at least bricks and mortar could reach his heart.

The carriage ground to a halt and one of the coachmen ran back to let down the steps. Hal jumped out first, but before he could even extend his hand to the girl the house doors had opened and a liveried footman had come forward to assist.

'Master Harry! Why, this is wonderful! His lordship will be delighted . . . and a young lady, too!'

'My wife,' Hal explained as Nicol alighted and glanced around.

'Madam!' The footman bowed gracefully, his powdered wig nearly touching the ground.

Hal smiled encouragingly, even taking Nicol's hand as they entered the lofty hallway from which rose an impressive flight of stairs. Another footman came forward to greet Hal warmly and lead them towards a set of beautifully polished doors.

'No need to stand on ceremony, Wilson,' Hal told him. 'I'd rather announce myself.'

'Your rooms will be prepared immediately, sir,' the footman assured him, and disappeared down a passage.

Nicol found herself being propelled into one of the grandest rooms she had ever seen, but for all its elegance there was a pleasant, intimate atmosphere created by a number of chairs drawn up in front of the roaring fire.

A gentleman rose as they entered, his expression faintly enquiring. When he saw Hal, his homely face lit with a smile of pure joy and he hurried forward, arms outstretched.

'My dear boy, how good it is to see you. We were becoming quite worried, you know.'

'I'm glad to be back,' Hal admitted, embracing his brother.

'And who is this?' Lord Ashton glanced questioningly at Nicol.

'My wife,' Hal announced, and if Nicol had not known better she would have thought it was with pride. 'Nicky, this is Arthur, and his wife Elizabeth.'

Nicolette found herself being unceremoniously hugged by her brother-in-law. She was pressed against his broad chest and heard his rich laugh. He was not at all like Hal in appearance, being stocky and fair, but the eyes that were smiling into her own were heartrendingly familiar.

'Oh, Hal, I'm so pleased!' exclaimed the slim, attractive woman. 'We had quite despaired of you taking a bride. But what on earth have you been up to, dear boy? You're looking quite worn.'

'Lord, yes!' added Ashton, drawing his brother towards a chair. 'For heaven's sake, sit down before you drop. Nicky—is it short for Nicolette?—why don't you join Elizabeth on the sofa?'

Nicol was surprised to find that Lord and Lady Ashton were so much older than Hal, almost an entire generation. She noticed a marked tendency on her ladyship's part to mother him, something he submitted to with surprisingly good grace. He was obviously tired to death and yet he smiled and replied to their questions patiently. He even managed to joke and only Nicol, exhausted herself, guessed the effort it was costing him. She blessed Lord Ashton for his perception when he suggested they both might like to rest before dinner, and rang for a servant to ensure their rooms were prepared.

Just as they were making their way towards the stairs, a small, dark-haired boy of about four or five came hurtling from the back of the house to wrap his arms around Hal's knees.

'Uncle Harry!' he cried. 'No one told me you were back. You've been away an awfully long time.'

'This is Elizabeth's nephew, her sister's boy,' Hal explained, lifting the child up and complimenting him on the way he had grown.

'Have you been fighting more battles?' the boy asked, reaching out his chubby hands to cup Hal's face.

'One or two...but I have someone for you to meet. Peter, this is your new aunt.'

The sight of the two dark heads so close together caused an ache of longing inside Nicol. Somehow it had never occurred to her that Hal might be fond of children. Suddenly, she could visualise him as a father as well as a lover, and the rift that had developed between them became even harder to bear.

He had turned towards her as he made the introduction and there was a rather questioning expression on his face. She was at ease with children and knew at once how to respond, seriously shaking the boy's plump little hand and promising to play with him another day.

Hal set Peter down, wincing slightly as he did so, and laughed as the child rushed off the way he had come.

He smiled approvingly at Nicol. 'You seem to like children.'

She nodded, not trusting herself to speak. She was thinking that she would love any child of his to distraction, but she could hardly tell him that.

At the top of the stairs Lady Ashton paused awkwardly. 'They've given you separate rooms but with an adjoining door. I hope that will be all right.'

'It's fine,' Hal replied, and, although he did not say as much, the impression given was that he preferred to be alone.

'You really do look terrible,' she told him. 'Perhaps Dr Hewitt should take a look at you. I can't think what you've been up to.'

'He's been shot and beaten, and last night he didn't sleep at all,' choked Nicol, suddenly finding herself embarrassingly close to tears.

Sensing her distress, her sister-in-law slipped a gentle arm around her shoulders and guided her along to the next door, entering the room with her. It was all too much. Days without sleep, concern for her husband's health and the agony of their estrangement had all taken their toll and Nicol found herself sobbing quite unrestrainedly. Elizabeth sat down beside her on the bed and, after a moment's hesitation, drew her into her arms.

'I love him so much,' wept Nicol, before going on to explain.

The older woman listened sympathetically and nodded her understanding. 'You really ought to talk to Arthur, you know. He, better than anyone, will be able to explain why Hal is like he is... He's not naturally a cold person. With us, even with Peter, he is extremely demonstrative and caring. It's just that he seems to have a grudge against pretty women. They could throw themselves at his feet and he'd walk right over them ... Perhaps, after you've talked to Ashton, you'll find it easier to understand. I don't know all the details myself, but in the past he's been badly hurt. Try to be patient with him, child, for he desperately needs someone like you.'

By this time Nicol had regained her composure and was attempting to dry her eyes. She was too exhausted to take in all that her sister-in-law said, but she knew she had found a friend, someone who cared for Hal, too.

'I should try to sleep,' Elizabeth advised. 'Things will look much brighter when you're not so tired.'

When one of the maids came to wake Nicol and help her dress for dinner, she really did feel better and was able to view her future with more optimism. Hal obviously still cared enough about her to bring her to his home, and if he did not love her at least he had not mentioned a divorce.

Divorce! The very word made her feel sick. If necessary, she would beg him to keep her with him, would suffer the sweet, aching torment of loving and not being loved in return; anything was preferable to never seeing him again. Perhaps if she was patient, if she was considerate and mature, they would at least be able to return to the easy friendship they had shared before.

She gave careful thought to what she should wear that evening, finally deciding on the most splendid of her new dresses—a rich yellow, cut enticingly low. She was determined to impress her husband with her new-found maturity, and to this end allowed the maid to dress her hair and pile it high on the top of her head, with just a few wispy curls escaping to frame her face.

When she viewed herself in the long mirror, she knew that she had not made a mistake. The colour of the dress enhanced the darkness of her hair and eyes and its neckline revealed a tantalising amount of cleavage. To complete the effect, she searched through her small jewel-case and selected a dainty emerald pendant that Hal had carried all the way from France. She glanced at herself one last time and gave a small smile of satisfaction; she had never looked better. She could only hope that Hal would approve.

As she passed his door on her way towards the stairs, she paused, wanting more than anything to go to him. She could picture him sleeping, long limbs sprawled and his hair appealingly tousled, and it was like a knife-thrust inside her for her to have to walk away.

She found her host in the drawing-room and, while they were waiting for Hal to put in an appearance, he offered to show her around.

Lady Ashton laughed at her enthusiasm and held out her shawl. 'It's an interesting house, I know, but it can be extremely cold, especially in December.'

Ashton Hall was certainly a splendid place, grand to the point of being a little intimidating. They passed through a series of rooms, each more elaborately furnished than the last and finally reached what her guide called the Long Gallery. Here, they passed row upon row of portraits, many yellow with age. Nicol paused before that of a young man wearing a dark periwig; there was something decidedly familiar about the stubborn set of his jaw and his merry grey eyes.

'He's like Hal, don't you think?' asked Ashton. 'Actually, it's my grandfather.'

She nodded thoughtfully. 'Yes, they're very much alike, only your grandfather seems more cheerful and carefree.'

'If you had known Hal when he was younger, you wouldn't have said that. He was a real handful, so full of life that people were automatically drawn to him. He was usually in some scrape or other—nothing serious, you understand, just high spirits.'

'On occasion I've seen him like that,' she admitted, 'but on the whole he's rather restrained. He's not an easy man to get close to.'

'Elizabeth has told me that things are not quite right between you. If there's anything at all I can do...?'

His face was so full of concern, so homely, and she had already seen how fond he was of Hal, that she began to tell him a little of what had happened.

'And I love him,' she said quietly, 'quite desperately, as a matter of fact. The trouble is, he cares nothing for me, and, after my running away with that dreadful man, who can blame him? It's just that I couldn't stand it, feeling as I do and knowing I'm only of interest to him in bed... And there's something else, too, something I'm not sure I should reveal even to you.'

'You mean the fact that he's a spy?'

'Then you know!'

He nodded seriously. 'I'm probably the only other person who does. I've not even spoken of it to Elizabeth... but if that's all, child, for heaven's sake don't let it come between you. He hates doing it and will be only too willing to give it up.'

'But I do feel he ought to have told me, and he's so close in other ways. I never know what he's thinking.'

'He's not always been like that,' he told her, smiling sadly. 'At one time there was no one more open and cheerful than he. As you can see, he's much younger than myself, almost twenty years. Really we're half-brothers. Hal's mother was very young and extremely lovely, and she absolutely adored him. My father doted on him, too—to be presented with a son when you're near fifty is quite something, and Hal was a son to be proud of.' He smiled a little wryly and totally without bitterness. 'In fact, I've often thought he should have inherited the title; it would have suited him far better than me. Mind, it probably will be his one day. Elizabeth and I have not been blessed with children and it's unlikely now that we shall be . . . But we were speaking of Hal. Did he tell you that he's been married before?'

She shook her head and he smiled knowingly.

'I didn't think he would have. It's not that he's deceitful or has anything to hide. He just doesn't seem able to talk about it. When he was barely twenty, he fell in love with an unusually beautiful girl. It was the romance of the season. She openly encouraged him, and he finally proposed—very much against my father's wishes, I might add. Perhaps he should have refused his permission, for Hal was still under age, but Father was never able to deny him anything. The marriage took place and Hal went off to Oaklands with his bride. It lasted six months! Louise was older and much more experienced and, throwing propriety to the winds, ran off with a dashing young Army officer.

'Hal was furious. Even in those days he had the devil of a temper, and he set off in hot pursuit. He was actually in sight of their carriage when it collided with another vehicle. Apparently Louise died in his arms, calling him every foul name under the sun. He was badly shaken, and at first I thought he was blaming himself, until one day he confessed that the whole six months of his marriage had been hell and that he would never be fooled by a woman again.'

'Morals of a cat, but I shouldn't have followed her...' Hal's words came back to Nicol and she realised that, on that night aboard the *Cassandra*, he had not been dreaming about her at all.

She had no real time to consider the matter, for Ashton was already continuing with his story, and, not wanting to miss anything about her enigmatic husband, she forced her attention back to the present.

'He bought himself a set of colours and went off to fight in America. I think it was rather a hard time for him. Father spoke out in the Lords against the war, and that must have placed him in a difficult position. While he was away the old man died, and then, surprisingly, Hal's mother. The Hal who returned home was very different from the sad young man who had gone away—harder, somehow, and much less inclined to talk. Oaklands was now completely his, and yet he showed little interest in the place, preferring to put in an agent to manage it and continue in the Army. Once or twice he joined us in London for the Season, but was as interested in the débutantes as a cat in a cabbage.

'About three years ago, the authorities discovered that he was virtually bilingual and a great deal of pressure was put on him to go to France. He was in

Paris when the King was executed and I think that finally set the seal on his disillusionment. I can remember him telling me that no one could witness what was happening there and still believe in either liberty or God. Quite suddenly, he sold his commission and went off to bury himself in the country.

'Then he arrived on an unexpected visit and obviously with something on his mind. Finally, he admitted that Pitt had asked him to go to the Vendée and report back on exactly what was happening there. He didn't much like the idea, but at the same time was concerned for his grandmother and thought a visit wouldn't go amiss. After discussing it with me, he decided to go, but only on the condition that he could be perfectly open with the old lady. What happened next you know better than I. He could never resist a fight, so I assume he was in your Royalist rebellion up to his neck, and surely there can have been no real conflict of interest—after all, we're fighting the Republicans ourselves.'

Nicol nodded and sighed miserably. 'I've behaved badly, and after what you've just told me I can't think I'll ever be forgiven. He never really trusted me and the way I've acted has only made things worse. He never professed love, you know. He was honest enough for that, but I wanted more. In fact, I'm still not sure that such a one-sided marriage can be at all successful.'

Ashton shrugged. 'I can only say I've never seen him look at another woman the way he does at you— as if he'd like to kill you and at the same time knows it would be like tearing out his heart.'

After that, he continued with the tour of the house in a much lighter mood, recounting tales of his boyhood, and of Hal's, too. Looking down the stairwell, he said, 'Hal tried to climb down over there on a discarded clothes-line. He fell and broke his arm. My God, did he yell! He was a difficult patient even then, as I recall. Oh, I can guess the time you've had with him. He's obviously still recovering, and to stop him doing too much must be a sorry chore.' He slipped his arm through hers and gave an encouraging squeeze. 'I shall have to have a serious talk with him. I'm sure he's not indifferent to you! I don't know why his wife's betrayal should have affected him so greatly; certainly he was no longer in love with her at the time. Perhaps it was because she seemed so perfect in the beginning. Hal was never one to do things by half, even falling in love, and she made him feel a fool.'

By the time they returned to the drawing-room Hal was already there, standing with his back to the windows, a glass of wine in his hand. He looked up as Nicol entered and smiled a little shyly. He was still very pale and there were lines of strain around his mouth, but in his fine clothes he presented a perfect picture of nonchalant elegance. His dark brown hair shone in the candlelight and his coat of dove-grey complemented the rather startling colour of his eyes. Pleasure flowed through her at the sight of him and showed plainly on her face.

He came towards her and took her hand, bowing over it in a formal kiss. 'You look enchanting, wife.'

His touch sent shivers of desire through her entire body. She knew then that she had been foolish to think that she could ever escape her feelings—without him she might as well be dead.

The meal was perfect, beautifully cooked and consisting of such a variety of dishes that it couldn't fail to satisfy. Nicol was hardly aware of what she ate or drank, conscious only of Hal's presence beside her. He, on the other hand, ate well and, the meal completed, lay back in his chair with a boyish sigh.

The two men did not linger long over their port and soon joined the ladies in the drawing-room. There was an unusual hesitancy about Hal and a barely concealed agitation that Nicol found puzzling.

'Why don't you take Nicol into the library and show her our family tree?' Lord Ashton suggested. 'There are some interesting miniatures in there, too.'

'Would you like that?' Hal asked, and, when she nodded, gently took her hand.

It was a natural, possessive gesture and once more she felt a stirring of hope. His hand was warm against her bare shoulders as he guided her into a book-lined room.

'What do you really think of the place?' he asked, softly closing the door behind them. 'I've always spent a large part of the year here and would like to continue doing so.'

'It's quite beautiful, if a little grand... Somehow the atmosphere is right.'

'That's almost exactly what Elizabeth said, and she loves it here. We none of us stand on ceremony, as you can see.'

'They're a charming couple.'

He smiled, obviously pleased with her remark. 'They like you, too.'

'They'd make an effort to like anyone you were married to.'

Walking across to a carved wooden box, he lifted out a large black book, placing it carefully upon the polished table-top.

'It's the family Bible,' he explained. 'It dates back to the Reformation. All our births, deaths and marriages are recorded here.'

He opened the cover and Nicol moved closer to study what was written there. She was acutely conscious of Hal's proximity and found her heart pounding like a drum.

'I know your Church considers marriage particularly binding,' he continued quietly, 'but in special circumstances it is possible to apply directly to the Pope.'

For a moment, Nicol froze, finding herself quite unable to breathe. The colour drained from her face and she looked away from him so that he would not see her tears.

'What I'm trying to say, Nicky, is that I don't want you to feel tied to me when you were forced into it by circumstances.' His voice was unusually husky, his hand unsteady as he ran his finger down the list of names, finally coming to rest against his own—'Henry Charles Anatole Grantly, Born 1759.'

'I want to put your name next to mine,' he said, turning to look questioningly into her face. 'I want you to remain my wife and be the mother of my children, but I won't hold you against your will... I'll even take you back to France if it's really what you want, although, God knows, life would have little meaning for me without you... Have I killed your love, Nicky? Have I, with my arrogance and my frozen heart?'

Reaching out, he took her by the shoulders, his fingers unconsciously biting into her flesh. There was such a look of anguish in his face that tears sprang unbidden to her eyes. Was he telling her that he loved her? Joy, pity and disbelief boiled inside her, so that for a moment she found it impossible to speak.

'I love you, Nicol,' he said huskily. 'I think I have done since the beginning, certainly after you nursed me so competently aboard ship. Oh, I fought against it and tried to deny it even to myself. I'd been hurt before, you see, and swore no other woman should have such power over me again.' He shook her gently, his mouth twisting into a bitter, tender smile. 'Oh, Nicky, Nicky, will you leave me no pride? I need you! I'm nothing without you! For God's sake, answer me and put me out of my misery!'

She couldn't—she was beyond words. Instead, she reached up to tenderly touch his pale cheek, the soft light of love radiating from her eyes. Then, with a stifled sob, she threw herself against him, holding him as if she would never let him go. He kissed her hair, her eyes, her throat, their tears mingling as their bodies entwined.

'Oh, at last, my Hal,' she whispered.

'After the way I treated you last night, I hardly dared hope,' he groaned, 'only I haven't seen the hate and condemnation I expected in your eyes.'

'Oh, my dearest, I could never hate you,' she admitted. 'There was a time when I tried, but I love you too much. I've been in agony thinking that you didn't care, that I was nothing more than a tiresome responsibility... And as for last night—if you think you raped me, then you're a fool.'

His eyes filled with hope as he searched his mind for some verification of this. Although he still couldn't remember, he could not doubt the love he saw in her eyes. His heart hammered with joy, and he wanted to cry his happiness aloud. She was his, totally and completely.

'I want you, Nicky,' he moaned after another minute of holding and caressing her, his lips toying beautifully with hers. 'Let's go to bed.'

She laughed light-heartedly for the first time in days. 'But what about your brother? We can't just disappear. What on earth would he think?'

'He'll be delighted,' he told her, sensing victory. 'In fact, I shall only be doing what he advised,' and, grinning like an idiot, he all but dragged her out into the hall. 'My wife and I have decided to retire,' he informed the surprised footman. 'Kindly pass that information on to his lordship.'

At the door of his bedroom, he turned to sweep her up into his arms.

'Be careful!' she laughed, concern for him momentarily tempering her joy. 'I'm sure you're not strong enough...'

'If I'm not, then *you* will have to make love to *me*,' he teased, tossing her playfully upon the bed. 'That dress is quite charming, my dear, but I think I would sooner see you without it!'

She scrambled to her feet and gently, teasingly, they began to undress each other, Nicol unbuttoning his shirt while he carefully removed her dress, letting it fall in a tumbled ring around her slender ankles. She gasped, the colour draining from her face when she saw the livid bruises which covered his body both above and below the strapping of bandages he still wore.

'Oh, Hal, I thought de Cruzat was going to kill you,' she faltered, the memory too unpleasant to prolong.

'You really do love me, don't you?' he said wonderingly, drawing her close and running his fingers through her hair. 'Even when you nursed me so tenderly, I still found it hard to believe. Then, just when I'd plucked up the courage to declare my feelings, you went off with that fiend de Cruzat... God, woman! Don't ever put me through that again!'

She marvelled at his insecurity, at his utter lack of conceit, and knew that he was going to need her re-assurance for a long time to come. Reaching up, she cupped his face in her hands, her eyes staring into his as if she would see into his very soul.

'I love you, Hal Grantly,' she insisted, and, drawing him closer, began convincing him in the only way she knew how.

EPILOGUE

A SOFT spring breeze rippled the grass and caused the golden daffodils to bob their heads in the pale sunlight. Nicol lay back in the garden chair and watched contentedly as Hal played with one of his spaniels. He seemed so much younger and more carefree, now that the trials and tension of their early marriage had become lost in the past. It was almost as though those happenings had been endured by another couple, only Hal's body would always bear the scars.

They had been married now for eighteen months. She was still discovering new things about him and, if anything, she loved him even more. The only cloud to mar their first days at Oaklands had been the death of Henri Jacquelein. Nicol, still raw from her experiences in France, had wept bitterly, and Hal too had been deeply affected, his soldier's mind rebelling against the tragic waste. Poor Monsieur Henri had never been able to overcome his natural chivalry, and had died while offering some outnumbered Republicans the opportunity to surrender.

Of late, matters were looking brighter for the Vendeans. Thanks to the efforts of men like Hal and several prominent émigrés, Pitt had finally agreed to finance a joint British and émigré landing in France. It was to be in Brittany rather than the Vendée, but the force was to fight its way south and join up with the Vendeans still fighting under François Charette.

Hal threw the stick for the dog one last time, and then walked over to join his wife. Resting his arm on the chair-back, he bent to brush his lips back and forth over hers, getting the feel of them before settling for a long rewarding kiss. She brought her arms up to encircle his neck and stretched up to meet his embrace, ignoring the nagging ache in her abdomen.

He drew back with a sigh and placed one large tanned hand over her swollen stomach. 'God, Nicky, I shall be glad when this child is born and I can love you as I really want to.'

'That might be sooner than you think,' she laughed. 'I do believe I've started.'

Five hours later, hearing the cries of the new-born child, Hal took the stairs two at a time and burst into his wife's bedroom.

'Mr Grantly,' the midwife growled. 'You've no right in here!'

'Damn it, I've every right! Is everything . . . is all well?'

His obvious agitation seemed to appease the woman and she smiled. 'You have a beautiful daughter, sir.'

'And Nicol?'

'I'm fine,' she said from the bed, and an instant later he was at her side.

Her face was pale and her hair damp with sweat, and yet he had never loved her more.

'We have a daughter, Hal, a daughter!' she exclaimed. 'I can hardly believe it.'

'Nor I.' He gazed in wonder at the small white bundle the midwife was holding out to him.

Two tiny pink feet were peeping out from under their cover, and he reached out his finger to touch one. It was a human being in miniature, something so perfect and helpless that he felt his heart would break with love for it.

'Go on, take her,' the midwife coaxed, placing the baby in his unaccustomed arms.

'I'd like to call her Henrietta,' Nicol said.

He turned to smile at her and for a moment they shared a memory. 'I think that's a lovely name.'

His attention returned to the child, to its small hands, as he studied each perfect finger in detail.

Nicol knew that he was hiding tears. 'You're not sorry she isn't a boy?'

He shook his head. 'I couldn't be happier.'

She knew exactly how he felt.

HISTORICAL BACKGROUND

THE French Revolution of 1789 was not embraced by the whole of the country and in several areas there was considerable resistance to it. The most organised and persistent was in western France, in the area known as the Vendée. There the landowning aristocrats were less harsh and had a better relationship with their tenants, many peasants even being allowed to shoot game.

Far from the influence of Paris, the Vendeans felt no need for a revolution, and were turned actively against it when the Republicans threatened their religion and their priests. In fact, their opposition, unlike that of the Bretons, was founded more on religious values than on political ideals.

The people of the Vendée liked and respected their landlords and actually went to them, asking them to lead their army against the Republicans. Many of the lesser nobility would have preferred quietly to coexist with the new régime and were only persuaded to oppose it by the pleas of the peasants.

In a countryside of narrow, twisting roads, the Vendeans were amazingly successful and by July of 1793, had cleared their area of Republicans. Unfortunately, this was not something that could last; the Republic's best Generals were sent against them and they were defeated at Cholet in October of that year. Many of their leaders were killed or so badly wounded that they later died, and command fell on Henri de la Roche Jacquelein, a young man of only twenty-one years.

The Vendean army, together with its followers, retreated to the Loire and managed to cross the river before the Republicans came up with them. This in itself was something of a miracle as the soldiers and camp-followers numbered some eighty thousand in all. Together they marched north, leaving François Charette and his men to continue the fight in the Vendée. They were joined by several thousand Bretons and, after many victories en route, finally reached the Normandy coast.

In early November, wanting to open a route to England and, hopefully, help and supplies, they made the mistake of attacking Granville. The town was too heavily defended and after attacking it for two days they were forced to retreat. The Army consisted mainly of peasants, and, being far from home, they lost heart, forcing their leaders to return to the Vendée. Help from England was not immediately forthcoming and, when Pitt finally did finance the landing at Quibéron, that too failed, mainly through the jealousies and ineptitude of the émigrés leading it.

In October 1795, the Comte D'Artois should have joined the Vendean Royalists and Charette had his army assembled on the beach at La Tranche to welcome him. When the time came for him to disembark, it was thought too dangerous, and although he spent several weeks on the Ile d'Yeu, to Charette's anger, he never set foot on the mainland. Without a figurehead, the Vendean Army lost heart and the end became inevitable.

The commanders of the Vendean Army were mostly very young, mainly in their twenties and thirties, and

the majority of them perished. Throughout their endeavours, they were staunchly supported by their wives
and families, and some of the women even took up
arms. However, the situation of any dependants must
have been desperate once their men had been killed,
and it is quite conceivable that the Comte in my story
would have wanted to see his daughter safely married
before he died.

SOLITAIRE – Lisa Gregory £3.50

Emptiness and heartache lay behind the facade of Jennifer Taylor's glittering Hollywood career. Bitter betrayal had driven her to become a successful actress, but now at the top, where else could she go?

SWEET SUMMER HEAT – Katherine Burton £2.99

Rebecca Whitney has a great future ahead of her until a sultry encounter with a former lover leaves her devastated...

THE LIGHT FANTASTIC – Peggy Nicholson £2.99

In this debut novel, Peggy Nicholson focuses on her own profession... Award-winning author Tripp Wetherby's fear of flying could ruin the promotional tour for his latest blockbuster. Rennie Markell is employed to cure his phobia, whatever it takes!

These three new titles will be out in bookshops from February 1990.

W❍RLDWIDE

Available from Boots, Martins, John Menzies, W.H. Smith, Woolworths and other paperback stockists.

2 NEW TITLES FOR JANUARY 1990

Mariah *by Sandra Canfield is the first novel in a sensational quartet of sisters in search of love…* Mariah's sensual and provocative behaviour contrasts enigmatically with her innocent and naive appearance… Only the maverick preacher can recognise her true character and show her the way to independence and true love.

£2.99

Faye is determined to make a success of the farm she has inherited — but she hadn't accounted for the bitter battle with neighbour, Seth Carradine, who was after the land himself. In desperation she turns to him for help, and an interesting bargain is struck. **Kentucky Woman** by Casey Douglas, best-selling author of Season of Enchantment. **£2.99**

WORLDWIDE

A Mother's Day Treat

This beautifully packaged set of 4 brand new Romances makes an ideal choice of Mother's Day gift.

BLUEBIRDS IN THE SPRING
Jeanne Allen
THE ONLY MAN
Rosemary Hammond
MUTUAL ATTRACTION
Margaret Mayo
RUNAWAY
Kate Walker

These top authors have been selected for their blend of styles, and with romance the key ingredient to all the storylines, what better way to treat your mother... or even yourself.

Available from February 1990.
Price £5.40

From: Boots, Martins, John Menzies, W.H. Smith, Woolworths and other paperback stockists.

TASTY FOOD COMPETITION!

How would you like a years supply of Silhouette Desire Romances ABSOLUTELY FREE? Well, you can win them! All you have to do is complete the word puzzle below and send it in to us by March. 31st. 1990. The first 5 correct entries picked out of the bag after that date will win **a years supply of Silhouette Desire Romances** (*six books every month - **worth over £90***) What could be easier?

H	O	L	L	A	N	D	A	I	S	E	R
E	Y	E	G	G	O	W	H	A	O	H	A
R	S	E	E	C	L	A	I	R	U	C	T
B	T	K	K	A	E	T	S	I	F	I	A
E	E	T	I	S	M	A	L	C	F	U	T
U	R	C	M	T	L	H	E	E	L	Q	O
G	S	I	U	T	F	O	N	O	E	D	U
N	H	L	S	O	T	O	N	E	F	M	I
I	S	R	S	O	M	A	C	W	A	A	L
R	I	A	E	E	T	I	R	J	A	E	L
E	F	G	L	L	P	T	O	T	V	R	E
M	O	U	S	S	E	E	O	D	O	C	P

CLAM	HOLLANDAISE	OYSTERS	SPICE
COD	JAM	PRAWN	STEAK
CREAM	LEEK	QUICHE	TART
ECLAIR	LEMON	RATATOUILLE	
EGG	MELON	RICE	**PLEASE TURN**
FISH	MERINGUE	RISOTTO	**OVER FOR**
GARLIC	MOUSSE	SALT	**DETAILS**
HERB	MUSSELS	SOUFFLE	**ON HOW**
			TO ENTER

HOW TO ENTER

All the words listed overleaf, below the word puzzle, are hidden in the grid. You can find them by reading the letters forward, backwards, up or down, or diagonally. When you find a word, circle it or put a line through it, the remaining letters (which you can read from left to right, from the top of the puzzle through to the bottom) will ask a romantic question.

After you have filled in all the words, don't forget to fill in your name and address in the space provided and pop this page in an envelope (you don't need a stamp) and post it today. Hurry - competition ends March 31st 1990.

Silhouette Competition,
FREEPOST,
P.O. Box 236,
Croydon,
Surrey. CR9 9EL

Only one entry per household

Hidden Question

Name _____

Address

_____ Postcode _____

SCOMP 8